DOC SAVAGE

The bronze giant, who with his five aides became world famous, whose name was as well known in the far regions of China and the jungles of Africa as in the skyscrapers of New York.

There were stories of Doc Savage's almost incredible strength; of his amazing scientific discoveries of strange weapons and dangerous exploits.

Doc had dedicated his life to aiding those faced by dangers with which they could not cope.

His name brought fear to those who sought to prey upon the unsuspecting. His name was praised by thousands he had saved.

DOC SAVAGE'S AMAZING CREW

"Ham," **Brigadier General Theodore Marley Brooks,** was never without his ominous, black sword cane.

"Monk," **Lieutenant Colonel Andrew Blodgett Mayfair,** just over five feet tall, yet over 260 pounds. His brutish exterior concealed the mind of a great scientist.

"Renny," **Colonel John Renwick,** his favorite sport was pounding his massive fists through heavy, paneled doors.

"Long Tom," **Major Thomas J. Roberts,** was the physical weakling of the crowd, but a genius at electricity.

"Johnny," **William Harper Littlejohn,** the scientist and greatest living expert on geology and archaeology.

**WITH THEIR LEADER, THEY WOULD
GO ANYWHERE, FIGHT ANYONE,
DARE EVERYTHING—SEEKING
EXCITEMENT AND PERILOUS
ADVENTURE!**

Bantam Books by Kenneth Robeson
Ask your bookseller for the books you have missed

Two Complete Adventures in One Volume

SATAN BLACK

and

CARGO UNKNOWN

Kenneth Robeson

BANTAM BOOKS
TORONTO · NEW YORK · LONDON

SATAN BLACK / CARGO UNKNOWN

*A Bantam Book / published by arrangement with
The Condé Nast Publications, Inc.*

PRINTING HISTORY

Satan Black *was originally published in*
Doc Savage Magazine, *November 1944.*
Copyright 1944 by Street & Smith Publications, Inc.
Copyright © renewed 1972 by The Condé Nast Publications, Inc.

Cargo Unknown *was originally published in*
Doc Savage Magazine, *April 1945.*
Copyright 1945 by Street & Smith Publications, Inc.
Copyright © renewed 1973 by The Condé Nast Publications, Inc.

Bantam edition / July 1980

ISBN 0-553-13421-3

Published simultaneously in the United States and Canada

PRINTED IN THE UNITED STATES OF AMERICA

0 9 8 7 6 5 4 3 2 1

Contents

SATAN BLACK

I.

The bronze man finally found a piece of rope. He had a worse time locating one than he had expected, and toward the last he searched with a haste that was near frenzy.

The rope was three-quarter-inch stuff about fifteen feet long, and it smelled of the anti-rust off the tools and the pipe. He found it on the fourth pipe-truck which he searched, although he had supposed there would be rope on every truck. Rope and chain were necessities on the big multi-ton pipe-trucks, one would think.

He clutched the rope, and he ran for the loaded pipe-truck that had broken an axle that afternoon. He ran desperately.

Early summer darkness lay over Arkansas, warm and amiable, and there was enough breeze to bring a slight odor, but not an unpleasant one, of the slough to the south.

The river was farther east. One couldn't say the river was a sound, but it was distinctly a presence and a fierce power. It wasn't a fierce-looking river. It was referred to more often as a ribbon of mud. Yet it was no ribbon, because a ribbon is something soft, something for a lady. This river was something for garfish that tasted of carrion, mud-cats, water-dogs; it was a repelling river, unlovely to look at and heart-breaking to deal with. It was a nasty, muddy, sulking presence in the eastern darkness.

The bronze man with his rope reached the pipe-truck with the snapped axle. He crawled under it. He knew exactly the spot he wanted, not under the truck itself, but under the pipe-trailer, beneath the mighty lengths of twenty-four-inch oil pipeline river-casing. This stuff wasn't the land casing, which was heavy enough; it was the special river casing.

The bronze man made himself a sling under the pipe. A hammock, a tight, snug little place to lie supported by the rope he'd been in such a wild haste to find. When he was done, and hauled up snug in the sling-hammock, one could look under the truck and not see him.

But if one happened to crawl under the truck, even partly under it, and poke around with a flashlight beam, he was sure to be seen. And once found, for a moment or two he would be helpless there. It was a good place to hide, but it wasn't a good place to be caught hiding. Not if one took into consideration the kind of a thing that was happening.

The bronze man lay very still. He coiled the end of the rope on his stomach. He wouldn't, he thought, care for more than half an hour of hanging like this. But it shouldn't take that long.

He listened to the night sounds, the crickets and the frogs and the owls, the rumbling of trucks in the distance, the heavy iron animal noises of bulldozers, the grinding of tripod-winches. The noises that go with the laying of a twenty-four-inch petroleum pipeline.

The noises sounded sharp and hearty enough. There was nothing sick-sounding about them, nothing at all.

There should have been.

Shortly another man came to the pipe-truck, coming idly, sauntering, pretending he was out for a walk. He was whistling softly so that no one would think he was trying to sneak or prowl. He reached the pipe-truck and leaned against the trailer duals and whistled. But he wasn't a good actor, and his whistling was unnatural.

The second man came more quietly. "Joe?" he said.

"Right."

"Nice night."

"Uh-huh," Joe said. "Got a flashlight?"

"What you want a flashlight for?"

"Want to take a look around."

"I ain't got one. Pack'll have one. Pack carries one alla time."

Pack came shortly. Another man was with him, a man called Dave. Pack said he had his flashlight. He said he'd look around.

"Want to see how bad that axle's broke," Joe said.

He didn't want to see how bad the axle was broken. He couldn't see anyway, because a truck axle was inside a housing, and anyway, if they broke, they broke. There wasn't such a thing as a bad break or a minor break. They just broke.

Joe put the flashlight beam into the pipe-truck cab. He put it under the truck, under the pipe, over the ground, around the wheels, in front of the truck, behind it, and he rammed the rod of light from the flash down each one of the load of twenty-four-inch riverweight pipes.

"Okay," he said. "We got the place to ourselves."

"That's why I put out the word for you to meet me here," Pack said. "Nobody around. Nobody got any reason to come around. Anyhow, this won't take long."

"Let's get it over with," Joe said. "This is the night I'd set aside to catch up on my sleep."

"Hell of a lot of sleep you'll get tonight."

"What do you mean?"

Pack was chairman of the meeting. Pack was sharper, more suave than the others. Possibly he was a little smarter. But none of them were dumb; they weren't honest, and they weren't stupid.

Pack said, "Go take another look around, Joe. Here's the flashlight."

"Dammit, we *took* a look around," Joe complained, but he moved off with the flashlight.

Pack said, "You guys keep listening and watching that light of Joe's. You might see or hear something Joe would miss."

"Say!" said the man called Dave. "What you trying to do, scare the hell out of us?"

Pack said, "I wouldn't want anybody to overhear this. Neither would you."

"Why not?"

"Wait until Joe takes another look around."

Joe had his look. He came back. He said, "Nobody around. Why so careful?"

"We got to kill a man," Pack said. "And we've got to do it quick."

No one said anything, not a word. The heat lightning winked redly in the distance, and an owl hooted in the slough. Far away, somebody began beating a pipe with a sledge, making a dull bell-like rhythm. Joe coughed. He said, "Here, Pack, is your flashlight." He wasn't casual. He wasn't even trying to be casual. He sounded about like any man would sound who had been told he was going to participate in a murder tonight. Startled, frightened, sick.

Pack said, "I don't like it either. But there's no other way out."

No one answered him for a while. Then Dave said, "Let me say something right now: I've never killed a man. It'll take a damned good reason to make me kill a man. A mighty damned good reason."

"You've got it," Pack told him.

"I doubt that! By Heaven, I doubt that!" The fear in Dave's voice crawled like a snake.

There was a silence. Probably the others were thinking about the way Dave sounded, wondering if there would be as much gut-torn terror in their own voices if they spoke.

Pack cleared his throat. "You yellow-bellied son!" he said softly. "Lost your insides right out on the ground, haven't you?"

Dave breathed inward and outward deeply, audibly, the way a sick man breathes.

"Take it easy," he said. "I'm all right."

"You sure as hell don't sound all right."

"I'm scared," Dave said.

"How scared?"

"Skip it!" Dave said hoarsely. "Don't push me. I'm all right. Just don't push me, is all!"

Again silence, until Joe said uneasily, "Dave will be all right. I know Dave."

Pack told Joe, "You'd better know him. You recommended him."

"Listen, take it easy," Joe pleaded.

Pack lit a cigarette. His hand shook, and he stared at the trembling hand. He grunted unpleasantly. "I'm jittery myself," he said.

It was a diplomatic statement.

"That's what I mean," Dave said eagerly. "I've got the jitters, is all. I didn't mean anything."

Pack shook out the match. He grinned in the darkness. He had deliberately made his hand shake, for there was actually no tremor in him and no touch of uncertainty. He had long suspected Dave was weak, and a moment ago he had made certain. Dave's weakness would have to be dealt with, but this was no time for that. With his little shaking of hand and his false admission of fear, Pack had avoided doing anything about it now.

Pack deliberately held silence for a while, letting the other three stew. The cruelty in Pack was more than a streak; it was the big thing in his nature, and he enjoyed it the way some men enjoy strong drink, others a meal and others a woman. Finally he spoke.

"Jones," he said. "The one they call Preach Jones. He's down in the paybook as Alvin Edgar Jones. Know him, any of you?"

The last question, did they know Jones?, was a master touch, a belt-punch.

"Jones!" Joe said hoarsely. "You mean it's Jones?"

"That's right."

They knew Jones. One or another of them had had Preach Jones in his hair at some time, but it was startling to discover, out of a clear sky, that they were to murder him. Preach Jones was not an invested minister of the gospel, nor even a preacher at all, so far as any organized religious group was concerned. He was merely a little man, with big soft eyes behind spectacles, who was always trying to carpenter other men's lives into a godly shape.

Oil pipeline construction is a hairy-chested job. This present Colbeck Construction Company project was no exception; tougher, if anything, because mostly there were old-timers on the job. The armed services had the young men. The fellows Colbeck Construction had hired were of the tough old school, from the days when pipe-joints were put together with threads, and tonged in place with brute sweat, when the men lived in tent camps and there were fights every night and a killing every week or so. The nice men, the engineers and the college products, were away fighting Japs and Germans.

Preach Jones was a saintly little nuisance with the ability to make you feel ashamed for saying a mouthful of cusswords. But he was nice. Somehow it inspired you to talk to him. You liked to talk to him; you found yourself telling him things that were close to your heart. He was a sympathetic listener.

Pack knew what the others were thinking.

"There is no other way out of it," Pack told them grimly. "So don't start thinking up arguments."

No one spoke.

Pack added, "The story is a long one, and we're not too sure of the details. All we know is that Preach Jones talked to Carl Boordling one time when Carl was sloppy drunk. You know how Carl was—when he got sloppy, he would get to thinking about his past, and it would scare him. Well, Jones happened to get hold of Carl, and out came the whole story."

Pack paused for emphasis.

"There was enough in what Carl told Jones to hang all of us and wreck everything," he added.

The fourth man whose name had not yet been used swore deeply and viciously. "Carl would do that! Damn a man who slops when he's drunk!"

Pack said, "Time is getting short. Jones is going to go along the hill road about nine o'clock. We can head him off there."

"We haven't more than a half hour," Joe said. "It's nearly eight-thirty."

"That's right," Pack agreed. "Joe, you and Dave will hide in the brush alongside the road. Guernsey, you stop Jones. I'll come up behind Jones and blackjack him. If he yells, Joe and Dave will close in quick. The idea is to get him without any noise, and get him out of there without hurting him too much. That's why I'll do the blackjacking myself. Don't any of you other guys hit him over the head or the heart. We don't want him killed."

Far away, toward the river, a steamboat whistle sounded mournfully. The dogs on farms for miles around, as if they had been waiting for such an excuse, began yapping.

Pack finished, "We'll take Jones back in the hills a ways and have a talk with him. We've got to know how much he's told."

There was another silence. Dave began to make his hard-breathing sounds again, deep and heavy, panting, as if the fear and nausea were animals in his chest over which he had no control. "Who—who—" Dave choked on the question, tried again with, "Who is going to—to—"

"We'll get to that," Pack told him. "Killing a man is easy at the time. It's just the before and after that gets your nanny."

"Take it easy, Dave," Joe said.

Pack turned away in the darkness. "Let's get going," he said. He spat.

II.

The bronze man slipped the knots in the rope which had held him against the pipe, concealed. He crawled out on the side of the pipe-truck where the moon-shadows were thick, and for a few moments kneaded the places where the rope had cramped him. He crawled back under the truck and got the rope, so that no one would have his suspicions aroused by finding it there.

He set off for the so-called hill road. There was no mistaking the road. It swept in easy curves up to the crest of the mountain which overlooked the vastness of the lowlands where the river and the marshes and the farmlands stretched. Ten minutes should bring him to it.

The man he wanted now was Jones.

He had not learned much, hiding there. Not as much as he had expected to learn. Not enough, standing by itself, to repay him for the tedious sherlocking by which he had learned there was to be a meeting at the broken-down pipe-truck tonight.

He tossed the rope on to a parked cat tractor, left it there. It had served its purpose.

Jones. Jones was the man he needed now.

He had not heard of Jones before. As a matter of fact, he had heard very little about anything. The sum total of what he had known before was hardly more than he had learned by roping himself under the truck and eavesdropping. So he was glad to hear of Jones.

Jones was something tangible. Jones was a door. If the door could be opened it might reveal the entire mystery.

The bronze man began running. He ran lightly, for a large man, with a long muscular spring in his legs and an easy agility over logs and through the brush. It was not too dark to tell fairly well where the thickest undergrowth lay, and avoid it.

He knew where the ridge road lay. The first thing he had done, one of the first things he always did in a matter of this kind, was look over the vicinity. The things he noted were the roads, the buildings, the paths, the short-cuts, and whenever possible he learned by inquiry the local names and nicknames for those places.

He had not, as yet, introduced himself to anyone, or stated his purpose to anyone. No one, as far as he was aware, knew who he was or why he was here. He had told no one. He had been careful not to ask enough questions to seem suspicious.

He had been quiet and inconspicuous. He had observed. It wasn't an accident that he had watched Pack quite a lot. Pack was the one name he'd known when he came.

Pack's full name was Lowell Packard. He was a welder. What else he was wasn't certain yet. His name had merely been given the bronze man as a possible suspect.

Watching Pack, the bronze man had seen him contact the other four, one at a time, and make the arrangements for the meeting tonight. With the aid of very good binoculars and a not inconsiderable skill at lip-reading, the bronze man had learned that they would meet at the truck, and when.

Pack was acting, the bronze man suspected strongly, at the behest of someone else. But he didn't know who. Nor did he know how Pack had reached the higher-up.

The bronze man came to the ridge road. He reached it near the foot of the hill, a poor place to waylay anyone. He reasoned that Pack and the others would be in wait further up the road.

The road was graveled. There was almost no grader ditch. Weeds grew up out of the gravel beside the road, rank and uncut. He lay in the weeds, waiting.

It seemed he waited no time at all before he heard footsteps coming. He dared not lift his head, because the weeds weren't tall.

The footsteps came rapidly. Then they paused. They came rapidly again, and this haste was followed by another pause. It was an unnatural way to walk.

The bronze man took a chance and lifted his head. He could see a figure, only the outlines of it. But he saw enough to know that the person was agitated, and stopping to listen every few paces.

When the figure came abreast, the bronze man came up silently out of the weeds and seized the person. He knew he'd made an error, that he had hold of a woman, but it was too late then.

Immediately he made a second error, when his impulse to be polite caused him to release the woman. He didn't quite release her. Just in time, he realized she had a gun in the waistband of her slacks.

She managed to draw the weapon, but he got hold of it. It was a revolver, a hammer model. He got his thumb-web between the hammer and the breech so the hammer could not fall. The hammer had a firing-spike on it which dug into his hand.

She said, "Jones, you fool! I'm Nola Morgan!"

The bronze man paid no attention, and kept working on her hand, not too roughly, until he had the gun. Just as he got it, she peeled his shin with a kick. She tried to run. He caught her.

Because he thought Jones might come along the road, and he still wanted to catch Jones, too, he hauled the woman off the road into the shadows.

"Take it easy." He made his voice gentle, so as not to frighten her more.

She surprised him then.

"Jones!" she said. "Jones, what do you think you are pulling?"

So she thought he was Jones.

"Be still," he said. "Listen for a minute."

He wanted her to be quiet until Jones came along, then he would grab Jones, and it would straighten itself all out, he hoped.

"This is going to get you nothing but trouble, Jones," she said.

"Shut up," he ordered.

She said, "Don't tell me what to do!"

He startled her by holding his fist, huge and bronze, close to her nose. "Look, how would you like to be hit with that?" he demanded. He wanted silence urgently.

Unimpressed, she demanded, "What are you pulling?"

He didn't answer. She was speaking in a low voice, and he decided to take a chance on hearing Jones coming before Jones heard them.

He had no idea who this girl was, any more than he could tell what she looked like in the darkness. He decided to fish for information, and dropped in his hook by saying, "Isn't this what you expected to happen?"

"I'm not too surprised," she said instantly.

"That's good."

"Listen, I told you I would pay you for the truth about the misericord," she said. "I will pay you. I'll even pay you more than I said."

"Are you sure it is the right misericord?" the bronze man asked.

"It's the one Carl Boordling made in the penitentiary," she said.

Carl Boordling? Who was Carl Boordling? The four men had mentioned him at their conference at the pipe-truck. Carl Boordling was the man who got sloppy in his cups and talked too much to Jones. Telling so much that the men felt they must now kill Jones because he had listened and was himself going to talk. The bronze man wished he knew more about Boordling.

"When was that?" he asked.

"Before he died," she said.

"Oh, before Boordling died," he said.

He was going slowly, picking his way, feeling.

Suddenly she demanded, "Was Boordling killed because of that misericord?"

"What makes you think that?"

"I don't know. Was he? Oh, I know the doctor at the penitentiary decided Boordling had committed suicide by drinking sodium sulphocyanate. They said he got it out of the chemical stock they used in the photographic class. But he could have been murdered, couldn't he?"

"Those penitentiary physicians are usually good men."

"But this one didn't know what was going on."

"Have you any proof?"

"That was one of the things you were going to give me, wasn't it?" she demanded.

He was cornered. She expected some kind of a direct answer. His mind raced, and he decided to try to evade the corner by putting her on the defensive again.

"We've got to be sure it is the same misericord," he said.

"It is! It's the one Boordling gave me, along with that strange note."

He said quickly, "What about the note? Let's see if it checks with what I know about it."

He tried to keep any hint of groping out of his voice.

"Why do you want to know?" she demanded.

"I have to be sure."

"Well, it's the right misericord—"

"The note. What did the note say?"

"The exact words were, 'This bloodthirsty looking trinket is not what it seems to be at all. It has a story to tell. Keep it, please, because it is not a gift, and it is important. You do not know me, so you can be sure this misericord isn't a gift. It is, incidentally, an exact copy of the one Napoleon Bonaparte owned. But that's not why I want you to keep it. Don't tell anyone about it, please.' "

The bronze man said, "That is a long note. You remember it quite well."

"I should as many times as I've read it."

"It sounds as if an educated man wrote it."

"Boordling was educated. He was an engineer for some electrical company once, wasn't he?"

Up the road, higher on the hill, there was a struggle and a low outcry.

Jones! They had caught Jones up there.

The bronze man was on his feet instantly. He gripped the young woman's arm and spoke to her with imperative haste.

"I'm not Jones!" he said. "They've caught Jones up there. They were lying in wait for him. They've got him. They're going to kill him. We've got to stop it. Now don't ask questions, and come with me."

He didn't really expect her to comply, but he was pleased when she did.

"All right," she said.

The bronze man left the road and headed for the sounds he had heard. The road mounted the hill in sweeping curves, and he was cutting across, saving time.

"Who are you?" the woman whispered.

"Quiet!" he said.

The going was fairly open. There was some buck-brush, a few redoaks, but mostly there was thick grass, sopping wet with dew. Such rock as there was was sandstone, and not very noisy when they stepped on it.

He heard sounds again. He gripped the girl's shoulder, pulling her to a stop, then down, whispering, "They're coming this way."

They crouched there, and soon the four men—Pack, Dave, Joe, Guernsey—came stumbling past, dragging a fifth limp figure.

"I think he's dead," Dave said. "Pack, I think you smashed his skull."

"Oh, put him down. He's just knocked out," Pack said. "Lay him down. This is as good a place as any to work on him."

They let Jones drop loosely on the sod. Then they waited. They were breathing heavily. Pack struck a match and lit a cigarette, then said, "You might as well smoke if you want to. It'll be a minute."

How frightened they were, and how dependent on Pack, was pitifully shown by the way all of them immediately lit cigarettes. Pack must have realized this, because he laughed.

Pack was the manager, the dominant force, as he said, "You did pretty good, Dave. I was worried about the way you were acting earlier."

"I'll make it," Dave said.

Suddenly there was a rushing, a scuffle, blows, grunts, a yell choked off. All was confusion for a moment. Then strained silence fell.

"Damn him!" Joe said. "He woke up and played possum and tried to get away."

"I told you he wasn't bad hurt," Pack said. Pack stood over Jones. "Jones, we'll kill you next time. You lay still and listen and answer questions, understand."

Jones had a good voice. It still had melody and roundness in spite of the strain and terror in the man.

"Who—who are you?" he asked. "Say, are you Pack? You sound like Pack."

"It's Pack," Pack said.

"Whew! Gee whizz! I thought a bunch of hijackers had waylaid me. Let me up, fellows."

Pack laughed, briefly and explosively. "Let him up, he says. Hear that? He thinks we're playing. Like hell he does."

Jones was silent for a moment. When he spoke, the little relief that had come into his voice was gone.

"What're you pulling on me?" he demanded uneasily.

"It's a case of *you* pulling something on *us*," Pack said. "Isn't it?"

Jones didn't answer.

Pack said, "Where were you going just now? Up to the Morgan house on the hill, weren't you?"

"Of course," Jones said. "What's wrong—"

"You're feeling pretty sassy," Pack told him.

"Naturally, I resent—"

Pack, using a conversational tone, said, "Some guys never learn."

There was a gasp, a moan, the moan more of mental than of physical agony. It was Jones, and after he moaned, he made various whimpering sounds of complete terror.

Pack said quietly, "Next time I'll put the knife in your guts and I don't mean maybe. Now I want straight talk out of you and no lip."

In the darkness where they were crouched, listening, the girl Nola Morgan put her lips close to the bronze man's ear and whispered sickly, "They must have stabbed him."

The bronze man said, "Sh-h-h," softly. There was nothing they could do about it now. The stupid thing he had done was to wait until something like this happened. As much as he had dealt with men whose emotions were made erratic by excitement, he should have known Pack might suddenly wound or kill Jones.

Pack was saying, "You were going up that hill to talk to Nola Morgan."

"I—I made a date with her," Jones said hoarsely. "She is a very attractive girl, and I am very fond—"

Pack snorted. "You never met her in your life. You've seen her, probably. But never met her. We could tell that from the way you talked to her over the telephone."

"You—telephone—?" Jones' voice had suddenly become as hollow as a voice could become.

Pack said, "We put a tap on your telephone line,

brother. We've had a tap on it ever since we found out Carl Boordling unburdened himself to you when he was tight."

"Oh!" Jones sounded sick. "You heard me trying to sell the information to Miss Morgan?"

"That's exactly what we heard. We were a little surprised at you, Jonesy. You're supposed to be a sanctimonious so-and-so, and it kind of upset us to hear you talking money to the Morgan girl the way you were talking it."

Jones thought about it, evidently, for a while.

"Look, I'll drop the whole thing," he offered.

"Now you're talking our language," Pack told him. "Except for one thing: The story has already gotten around."

"It couldn't!" Jones gasped. "I haven't told anybody."

Pack grunted. He was pleased. There had been a kind of absolute truth in Jones' statement, a finality. He hadn't told anyone. A man as scared as Jones simply could not have gotten that much truth-sound into a lie.

"That's all, brother," Pack said. He had the knife.

III.

The bronze man ran, then dived for Pack. He hadn't seen Pack's knife yet, could not even see in the murk what Pack was doing. But he knew enough from the man's tone.

He came down on Pack from the side, hitting the man, driving him down into the grass. He hit Pack on the side of the neck, partly on the jaw, and grasped Pack's knife arm and twisted it. He twisted to break the arm rather than get the knife, felt the padded snap as the bones, first the radius and then the ulna, broke. Pack screamed, as any man would scream, with the full rush of his lungs and his vocal cords making nothing but noise.

The bronze man clutched at Jones. Jones was moving. Jones was very scared. They hadn't tied him, and he wanted to get away from there.

Jones fought madly when he was seized.

"Stop it!" the bronze man said. "I'm helping you."

Jones kept fighting. He fought now, more than he had before. The bronze man ran with him. Jones tried to trip him. The bronze man slugged Jones, using a short punch with his right hand.

The blow hit Jones on the throat, and for the next five minutes, Jones made a continuous series of gagging noises as he tried to get his paralyzed neck muscles to function.

A gun exploded, making a winking of reddish light and the thunderous amount of noise that a first shot from a gun always seems to make.

The bronze man shouted, "Close in! Get them! Arrest them!"

His voice had remarkable power. It was a trained voice, and he gave it all the volume he conveniently could, hoping to frighten the four men.

The yell might have had some effect. It was hard to tell. Certainly it didn't stop the shooting. There was more of that, a loud banging of guns and noise of bullets knocking about in the trees.

The bronze man reached the girl, "Run," he said.

"I know these woods," she said, in a much quieter voice than he expected. "This way."

She led the route. She was fast for a girl, and because she seemed to know exactly where she was putting her feet with each step, she gave him a run for a quarter of a mile.

A few bullets followed them. Pack and his men could hear them, of course. But the trees were thick, the rocks big, and it was dark.

She was leading the route downhill.

"Don't you live on top of the hill?" the bronze man demanded.

"Yes. But that's exactly the way they'll expect us to go," she said. "They might head us off."

"They didn't know you were along," he said.

She stopped. "They didn't, did they? That makes me feel foolish."

"Better keep going."

"Where are we going?"

"I have a trailer about a mile from here. That will do."

The bronze man had obtained the trailer his first day here. There had been difficulty about getting a house-trailer, because of the war-time scarcity. But he had insisted on the trailer, because it was the most inconspicuous way of living on this pipeline construction job. Most of the workmen lived in house-trailers. He had insisted, and he had gotten the trailer, but he was startled when it arrived. It was strictly a de luxe job, something that belonged in a Palm Beach trailer park instead of a rough and tough pipeline job. He had a suspicion that it might be making him noticeable.

Nola Morgan looked around the trailer and was impressed enough to say, "It's nice."

So was she, the bronze man thought. He hadn't been expecting anyone like her. She was tall and smooth and golden. She had a flashing vitality, an aliveness, and no makeup. She wore slacks and a waist and a field jacket and a large handkerchief over her hair.

When he realized he was staring, he stopped it. He put Jones on the bed.

Jones was a round, fat, jolly-looking man. He looked like a cherub, a salesman in a bakery, a little fat Santa Claus in a department store. His pockets held a total of fourteen wooden pencils differing in color, size and length, a billfold containing twelve one-dollar bills; a draft card classification 1-A (H), a Bible, several religious tracts, and sales tax mill-tokens from Missouri and Kansas.

"Not very illuminating," the bronze man said.

Nola Morgan had watched his searching of Jones. "Do you have a legal right to do that?" she demanded.

Her sharpness irritated him. "Is that important?" he

said. He knew she did not trust him. It followed that she would not talk freely.

Jones was conscious. The last sound he had made had been the gagging and hacking as he tried to relieve his throat from the paralyzing effects of the blow with which the bronze man had silenced him during the rescue on the hill. He had not spoken since.

"Jones," the bronze man said.

Jones stared at him. He stared fixedly, strangely. He did not speak.

"Want to talk to us about a misericord?" the bronze man asked.

Jones cleared his throat. "I think I know who you are."

"Could be."

"Yes, sir, there is not a bit of doubt in my mind about who you are. I've seen pictures of you. I've heard of you, too."

"Want to talk freely?"

"No! No, I don't!" Jones closed his eyes for a moment, then shuddered. "The fact that you are here—a man of your consequence here, investigating, incognito—proves to me that this affair is a great deal more vast than I imagined. I do not want anything more to do with an affair of such enormity." He looked steadily at the bronze man. "I haven't another word to say."

"You're in pretty deep to back out."

Jones nodded slightly. He shrugged. The gestures meant he'd made up his mind.

There was tape in the first-aid kit in the galley locker. The bronze man tore strips and sealed Jones' mouth, after making sure there was no impediment in his nasal passages which would keep him from breathing. He tied Jones with the clothesline, hand and foot.

Then he gestured to the girl that she was to go outside with him. She was puzzled, but she followed.

The darkness was still, musky. The heat lightning jumped with more liveliness in the distance. The night had settled down to a calm. The noises of the actual construction near the river were far away and peaceful.

"Why did you do that—tie him and leave him in there?" the girl demanded.

"They may follow us here. If they do, we had better be outside."

"You think they will?" she asked, suddenly uneasy.

"Let's make sure."

"What did he mean—he recognized you?"

"He was possibly mistaken."

"Oh, no, he wasn't!" she said sharply. "He recognized you. He said he'd seen your picture and heard of you. Who are you?"

"That doesn't matter," he said.

"Who are you?" she asked sharply.

He stood in the murk frowning and wishing he knew more about handling women. They mystified him as a class and invariably baffled him as individuals.

He had no intention of telling her who he was. He had taken infinite pains to conceal his identity.

He had even changed his personal appearance. His hair was different; this dull black was not its normal color. The muddy brown of his eyes was not normal, either. The change in eye-tint he had managed with plastic contact lenses which fitted directly against the eye. These were tinted. He had managed a stoop to look less tall and a slouching walk that was also a help. His skin was unchanged, because its natural deep bronze was too hard to change with dye. There was no skin dye that would stand up dependably under weather, wear, strong soaps and the gasoline or tetrachloride which pipeline workers used to get grease off their hands. It had been his intention to get a job in one of the pipe-line crews.

He said, "We have some time to talk now. Suppose you tell me a few things."

"I asked who you are," she said sharply. "Aren't you going to answer that?"

"No."

"Don't expect anything out of me, then," she said.

He said patiently, "If I knew more about you, who you are and what is your connection with the affair, I might feel free to tell you a great deal you do not know."

"I'm not tempted," she said. But she was intrigued

by the idea that he might tell her much that she did not know. He could sense her interest. He knew also that she was trying to hide her interest, and this made him angry. He was playing games himself—but that didn't keep him from getting impatient.

He demanded, "What were you doing on that road tonight?"

Startled, she answered, "I wanted to make sure Jones came alone to talk to me. I hid at the foot of the hill road, where the road turns off the highway, to watch him go past. He went past alone. I waited long enough for him to get well ahead, then headed for the house to meet him. That was when you caught me."

"Why was it important he come alone?"

"I was scared," she said. "And if you think I am going to keep on talking to you without knowing who you—"

He gripped her shoulder, said hastily, imperatively, "Get down! Somebody's here!" He had heard a small sound from the darkness nearby.

"Who is it?" She sounded frightened.

"Wait here," he whispered. "Keep down flat."

The bronze man crawled, a few inches at a time, in the direction of whatever it was he had heard. He came to a small ravine. He lay there, waiting, knowing he must be close to whoever had made the noise. As for the sound, he had decided it had been a man who had tried to sneeze and who had almost stifled it.

He was right. Close at hand, a man said in a low cautious voice, "God bless it, I'm going to have to sneeze again!"

"Rub your upper lip like the devil," someone whispered. "That might help."

After a while, the other said, "I think it's going to help."

"It's these dang weeds growing around here, probably. I don't see the sense of waiting here in this ditch, anyhow. How much longer we gonna do this?"

"Until something happens, I guess."

"Suppose nothing does?"

"In that case, the sheriff said to walk in and ask questions of whoever we found."

"We're going to sound silly as hell, asking questions without knowing what to ask about."

"You said it."

"Did you hear this telephone call the sheriff got?"

"No, he took it himself. The sheriff doesn't excite easy, and this got him stirred up, so there must be something to it."

"Man or woman on the phone?"

"That was a funny part of it. It was either a woman trying to sound like a man, or a man trying to sound like a woman, the sheriff said. He wasn't sure which."

"Queer business."

"Uh-huh. This party on the phone said there was going to be a murder around that trailer tonight, and to watch it. It was queer, all right."

They lapsed into silence. In the distance, far away where they were beginning to put the pipeline across the river, men began beating a pipe with sledges. They beat the pipe with a regular mechanical cadence.

One of the men in the ditch complained, "I wish they'd get that damned pipeline built through here. There's been more stinking trouble since construction started."

"It sure sitrred up the Colbecks and the Morgans."

"When old Erasmus Morgan was murdered, it stirred up a hornet's nest, all right."

"You think Bill Colbeck killed Erasmus Morgan?"

"I doubt it. He had an alibi."

"I know. But sometimes I wonder."

"Listen, Colbeck isn't enough of a damned fool to kill a Morgan and open that old feud. Colbeck Construction Company is building this line, and it's going to go broke if this trouble keeps up."

"It won't go broke as long as Art Strain is around to throw more money into the concern."

The other deputy—the pair were obviously sheriff's deputies—chuckled. "That's quite a state of affairs. The general manager of a company furnishing money to keep it going."

"Well, it's no skin off my nose, and all I wish is that

the danged pipeline was built. I hear the army and navy needs the oil this line will take to the east coast. I hear it's what held up the invasion."

There came from the trailer a noise that was neither scream nor words, but a little of each, with a gurgling overtone of death. Mostly it was a nasal noise, something a man would make through his nostrils alone, if his mouth was sealed. There was a complete, utter finality about the noise, a finished horror, an ending. The man who made that noise had died and you knew it.

The men from the sheriff's office piled out of the ditch, all but trampling the bronze man. The pair raced to the trailer, burst inside with flashlights in their hands. They cast the flashlight beams around.

"Oh, mother!" One of the deputies said suddenly, and he came to the trailer door and was sick at his stomach.

The other deputy said, "It's that little fat guy named Jones. One of the pipeliners." He whistled in wonder. "My God, they sure cut his throat from here to there."

IV.

The bronze man listened for some sign from Nola Morgan, but none came. He watched the deputies throw their flashlight beams around suspiciously, saw the light hit the exact spot where he had left the girl. She wasn't there. She had gone, either of her own accord or under force.

One deputy started to dash off into the darkness. The other shouted, "Where you going, Sam?" Sam said he was going to catch the blankety-blank that used the knife.

The other deputy said, "You'll get an intestine shot

out, too. Come back here, you fool. Let's use the telephone in here and call for help."

"Is there a telephone in the trailer?"

"Sure."

Sam came back and stood in the trailer door. He did not go inside, but stood in the door. After he had looked inside, he was sick again. He swore at his nausea.

"That knife on the floor; that's the one, ain't it?" he asked.

"Sure. It matches the other cutlery."

The bronze man stiffened. The trailer, which was far more ornate than he had wanted, was equipped with silverware and cutlery in matching chrome and plastic. He had used the knives in cooking. His fingerprints would be on them.

Uneasiness began to crawl through his nerves. The men from the sheriff's office had been drawn here by an anonymous telephone call. They had been promised a murder. The murder had eventuated. Jones was dead, and the bronze man's knife had been used. There was reason to be scared.

The sheriff's man in the trailer was saying over the telephone, "Sure, sure, of course he was killed by whoever was living in the trailer. The guy who lives here came home a while ago and unlocked the place and went in. There was somebody with him, probably this Jones who got his throat cut."

He paused to get a question from the other end of the wire.

"He's a big guy, if I remember," he said. "Kind of a deeply tanned skin. Seems to have been around a lot, but not doing much of anything."

The bronze man eased away. The neighborhood was no place for him to be caught.

What had happened to Nola Morgan he did not know. He did not think it was anything violent. And his conviction was that she was not in the neighborhood.

He went to the highway, reasoning that an alarm had not yet been broadcast, and began to run. He ran half a mile without slackening speed, and turned in at a private residence.

He had a car in the garage which he had rented at the private home. He had driven the car not at all since arriving in the vicinity, and he did not believe that anyone would connect the machine with him.

He drove west on the highway, then north about ten miles to a town of about six thousand. It was an old-fashioned town, a river town. He had looked the place over previously. It still had the old-fashioned brick pavement on the river bank with the big bollards and great rusting iron rings where the steamboats once tied up. Now it slept in the night.

The oldest hotel was still the best. A great old brick thing with a certain majesty in its dull red turrets and old-fashioned bric-a-brac.

He entered by a side door, waited in the shadows until the elevator operator and the night clerk had their attention on a pinball machine, and went upstairs.

He had a room which he'd gotten his first day in Arkansas. He let himself in, closed the door and went to the telephone.

He called Bill Colbeck and Arthur Strain and told them to come to his room immediately.

Bill Colbeck was a big man with a square, honest-John face. He had big bones and big muscles and an open-eyed look and a contagious grin and a big infectious donkey laugh. He made you think of cactus and sagebrush, drilling tools and wildcat oil wells.

He looked at the bronze man and said, "Who the devil are you? I don't know you."

"Come in and sit down," the bronze man said.

Bill Colbeck came in and sat with a leg cocked over the arm of a chair. He examined the bronze man curiously. "You're big enough," he said. "The more a man looks at you, the bigger you get."

"You own Colbeck Construction Company?" the bronze man said.

"That's the rumor."

"Is it a stock company? Are there other stock-holders?"

"Colbeck Construction is me," Colbeck said. "My money and my blood and my tears, more of the last than anything."

Arthur Strain arrived. He was as much a man for the luxury of the city as Colbeck was a man for the hardbitten open places. His clothes were soft, his gestures were polished, his voice cultured.

"You telephoned me rather imperatively, I believe," he said.

"Come in," said the bronze man.

Bill Colbeck exclaimed, "So he got you out of bed too, Art! What goes on?"

"I have no idea."

Colbeck nodded at the bronze man. "Did you ever see a bigger guy? I mean a bigger guy who didn't pack any fat?"

Arthur Strain smiled. He was a man whose manners did not permit him to comment on the appearance of another, unless in a complimentary tone. And he wasn't a man who would use compliments, except to his friends or for business reasons.

"Would you like to get along with whatever is on your mind?" Strain asked the bronze man. "After all, it's two o'clock in the morning, and we have a pipeline to build."

Colbeck slapped a knee. "Sure, get going. I don't climb out of bed past midnight for everybody." He sounded somewhat angry, as if he was wondering just what had persuaded him to get up anyway.

"Jones was murdered tonight," the bronze man said.

He dropped the remark casually, then watched their faces. He saw no emotions that should not normally have been shown, which could mean nothing, of course.

Anyway, he had their interest.

He said, "A large, modern pipeline is being constructed from the Mid-continent oil fields to the Atlantic Coast. The project is too enormous for a private concern, so the government is handling it. A number of different contracting firms received contracts to construct in total the various sections of the line. The

Arkansas and southern Missouri section was awarded the Colbeck Construction Company, which you gentlemen represent in the capacity of owner and executive general manager."

Bill Colbeck, who owned the company, showed his teeth slightly in something that wasn't quite a grin. "What's the childish word-picture of the situation for?" he demanded.

"That isn't all the picture," the bronze man said. "The rest of it is this: The Colbeck Construction Company isn't delivering on its contracts. It is falling down. It is—"

"Damn you, don't tell me I'm falling down!" Bill Colbeck said. His face had suddenly darkened with rage.

"—is in the unenviable position of having failed to meet three of its forfeit dates on the contract," the bronze man continued. "When the contract was let to Colbeck Construction for its share of the pipeline, it agreed to complete certain sections by certain dates, or forfeit penalty sums. Three times such penalties have been paid. As a matter of fact, none of the contracted sections have been finished on time."

Bill Colbeck was livid with wrath. This contract penalty forfeiture was obviously a tender subject with him.

"What the hell business is it of yours?" he yelled. "If we never get done, it's no skin off your nose!"

"Bill!" admonished Arthur Strain. "Take it easy."

"Easy, hell!" Colbeck shouted. "Who is this damned guy to come in here and call us out of bed in the middle of the night? What kind of fools are we to come down here and listen to his gas?"

"Bill, Bill!" Arthur Strain said sharply. "You sound like a fool!"

Bill Colbeck whirled on him and bellowed, "Who are you calling a fool? By God, general manager or not, someday I'm going to fire you off the job!"

Arthur Strain's mouth tightened downward at the corners, remained so for a moment. Then he smiled, and said, "Oh, keep your shirt on, Bill. If you could see the way you look, you'd laugh."

Colbeck grunted. He did not apologize to Strain with

words, but his manner conveyed that he was sorry for his loudness and his near threats, and that he didn't really mean it.

"Who are you?" Colbeck demanded of the bronze man.

"This pipeline," the bronze man said, "happens to be very important just now. The amount of fuel oil, aviation gasoline, plain gasoline, and other fuel this line will carry to the Atlantic Coast is controlling the progress of the war."

Strain frowned at the bronze man. "Who are you? If this stuff you are telling us is straight, you must be somebody important."

"That comes next," the bronze man admitted.

He went to the window and pulled down the old-fashioned roller shade, pulled it down as far as it would go. At first, there seemed to be nothing rolled up in the shade. But he reached up behind the shade, and carefully pulled off an envelope of thin paper. The envelope had been colored carefully with ordinary crayon so that it was about the tint of the ancient shade—when the shade was pulled down, the envelope was not on the inside, but the outside, and it would take a sharp eye to discover it in the moment it whisked into view over the back side of the shade.

He handed the envelope to Bill Colbeck, who looked at the single sheet of onionskin inside.

"I'll be damned!" Colbeck blurted. He looked at Strain. "Art, we seem to rate important attention."

"Who is he?" Strain demanded.

"Ever hear of Doc Savage?"

For a moment, Arthur Strain's face was very blank. Then he stood up quickly and put out a hand to the bronze man.

"This makes me feel somewhat foolish, Mr. Savage," he said. "I'm glad to meet you."

Bill Colbeck stared at the bronze man. "I suppose the War Department sent you down here?"

"That's right," Doc Savage agreed.

"What the hell for?"

"To see why you aren't completing your part of the

pipeline on time," the bronze man said briefly. "And to see that progress improves."

Colbeck scowled. "Simple as that, eh?"

Colbeck was sullen and angry. He had been talking crudely, but he wasn't a crude man. He was just taking pains to be somewhat insulting.

Doc Savage said, "Suppose you tell me how simple it is. Let's have your story."

"Giving me orders now?" Colbeck asked sharply.

The bronze man gestured at the document. "Take another look at that. Next to the last paragraph."

Colbeck said, "What the hell do I care what Washington writes on a piece of paper." But he examined the document again. Apparently he had missed the indicated paragraph. Rereading it again, and understanding it, he looked sick.

"What's the matter, Bill?" Arthur Strain demanded.

"According to this, this Doc Savage can do just about what he wants to with this job—shut it down entirely, if he wishes."

"Naturally," Strain said.

"What do you mean, naturally?"

"No man of the caliber of Mr. Savage is going to appear on a job without authority. Bill, I'm afraid you're not awake to just who Mr. Savage is."

Colbeck said uneasily, "Oh, I've heard of a Doc Savage vaguely, as a kind of international figure who has been mixed up in some kind of excitement a time or two."

Strain laughed. "That sounds a bit like the little boy who looked at the elephant and said, "Oh look, momma, a mouse.""

Doc Savage asked, "Are you gentlemen willing to give me a summary of the situation here?"

Colbeck hesitated. Strain looked at Colbeck and waited, and then said, "Better tell him everything you know, Bill. You'll be glad of it later."

Colbeck must have already made up his mind to speak freely, because he suddenly began disclosing information. After the first few words, he spoke in an easier voice.

"To understand the background of this trouble," he said, "forget the war. Forget that this pipeline we're building is more vital to the war, and the future of America, right now than fifty battleships or a few thousand airplanes. Forget all that. Think of me as Bill Colbeck, a lad who came from a long line of Colbecks who have lived in this part of Arkansas since the days of Arkansas Post, the first settlement in Arkansas, long before the Louisiana Purchase. I'm Bill Colbeck, and I'm building a pipeline through Morgan country."

"What has a Colbeck building a pipeline through Morgan country got to do with it?" Doc asked.

"That takes a little explanation," Colbeck said. "Sit back and listen."

Colbeck had a good deal of family pride, although he didn't look or talk like a man who would have. A confident, solid emphasis came into his tone when he spoke of his ancestors and their doings.

The Colbecks had come to Arkansas from England via Virginia, Kentucky and points between. Old great-great-Grandfather Hoit Colbeck had been assistant to the Territorial Governor when it belonged to the Missouri Territory, and had formed some of its earlier county organizations. He had also made an enemy of the first Morgan.

"The Morgans came in here from New England in 1815," Colbeck said sourly. "They were snobs, but they were capable and they were aristocrats. Old Hoit Colbeck bought a slave from the Morgans and it turned out the slave had the plague and the Morgans knew it, or Hoit thought they did. Anyway, Andrew Alstar Morgan and Hoit Colbeck had words, and Hoit shot and killed Andrew Alstar Morgan. A Morgan took up the quarrel by shooting at Hoit Colbeck and a Colbeck killed that Morgan. Then Morgans killed some Colbecks. It got worse and worse, and it got passed down from one generation to another. Colbeck kids were brought up to hate Morgans, and Morgan kids were brought up to hate Colbecks.

"In the Civil War, Colbecks fought on the North and Morgans on the South. And in 1868, in that fuss over whether Isaac Murphy was governor or not, Colbecks and Morgans were pitted against each other. The Colbecks were Republicans and the Morgans were rebels. It went on like that through the so-called gay nineties, and the World War and the boom and the depression. The Colbecks were New Dealers and the Morgans were old-line individualists, and they hated each other's guts and said so. Now and then, all through those years, a Colbeck or a Morgan would get killed by the other side."

Colbeck stopped for a moment, staring at Doc Savage.

"Don't get the idea this is one of those mountaineer feuds," he said.

Arthur Strain said dryly, "Anyway, the participants do not necessarily live in the mountains."

That angered Colbeck. He shouted, "It's no hillbilly Hatfield-McCoy feud!"

Strain shrugged. "Skip it."

Colbeck shoved out his jaw as if he wanted to say more, decided to drop the point, and wheeled back to Doc Savage.

"Take this pipeline contract. It goes through Morgan country. Through Morgan plantations. Through counties which have Morgan sheriffs and towns with Morgan mayors. Through Morgan farms and Morgan hills. Morgans to the right and to the left of you." He scowled at the bronze man. "And that's not intended to be funny."

"Take it easy, Bill," Art Strain said.

Bill Colbeck sat on the edge of the bed. He stared soberly at the floor, and for a moment, when his belligerent attitude was relaxed, he seemed scared and tired. The change was brief, but it was a collapse; the tough go-getter sank for a moment, leaving a terrified, helpless man. But Colbeck immediately gripped his emotions and jammed them back into hiding.

He said, "The grandest Morgan of them all was old Erasmus Morgan. He was a great guy. Santa Claus had nothing on him. And I'm not kidding.

"Erasmus Morgan was the head Morgan, the president of the company, the shepherd of the flock, the first goose in the flight. He was their book of wisdom, and their example. And again let me say I'm not kidding, because old Erasmus Morgan was swell. I'm not being sarcastic. Erasmus Morgan was the leading citizen of Arkansas, for my money—for my money, the leading member of the human race."

Arthur Strain said quietly, "Maybe you're laying it on a little thick, Bill. Old Morgan was okay. But he wasn't Jehovah and the seven angels."

"He was for my money," Colbeck said grimly.

For a moment, the terror crawled across Colbeck's face again.

"He was murdered," Colbeck said. "And it looked for a while like it was going to get proved that I did it."

V.

Outside in the street, a car passed. It was the first automobile that had gone by since they had been in the room, and it traveled rapidly.

Bill Colbeck had his face in his hands. He seemed to have run out of words.

Arthur Strain, speaking gently, began explaining about the death of Erasmus Morgan. Old Morgan had gone one night to a meeting of land-owners through whose property the pipeline was being constructed.

The meeting that night had been Erasmus Morgan's idea, and typical of his benevolence. It had been a get-together to compare notes, to insure that all the land-owners were getting an equal and fair damage payment. Pipelines had been known to pay one farmer fifty cents a rod damage and pay his neighbor twenty dollars a rod, and the land the same.

Colbeck Construction Company had been discussed

and cussed at this meeting. It would have been at any meeting of Morgan majority. There had been no Morgan-Colbeck violence for a few years, but legends and talk last longer than a few years, so there had been some uncomplimentary talk about Colbecks.

Erasmus Morgan left the meeting in his car. He was very old, but he drove the car himself. He was found shot, in his charred car. The car had been run off the road, down an embankment, and apparently set afire. The fire had not consumed much, having died after the gasoline in the fuel tank was exhausted.

The bullet had been taken from Erasmus Morgan's body, and compared with the barrel flaws in a gun found nearby. This gun had fired the bullet. The gun belonged to Bill Colbeck.

Some of Bill Colbeck's fingerprints had been found on Erasmus Morgan's car.

Bill Colbeck looked up at this point in Strain's story.

"I didn't do it!" he growled. "It was the most beautiful frame you ever saw!"

"Bill was with me at the time the murder had to have been committed," Arthur Strain said. "He was also with the governor of the state, the attorney-general, and some other big-wigs. We were at a dinner, and there was a poker game afterward. So Bill had an alibi. God help him if he hadn't."

Bill Colbeck had taken to frowning at the floor again. His face was twisted, fierce, and afraid.

"You can imagine what happened to the Colbeck-Morgan feeling after that," he said. "Right then, this pipeline started having trouble."

Doc asked, "You blame your delays on this feud?"

"Sure."

"Bill is a Colbeck," Strain said. "And Colbeck Construction Company means Colbeck to all the Morgans. They're not unpatriotic, and they're not ignorant. They are just hell-bent on paying-off somebody for old Erasmus Morgan's death."

"Have you any direct evidence Morgans are causing the delays."

"Plenty."

"Specific examples?"

"By the bushel. They sit around in the beer places and the honky-tonks and laugh about it and tell what they're going to do to Colbeck Construction. We've had Morgans drive cat tractors into the river and pile trucks against trees. We've tried to fire all the Morgans off the work gangs, but there must be some left."

Doc Savage was silent for a while. When he spoke, it was in pursuit of an entirely different subject.

"Who was Carl Boordling?" the bronze man demanded.

Bill Colbeck frowned, shook his head. But Arthur Strain showed surprise, then said, "If I'm right, I think he was a fellow who was picked up for killing a man in a beer joint brawl out on Taney road. He got a quick trial and sentence to the penitentiary, and died of some kind of poisoning, self-administered, shortly after they sent him to the pen."

"That all you know?"

"I don't even know that. I'm just pulling on my memory of what I read."

"Then you actually know of no conncection the man had with this affair?"

"No."

"What about the misericord?"

"The what?"

"Misericord."

"What the hell's a misericord?"

Doc Savage shifted to another question, demanding, "What connection did Smith have with it?"

He was not putting the inquiries so much with the expectation of getting important answers as with the idea that, if he touched something important, it would show on the faces of the men. He wasn't learning much.

Arthur Strain shook his head. But Bill Colbeck jumped up suddenly, saying, "Didn't you say somebody named Jones was killed?"

"Murdered."

"What about it?"

There were footsteps in the hallway, hurried ones.

They came directly to the door of the room, and a hand seized the knob and tried the locked door.

"Open up!" a harsh voice said.

"Who is it?" Doc asked quietly.

"Tom Scott Morgan. The Sheriff," the voice said. And a shoulder began hitting the door, making the panels crack and bulge.

Doc said, "It might be spectacular to break down the door, but there's not much object to it." He went over and unlocked the door.

Four men—a town policeman, a state policeman and two men from the Sheriff's office, was the way Doc indexed them—came crowding into the room with the belligerent manner of men who were frightened but determined not to show it. Nola Morgan followed them, looking grimly determined.

The sheriff, a lean man with a capable manner, examined Doc Savage briefly. He indicated Doc.

"This the one?" he asked Nola Morgan.

"Yes."

"You sure?"

Nola Morgan met Doc Savage's gaze for a moment. She made an obvious business of showing him she wasn't going to be bulldozed. But in the end she looked away uncomfortably.

"I'm sure he is the man I met on the hill road," she said.

"He carried Jones and put him in the trailer?" the sheriff demanded.

"Yes."

"And then he went outdoors with you?"

"He did. He said we should stand out in the darkness and listen for someone coming, although there hadn't been the slightest indication that anyone had followed us."

"Then what happened?"

"He pretended to hear a sound. He left me, saying someone was close and he was going to investigate. That was a trick. His plan was to get away from me, sneak around to the back of the trailer, reach in through the window and stab Jones to death. That is what he did."

The sheriff turned to Doc Savage. He was a wheaty looking man with blue eyes and very even, very solid-looking white teeth. A substantial and determined man, horrified at murder, but grimly pleased to be able to make a logical arrest so early.

"You own that trailer?" he asked.

"I have been living in it," Doc said.

"All right. That's enough. The Prosecuting Attorney can ask you questions." The sheriff indicated himself, continuing, "You probably don't know me, but I'm T.S. Morgan, county sheriff. You're under arrest. The charge is suspicion of having murdered a man named Jones."

The county jail and the sheriff's living quarters were together in a two-story red brick building on Flatland Street near the riverfront. The county was not populous, and the run of captured criminals far from high grade, so the jail was the smallest and nastiest looking building in the neighborhood, a position it maintained by a narrow margin, since it was located in a section of warehouses.

The business of clapping Doc Savage into the ancient, but efficient calaboose was done with speed.

The sun was just coming up at the time. Sunlight, as a matter of fact, was slanting into the windows of a rat-nest rooming house across the street, and making the dirty panes somewhat less than transparent.

The man called Pack had been sitting on a straight hard chair in front of the window for hours, and his patience was low. He cursed the blinding sun bitterly. "I wait here all night, and then the damned sun gets in my eyes!" was his text.

Guernsey, the man who was not a conversationalist, said, "It was him."

"You sure it was Savage?"

"Yep." Guernsey was at the other window.

"Handcuffed?"

"Yep. State troopers had their guns out, too."

Pack leaned back in the chair, closing his eyes tightly and holding them shut while he slowly got out a cigarette and put it between his lips. "That's better," he said. He opened his eyes and lit the cigarette. "Come on, Guernsey."

They left the rooming house by the side door, sauntered two blocks north and one east, and climbed into a car they had left there. Pack drove.

"I sweat a quart of blood," Pack growled. "I don't like these damned elaborate schemes."

"They're wonderful if they work," Guernsey said briefly.

"Yeah, like a watch. And what happens to a watch if one wheel falls out. Just one little cog off a wheel will jim the works."

"No wheels fell out."

Pack glanced at Guernsey. Of all the men working in this tense and almost continuously nerve-wracking affair, Guernsey was the one Pack respected the most. Guernsey rarely had much to say when he was in a crowd, but what he did say was sensible, and Pack had noticed that men would listen to Guernsey and accept his sense.

Guernsey would talk when alone with another man. Not excessively, but enough to make him a pleasant companion. Guernsey was a coldly calculating crook under his taciturn exterior, Pack was convinced.

Pack had plans for Guernsey. After this present frightening affair was concluded, and if they emerged with their lives, Pack intended to persuade Guernsey to work with him. They would make a good pair.

Pack chewed the cud of his plans for the future as he drove along. His ideas for the future did not include anything on the scale of this present thing. Pack felt this was to be the biggest thing in his career. He had no regrets. There was too much apprehension, agony, shock and devilish plot-counterplot involved here. Too many chances of dying violently.

"Going to be a nice day," Guernsey volunteered quietly.

"Looks like it might be," Pack agreed. A great guy, this Guernsey, he thought.

They met Joe outside a ramshackle cabin on the bluffs north of the river, about two miles from the spot where Colbeck Construction was trying to put the big pipeline across the sullen river. Joe was stalking a rooster with a long club.

Joe said, "We'll have chicken for breakfast if I can get that doggone rooster."

Pack wasn't interested in breakfast. He asked, "How's Dave?"

"Dave? Still asleep, I guess."

"Is he over his jitters yet?"

Joe looked uncomfortable. "Oh, Dave will be all right. Don't worry about it."

Pack reached out suddenly and grabbed Joe's coat front. He yanked Joe close by the fistful of cloth. "Listen!" he said harshly. "I didn't like the way Dave got the shakes last night. I don't like the idea of a man who might go limber on us. Now listen to this! If Dave goes sour on us, I'm going to hold you personally responsible!"

Joe had seized the other man's hand which was entangled with his coat, but on second thought he had not tried to free himself. He was afraid of Pack when the man was aroused.

"Dave is all right," Joe repeated.

Pack released him. "Remember what I said."

They went into the shack. It was a hovel. They had rented it from a shiftless white man who had the respect of neither the whites nor the Negroes in the neighborhood, and the place still had the same furniture and the same filth.

Pack shook Dave awake, and Dave sat up on the edge of the cot. Dave was groggy. He kept yawning and rubbing his face. Pack picked up a bottle half filled with small white capsules which stood on the floor beside the coat. It was barbital.

"At least, that stuff is better than whisky." Pack tossed the bottle on the cot. "Could you use a drink, Dave?"

"Not me. Beer is my speed," Dave said.

Pack nodded. "That's good. Stick to beer today."

He gave them their orders for the day.

* * *

The duties assigned Dave were typical for the day. He had a certain section of highway, and the west end of the town, for his territory.

The midnight-eight shift was just coming off duty. The pipeline construction was proceeding in three shifts, the clock around, because of the urgency of the job. The more dependable midnight-eighters had gone home to sleep as soon as their duty tour ended. Dave wasn't interested in those. The type of men he wanted were the ones who floated into the joints for a drink of three point two, or harder stuff. The morning-drinkers. The loud-mouths.

Dave had his routine fairly clear in his mind.

First, he struck up an acquaintance with five men in a booth.

"They've got the guy who killed old Erasmus Morgan in jail, but I hear they're going to turn him loose," he said.

There were Morgan men in the booth. They stared at him. One said, "So they finally hung it on Bill Colbeck, eh?"

Dave shook his head. "Not Bill Colbeck. Not directly, anyhow. The guy was working for Colbeck. He did the job for Colbeck. They arrested him in the hotel with Bill Colbeck about three or four o'clock this morning."

Without a word, a Morgan man got up and went to the telephone. He talked over the phone a while, then came back. "They arrested a guy for killing Preach Jones," he said. "Arrested him in Colbeck's hotel."

Dave said, "Yeah. The guy tried to kill Nola Morgan earlier in the night. She got away from him. He killed Preach Jones for interfering with his attempt on Nola Morgan's life. Nola Morgan got the sheriff, and they went to Colbeck's hotel and arrested the guy before he could get money enough from Colbeck to skip the country."

He let that soak in for a while.

"They'll turn the guy loose," he said bitterly. "I don't see why the hell there ain't some men with hair on their chests around here. Something oughta be done about that guy."

He left the booth, sure that the seed was planted.

He worked hard until mid-afternoon telling the same story in different places. By noon, three men had told the same story to him, with variations and exaggerations. By three o'clock, he had heard a score of muttered suggestions that a mob should do something about it.

Dave joined Pack, Joe and Guernsey at the filthy shack. Joe was a little tight.

Pack listened to them report.

"That's good," Pack said. "That's fine. We've got the ball rolling."

"They'll lynch the big bronze guy, whoever he is," Dave said.

"They won't get a chance," Pack said. "Get some sleep. I'll wake you."

At nine o'clock, it was very dark. Pack entered the shack quietly and awakened Joe, Dave and Guernsey. While they dressed, thunder whooped and gobbled in the distance.

Guernsey muttered, "Going to rain again."

It had been a very wet spring, which accounted for some of the trouble they were having getting the pipeline across the river.

Pack handed them rifles. One apiece. Short saddle guns.

He also gave each of them a cylindrical metal affair, the nature and functioning of which he explained carefully with: "These gadgets are silencers made out of automobile mufflers. You'll find the piece of gas pipe in each one will slip on the end of the rifle barrel. The rifle sights have been raised enough to be used over the silencers."

"They're clumsy as the dickens," Joe said.

"Sure, but they're the best we could do. You'll be shooting from a rest, with plenty of time to get set, anyway. They'll do the job."

They dismantled the rifles, and put them, with the remarkable homemade silencers, in suitcases. They took the suitcase to the pesthole of a room-house across the street from the jail.

Pack went to the window. Below him in the street, there were a number of men and a few women standing staring at the jail. There were small groups, no large crowd as yet, and no loud talk, no shouting.

There'll be no mob attack on that jail tonight, Pack reflected. They're not shouting, and mobs shout and mill and work themselves up into a frenzy.

Guernsey was beside Pack.

"I can see him," Guernsey said. "Second cell from the left."

Pack stared, but his own eyes were less able than Guernsey's and wouldn't let him be sure. He opened his suitcase, in which he had put a pair of binoculars, and used those.

"You're right," he told Guernsey.

Guernsey looked at their weapons. "I don't give a damn how good these silencers are, they're going to make some noise. We can't shoot."

Pack knew this was true. He gave orders to Dave and Joe.

"Go down in the street," he told Dave and Joe. "Start talking loud. Get together, and not too far from this window, and start yelling your heads off making speeches to the crowd."

Dave and Joe livened up considerably at this news that they were not to take part in the actual trigger-pulling.

Pack added, "Don't start your speech-making at the same time. One begin, then later the other. That'll be more natural."

Dave and Joe went out and downstairs. The next ten minutes was a dragging age in the room. Then they could hear Joe making his speech, yelling for violence against the man in the jail.

A second man started speech-making, and Pack laughed. "That's not Dave," he said. "Some other guy got the fever."

Guernsey nodded. He was watching the jail windows across the street. He could distinguish the figure of Doc Savage, or rather the silhouette of the figure, in one of the cells.

The bronze man moved in the cell, and Pack and

Guernsey saw that it was indeed he. They could distinguish his features, the bronze color of his skin, in the lighted cell.

They watched the bronze man move out of sight. Then, a moment later, the dark silhouette of him appeared in front of the window.

"Now is as good as any," Pack said.

Guernsey breathed, "Hold it a minute! My gun isn't set up quite right. I can't see the sights."

He fooled with the rifle, squinting, moving the piece. The dimness of the light in the hotel room—there was no actual light in the room other than what came in from the streetlights—made aiming at the bronze man difficult.

"Okay," Guernsey said.

Then the bronze man moved. His silhouette moved away from in front of the window, vanishing somewhere to the side of the cell.

Pack spoke fiercely, patiently.

"He'll be back at the window to see about the noise in the street," he said. "We can wait."

VI.

It was raining in New York City. Colonel John Renwick, the engineer, awakened with the glare of electric light in his eyes. He was befuddled with sleep, and his first reaction was shame at being caught asleep, so he said automatically, "I was sitting here thinking."

The man who had turned on the lights laughed. "The way you were snoring, it sounded like bombers flying through the office."

Renny Renwick had a long face that was perpetually sober. "Oh, hello, Monk."

Monk Mayfair closed the office door. He had his

pockets stuffed with the morning newspapers, all editions. He was a very short, very wide, and surprisingly homely man, but with a pleasant quality about his ugliness.

"Ham come down yet this morning?" Monk asked.

"No."

"You work all night in the office here?"

"Just about, I guess," Renny admitted.

"I'm glad I'm not an engineer," Monk told him pityingly. "It must be great, sitting up all night beating your brains together to find out how many pounds of steel it will take to build umpteen miles of special invasion railroad."

"Anyhow, I got that one job done," Renny said with relief.

The office—it was the reception room, actually—was large and modernistic except for the incongruous intrusion of an enormous and elaborately inlaid table of somewhat oriental design, and an oversized safe of a vintage forty years back. The room, impressive as it was, was the smallest of a suite of three rooms which comprised the entire eighty-sixth floor of the building. The other two rooms were the library and the laboratory. The place was Doc Savage's New York headquarters.

Monk hauled out a chair on the other side of the inlaid table, pushed aside a stack of Renny's blueprints, and spread out his morning papers. He began on the comic strips.

Renny, looking idly at Monk, had a thought which he frequently had, namely: Monk did not look as if he could possibly be one of the world's leading industrial chemists; he bore a much greater resemblance to an amiable ape which someone had shaved and dressed up in baggy clothes. But it was a mistake to underestimate Monk's brains.

Renny had worked with Monk Mayfair for a long time and he had learned that Monk could be depended upon in any situation which needed a man's character and courage.

Renny Renwick, with Monk Mayfair, Ham Brooks, Johnny Littlejohn, and Long Tom Roberts—there were five of them, all told—were the Doc Savage group. These five had worked with the bronze man over a long period of time.

I wonder, Renny reflected, how we ever came to get together. There is as much difference among us, really, as there is in a group of cats and dogs. We look different, we act different, we think differently, and no two of us have the bond of the same profession. The one thing we have in common is a thirst for excitement. And that's a childish thing for grown men to have in common, when you stop to think about it.

No, there was another thing in common. Their bond with Savage. It wasn't a hold which the bronze man had on them, but it was a tie hard to define. If I were to name the principal ingredient in the glue that holds us together, Renny thought, I'd say it was respect. Respect for each other's ability, and a not inconsiderable respect for Doc Savage, who was as unusual as he was human.

Monk finished his comic strips, grunted amiably, and spread the front pages out on the table.

"Any word from Doc?" he asked.

"No," Renny said.

"This makes eight days, doesn't it?"

"That's right."

"I wonder where Doc went?"

"Holy cow, don't start on that before breakfast!" Renny said. Renny had a deep, bull-throated voice that boomed. "Let's go eat, or have you?"

"No, I thought we'd wait for Ham and all go down together," Monk explained. He leaned back and grinned delightedly at the ceiling. "I'll tell you a secret. I fixed old Ham. I cut his water off. I introduced him to a beautiful blonde named Mabis, and Mabis has a very jealous Marine for a boy friend. This Marine of Mabis's is corps boxing champ, and noted for punching guys in the kisser when they fool around Mabis. I just happened to know the Marine was to make a speech at the International Club benefit last night, and I just happened to buy two tickets to the benefit and give them to Ham, and he took the bait. He was going to squire Mabis to the benefit. I wonder what happened."

"Holy cow!" Renny muttered. "Let's go eat."

"Without Ham?"

"You think I want to listen to you two squabble all through breakfast?"

"It should be worth hearing," Monk said gleefully. He pushed the newspapers into the wastebasket, and got to his feet. "All right, let's go. But I wonder what's keeping Ham?"

The eighty-sixth floor headquarters was equipped with many gadgets, practical and impractical, because Doc Savage had a weakness for gadgets. One of the gadgets was a private elevator which traveled at a rate of speed that would scare the daylights out of almost anyone. Renny and Monk rode it down to the lobby.

"Someday something is going to go wrong with that elevator and it'll be the death of all of us," Renny grumbled.

Monk grinned. "That's one of Doc's lemons. He invented the special mechanism to service skyscrapers, and they aren't building skyscrapers any more."

"After the war, they'll be built."

"Nah, after the war people will live in the country and fly airplanes to work."

Renny grunted. Using what for money, he was tempted to ask. What about this unbelievable national debt? He was no economist, but of late the subject had been bothering him, just as it must have secretly been bothering every other American with foresight farther than the end of his nose. But he didn't care about starting an argument with Monk, who belonged to the live-today-worry-about-tomorrow-when-it's-here school.

Monk stepped through the revolving door to the street. Renny was close behind him.

Wind buffeted them, and thin misting rain wet their faces instantly. The restaurant was close. They began running, and two men were suddenly running alongside them. Two strangers.

One stranger took Renny's arm, the other took Monk's arm, and each stranger exhibited a newspaper-wrapped package he carried in his free hand.

"There's a gun in this newspaper," Renny's stranger told him. "Better take my word for it."

Renny heard Monk say, "What's that? What'd you say?"

"Don't put your hands up," Monk's stranger told him. "Just be damned careful to do what I tell you."

Renny knew what Monk was sure to do. He did the same thing himself. He chopped down fast, as fast as he possibly could, with his arm which the stranger was not holding. He chopped at the package, and hit it, and knocked the package away from him.

The gun in the package exploded, its bullet hit the sidewalk and made a bright metallic smear, glanced and made a round hole and a long crack in a plate glass window.

Renny gave all his attention to the packaged gun. He seized it with both hands, fell upon it, twisted, fought for it and it alone.

Renny was a big man. He was nearly as tall as Doc Savage, and somewhat heavier than Doc. Renny's fists were abnormally large and full of strength.

He got the gun. He clubbed at the stranger. The latter dodged, and, frightened by the violence, began going away. As he went, he yelled, "Shoot 'im! For God's sake, shoot 'im!"

Renny veered to help Monk. But that wasn't necessary; Monk had his man down and was beating him over the face and skull with the package.

"Watch out! Gunplay!" Renny gasped. When Monk didn't seem to hear him, or at least paid no attention, Renny seized the homely chemist and yelled, "Watch out!"

Monk straightened, growling, "Where?" Then he muttered, "Oh, oh!" And he leaped, doubled over and zig-zagging, for the entrance of the nearest store.

From a car parked at the curbing about forty feet away, a man had stepped with a short old-fashioned lever-action rifle. He was trying to draw a bead on them. He fired too quickly, and missed.

Renny and Monk piled into the doorway, Monk first, Renny stumbling over him. Monk dropped the package containing the gun his stranger had held. He grabbed at the one Renny had. Renny said, "Get away!" He tore the wrappings off the weapon, disclosing a new-looking revolver.

Monk always got excited in a fight. It amused Renny. Renny said, "Put your head out and see if they'll shoot."

Monk, in a dither, actually started to do it. He caught himself. "Why, blast you!" he muttered. Renny laughed.

There was no humor in Renny's laugh. It was just a kind of uncaring, desperate feeling he got when there was intense excitement. Ordinarily he was a taciturn and somewhat sour fellow, but excitement seemed to make him drunk. Afterward he would look back on the emotional binge with pleasure.

An automobile engine started. There was considerable excitement in the street, but they heard the engine going over the uproar. It didn't start the way an ordinary motorist would have started. It roared and tires squealed. It could be a scared motorist leaving. Renny took a chance that it wasn't. He put his head out.

The two strangers were in the automobile with the rifleman and they were leaving.

Renny aimed deliberately, making a snap decision to shoot at the tires first, while they were near enough to make a fair target. Later he could try for the men. The gun made fire and noise in his big fist. The car tire made a loud whistling, then a mushy bang as it blew out.

The car was turning at the time. It reeled, failed to make the corner, heaved across the sidewalk, and broke off a fireplug. It stopped above the smashed fire hydrant, and the mounting roaring geyser of water slowly turned it over.

The three men came out of the machine. They didn't do any shooting. They ran. There was a subway entrance ahead.

The trio popped down the subway kiosk.

"Come on!" Renny yelled. "We may have them trapped."

He sprinted across the street with Monk, and they could hear the slowly increasing rumble of a subway train in the tunnel. It was leaving. As they pounded down the steps, they saw the last coaches of the subway train leaving.

Monk yelled, "How can we stop that train? Aren't there switches or something in the stations? What about the signal system—how can we stop it with that?"

"I don't know," Renny said.

"Dammit, you're an engineer, you should know!" Monk said wildly. "Where's something I can drop on the third rail and short-circuit the power."

He dashed about frantically, finally seized a metal lid off the pop-cooler in the subway station newsstand, and leaped down on to the tracks. He tossed the lid on to the third rail and the wheel-rail. The result was fire, smoke, cracking spark, and stink. Nothing more. The tin sheet hadn't had enough conductivity to short-circuit the power.

Monk climbed on the platform, disgusted.

"Let's look at the car," Renny said. "The police will be here in a minute. We'll put out an alarm."

Climbing the stairs to the street, Monk muttered, "If anybody had told me a thing like that would happen right on a New York street, I'd have called them nuts."

"Did you know any of the three?"

"Never saw them before in my life."

"They knew us."

"Depends on what you mean knew. Recognized us, of course. But I don't think they had ever met us before."

"What were they up to?"

"Don't ask me," Monk said. "It's as much a mystery to me as to you."

"Did you get hurt?"

Monk shook his head. "'Skinned up a little, is all. And I won't be able to sleep right for a week or two, probably."

Renny shuddered. "I never tried that commando tactic of knocking a gun aside before, and right now it would take quite a bit to hire me to try it again."

"Me, too," Monk agreed uneasily.

Reaction was setting in. A few moments ago, when it was necessary, they had gone through with what seemed essential at the moment, and done so with a certain verve. Now they had time to think. It was like being shot at—when it happened, you ducked and were startled. Later you got to thinking about the hole the bullet could have made.

That was the bad part. Fear, like the measles, took a little time to develop. They came out on the sidewalk. A crowd was around the upset car and they were dragging a man out of the machine. "Holy cow!" Renny said, staring unbelievingly.

"Ham!" Monk said. "It's Ham Brooks! They had Ham in that car!"

Ham Brooks was their friend, also a Doc Savage associate. Ham was a lawyer, his full name with trimmings being Brigadier General Theodore Marley Brooks. He didn't like the nickname of Ham, or professed not to, and so everyone who knew him well called him that.

He glared at Monk and said, "Don't stand there and gape at me! Cut me loose!"

Monk got out his pocket knife and sawed through the ropes. He helped Ham to his feet. Ham didn't seem to be harmed.

The crowd was growing. Someone recognized Renny, and the word went around about who they were.

Ham said, "Let's get out of here! I've got something important to tell you."

Renny said, "Let's duck into the building. I'll call the police from there."

They found seclusion inside the office building where Doc had his headquarters. Renny picked up a telephone.

"Make that call snappy," Ham advised him. "We haven't any time to waste."

Renny nodded. He got a police lieutenant he knew, and sketched what had happened, described the three men who had tried to waylay them, and where they had last been seen. "Pick them up if you can," he said.

"They tried to kill us. I don't know why yet. I'll give you more information when I get it."

Ham was talking before the receiver was on the hook.

"Here's what I know," Ham said rapidly. "I got a telephone call. Man with a shrill voice, or a deep-throated woman's voice. I couldn't tell which. Said Doc Savage was in trouble, needed our help. Said Doc might be dead already. Asked me to get over to North Jersey airport immediately for the full story."

Ham stared at them uneasily. "You can imagine how that hit me. I dressed in a hurry and charged out of my apartment house, and those three guys were waiting. They had guns. They got me in the car, and came down here to waylay you two. They had me in the back, a laprobe thrown over me, tied up so I couldn't make a sound, and I wouldn't have dared make one if I could."

Renny asked, "Think the phone call was a gag to get you excited and cause you to rush out into their waiting hands?"

"I do not."

"Why?"

"The way they talked. They hadn't figured on me getting out of the apartment until later in the day, about the time I usually get up."

"They knew when you usually get up?"

"Yes. That means they've had their eye on us for several days."

"I don't get this," Renny said.

"It's part of some kind of trouble Doc is in."

Monk said, "We'll take the big car. It's faster."

The big car was a sedan, black, overpowered with a souped-up motor. Renny drove. He took Eighth Avenue north, then Broadway, then George Washington Bridge into New Jersey.

Monk said, "That was the darndest mess there in front of the building for a while." And then he was silent, thinking about what a mess it had been, and how they could have been shot down. He began to per-

spire a little, and took out a handkerchief sheepishly
and wiped his face.

"Scared now, eh?" Ham asked.

Monk was scared, but he put his handkerchief away,
and examined Ham thoughtfully, noticing for the first
time that Ham had a discolored eye.

"You didn't tell us they beat you up," Monk said.

"Eh?"

"Your eye."

"Oh, I got that last night," Ham said. Then he
scowled at Monk. "Yes, last night. And I intended to
take that matter up with you. By any chance, did you
know that Mabis had a slightly more than casual acquaintance with a big lug of a Marine?"

"Me?" Monk didn't succeed in looking innocent.
"Did she?"

"Brother, I'll put that down in my book," Ham
promised unpleasantly.

Monk was uncomfortably silent. The gag had
seemed funny when he had pulled it on Ham, but now
it seemed pretty juvenile. He was ashamed of it, as he
was frequently ashamed of his practical jokes afterward. Too many of them, it often struck him, were of
the variety a ten-year-old would perpetrate. But they
always looked good, if not too adult, at the time. There
was also some addded pleasure in the fact that the more
childish the gag, the more it got under Ham's skin.

Nothing more was said for a while. All three of
them were having nerves. What had happened was not
conducive to a placid feeling. They had, in plain truth,
had the devil scared out of them, and they had no idea
what it was all about.

When they drew near the airport, Renny said uneasily, "Keep your eyes open."

The airport was peaceful. They parked and remained in the car for a while, watching.

"I'll inquire at the line shack," Renny said. "You
fellows stay in the car and be ready to help me out if
this is another joker."

Renny walked to the line shack. The only occupant
was a thin, disgusted-looking man who was making
pencil marks on a stack of government forms.

"Is there someone around here who wants to see Ham Brooks?" Renny asked.

"Brooks? Brooks?" The man thought for a moment. "Oh." He dug around in the forms and came up with an envelope. "You Brooks?"

"He's in the car outside."

"Well, give this to him." The man extended the envelope.

"Where'd it come from?" Renny asked.

"Girl left it."

"What girl?"

The man eyed Renny intently. "Girl who flew in here about six o'clock this morning. Private plane, nice little job." He grinned slightly. "They were both nice little jobs, the girl and the plane. She paid the night man five dollars to use his car, drove off in it, and came back in about ten minutes in a hurry. She was acting kind of funny when she came back. Said she wouldn't need the car. Night man offered her the five bucks back, but she wouldn't take it. She used the telephone."

"Whom did she call?"

"I don't know."

"How many calls?"

"One."

Renny picked up the telephone, and got hold of the long-distance operator and said, to avoid an argument with the operator, "There was a call made to a Ham Brooks in New York City a couple of hours ago. Will you verify the charges, please."

The operator looked it up, said, "Ninety-eight cents."

Renny thanked her. He had what he wanted. The call the girl had made probably had been to Ham.

"What happened to the girl?" he asked the thin man.

The thin man was suspicious and doubtful by now. "What's going on? You a cop?"

Renny produced his billfold and dug out a couple of cards, which he tossed on the table. "Look those over. I'll be back in a minute."

He went outside, took the envelope to Ham. "Here's what we drew."

Ham tore open the envelope, unfolded the single sheet of paper inside. They read:

I SAW SOME MEN I'VE SEEN AROUND HOME AND I KNOW THEY WERE WATCHING HERE AT THE AIRPORT FOR ME. I'M AFRAID TO WAIT. DOC SAVAGE IS AT THE COLBECK CONSTRUCTION COMPANY PIPELINE JOB WHERE IT CROSSES THE RIVER IN ARKANSAS. HE IS IN SERIOUS TROUBLE, SOME OF WHICH IS MY FAULT. YOU HAD BETTER COME HELP HIM.

There was no signature.

"A girl left it," Renny explained. "Let's go ask the fellow in the line shack more about the girl."

The thin man was frowning at the two cards Renny had given him. He handed them to Renny. "So you're a cop," he said.

Technically, the cards identified Renny as a special state investigator, which was not the same thing as a policeman. Renny let it go.

"What became of the girl?" he asked.

"Well, she acted funny, as I said. She walked around the place two or three times, and then she had me fill up her tank with gas, and she took off."

Renny said, "Did it look to you like she started off in the car, saw someone who scared her, then came back here, saw whoever had scared her was still around, and decided to get out?"

"I figured it was something like that," the thin man admitted. "I didn't know what to do. I couldn't very well hold the girl. Her airman's identification card was okay. So was her license. She had an instrument rating."

"Let's see your sheet."

The thin man got out his book. Private fliers, because of war restrictions, could operate only from designated airports, from which they had to sign in and out.

Renny examined the signature on the book.

"Nola Morgan," he said. "I never heard of her."

"Where did she check out for?" Monk asked.

"Pittsburgh," Renny said.

"That means she's headed back for Arkansas."

"Probably."

Ham Brooks thoughtfully pocketed the note Nola Morgan had left. "If you ask me, we'd better do the same thing."

VII.

It was from the air that the river looked most like the kind of a river it was. From any altitude above five thousand feet it resembled a brown snake, sullen, lazy, dissatisfied, fretful, threatening. You got a feeling of foulness about the river.

The river had overflowed that spring, and the vegetation and crops on the overflow land had an unhealthy yellow cast, whereas the hill country and the uplands were furred with hearty green. It was as if the river had contaminated the country through which it flowed, sickened whatever was close to it.

Renny was flying. He was flying sheepishly, because he had made a bobble in his dead-reckoning navigation and hit the river fifty miles from his intended destination. He suspected he had bungled the computer gadget when he set up the triangle of velocities for his flight course. It was a mistake a WTS student wouldn't have made, and Renny was an engineer, and he was ashamed of it.

Anyway, they had hit the river at a power dam, a long wall of concrete which barred the progress of the brown river snake and fattened it for miles upstream. This wasn't where they were supposed to hit it, but it was a landmark easy to identify. Renny had turned downstream.

"There's the town," Ham said finally. "Isn't that the pipeline just beyond it?"

Renny muttered that with his navigating, he wouldn't be too surprised if it was the Burma Road. He eased the throttles out and slanted down toward the pipeline job.

With an engineer's practiced curiosity, Renny examined the pipeline work. He frowned, dived the ship, and sailed along a few hundred feet above the line. He banked back toward the river.

The job down there wasn't going well, he knew immediately. First, it was strung out too much. Laying a pipeline was a regular operation. First, the survey crew laid out the line, and the aerial photos were taken. Then the claim agents bought up the right-of-way and cleared titles.

The soil-checker would come through, checking the earth for alkali or other chemical content injurious to pipe. Wherever alkali was found, the pipe would be re-routed to avoid these "hot" spots.

The ditching machines next, then the pipe-stringers, the tacker, the welders, the paralite and papering crew, the backfillers, the fencing crew—all these last in a compact group, probably spread out over no more than three or four miles of line.

Renny grimaced. Visibility was about twenty miles to the west, and it looked to him as if the pipe wasn't even in the ditch that far back.

The river crossing made him uncomfortable to look at it. He hated to see an engineering job bungled.

"There's plenty of trouble down there," he said.

Ham and Monk were surprised. The construction job, to their inexperienced eyes, had looked large, efficient and impressive.

"What's the matter with it?" Monk demanded.

"The whole job is shot to blazes," Renny explained. "No coordination. Take right across the river—the stringer crews aren't a bit ahead of the connection crew. And you can see, all the way down the line, where it isn't clicking."

He scowled at the ground for a while, banking the plane back.

"Crews are short-handed, too," he muttered. "Looks as if something was keeping them from work."

"If there's trouble, Doc is probably here somewhere," Ham said.

"We'll find out," Renny said grimly. "This is a damned mess! Holy cow! Did you know the fuel from this line has to be reaching the invasion shove-off bases before we can start the last big punch to end this war?"

Monk and Ham hadn't known that. They had been doing odd jobs of specialized nature for the War Department and the general staff, but this was an engineering and supply problem, so they hadn't known. The War Department wasn't noted for broadcasting such information, anyway.

The airport was a municipal one, suffering from the usual war-time doldrums. There were three shed-hangars and a seedy individual to take care of the line shack and the gasoline pumps.

"You ain't staying?" the seedy attendant asked.

"Why not?" Renny demanded, surprised by the man's unexpected curiosity.

"You ain't newspapermen, or government agents, or something?" the man inquired.

Renny growled, "Brother, who appointed you to ask—"

A man came out of the line shack saying, "I did. Keep your hair on straight, friend." The man was tall, wiry, and he carried a shotgun casually across his arm. He was followed by another man, shorter, less flexible-looking, also with a shotgun. Both wore hunting clothes.

"Who are you and what's your business here?" the first man asked bluntly.

Renny didn't like the manner of either man. As men, they were decent looking. But their attitude certainly wasn't pleasant. Renny said, "I don't see any badges on you two birds. Show us a badge, and we might talk to you."

"Maybe we don't need any badges," the man said. "Who are you three? Some more Colbeck men?"

"What do you mean—Colbeck men?" Renny demanded.

"I'm asking the questions."

Renny, in an ugly tone that suddenly got to rumbling, said, "You're the one who's getting his teeth kicked out in about three seconds."

"Friend, I wouldn't advise you—"

"On your way!" Renny said. "Get going, you bums!"

"Listen—"

Renny said ominously, "Beat it, brother! Right now."

The two men stared at Renny, who was not a sight to inspire peace in their minds. They were in an uncomfortable spot, with their bluff called.

One of them said to the other, "No need of getting ourselves skinned up by tackling three of them. Come on. They're Colbecks, all right."

The pair walked off. They had the long healthy stride of men who had done a lot of foot traveling over hills and country roads.

Renny wheeled on the seedy old airport attendant. "Who were those two?"

"Chester and Jim Morgan, my second-cousins," the old man snapped. "They're not afraid to have you know who they are."

"What'd they mean—were we Colbecks?"

"Are you?"

Exasperated, Renny yelled, "I asked you! Now answer my questions!"

The old man scowled at Renny, then deliberately spat on the ground. "Nuts to you and the rest of the Colbecks," he said. He turned and stalked into the line shack, slamming the door.

Renny, angered, seized the door knob with the intention of following the old fellow. The door was locked. Renny rattled the knob. "Open up!"

Inside the line shack, the old man said quietly and purposefully, "You try to bust that door down and I'll shoot you dead in your tracks, and I'll get away with calling it self-defense, too."

Monk grimaced. "Sounds as if he wanted us to try it."

"Where do we get a taxi?" Renny asked the old man.

"Walk," the old man said.

They walked. It was about a mile. They passed two pipeline trucks piled in the ditch, one of them with a load of four forty-foot joints of twenty-four-inch river-weight pipe.

Renny, at the second truck, said, "Wait a minute." He went over and probed and poked for a while, then indicated the pipe-trailer coupling. "Parted. Made the truck go into the ditch," he said. He rubbed a finger over the greasy friction surfaces of the coupling. "Been wiped off," he added. "There should be grease on that." He got down and felt and searched carefully on the underside. "Holy cow!"

He showed them his fingers. He rubbed the fingers together. "Emery dust," he said. "You can feel it. The stuff was put on the coupling so it would cut out. This is a special compound used for metal-cutting."

"Deliberate?" Monk asked.

"Why not? It was wiped off, wasn't it?"

Monk waved an arm at the other damaged truck. "Two trucks knocked out on this short stretch of road. "What's somebody trying to do—butcher this construction job?"

"Let's find out," Renny said. "And while we're doing it, we might get a line on Doc Savage."

They reached the outskirts of town. Only four cars passed them, and each of these was loaded with suitcases or the kind of light-housekeeping furniture which pipeline workers carry with them from one location to another.

They passed through a region of fairly nice residences. Then filling-stations began to appear, and the usual average of rooming-houses.

Renny stopped. "There's a guy loading his stuff into his car. Texas license on the car. And he looks like a pipeliner." He glanced at Monk and Ham. "I'm going to see if I can find out whether the workmen are pulling out, and why."

"Probably get your nose flattened," Monk said.

Renny entered the yard. The house was two-storied, weather-boarded, a vintage probably thirty-five years back. There was a fat fortyish man and a fat younger man and a woman loading stuff into an elderly sedan.

"Leaving?" Renny asked.

All three stopped working. They stared at him. The older fat man said, "Get along, buddy. You haven't lost anything here."

Renny scowled. "You insult people kind of sudden, don't you?"

The younger man said, "Look, Morgan or Colbeck or whichever you are, we don't want any part of this mess. We're getting out."

"Quitting?" Renny asked.

"Yeah. And if you mean are we scared, that's right, too."

"What's the trouble?" Renny persisted.

Both men spat on the ground simultaneously.

"Are you kidding!" one said. And they both went back to carrying suitcases, cardboard boxes, and a baby crib out of the house.

The woman stood staring at Renny for a while, then cried shrewishly, "You git! You leave us alone, you hear!"

Renny went back to Monk and Ham.

"Everybody seems to be in a stew," he said. "Let's find out whoever is bossing this pipeline job and get the lowdown."

The office had been makeshifted out of a suite of sample rooms on the balcony floor of the old hotel that was still the best hotel in town. A cardboard sign with *Colbeck Construction Company* lettered on it with crayon marked the door.

Big Bill Colbeck, with strain showing all over his honest-John face, stood flatfooted behind his desk and said, "Yes, I'm Colbeck. Yes, I own the company, or what was the company. What do you want?"

Renny introduced Monk, Ham and himself. "We're associated with Doc Savage," he added.

"Damn my soul!" Colbeck said violently. He strode to a connecting door, shouted, "Art! Oh Art, come in here. The Philistines are with us again."

Arthur Strain came in, a long man who looked soft without any fat. He wore tweeds and everything that went with them, down to a knobby brair pipe which gave off the aroma of good Irish-blended tobacco that was hard to get these days.

"These three guys are friends of Doc Savage," Colbeck told him.

Stain extended his hand. "Glad to meet you gentlemen. I hope you can help us." When he had finished shaking hands, he asked, "Have you seen Doc Savage yet?"

"We don't know where he is," Renny said. "Do you?"

"In jail."

"How come?"

"Sit down," Strain suggested, "and I'll tell you about it."

Arthur Strain proved to have a gift for clear expression. He painted a word picture swiftly, emphasizing the points that were important. How the construction of the pipeline had dragged mysteriously until Colbeck Construction had been forced to forfeit three of its penalties for failing to have agreed-upon amounts of pipeline built by agreed-upon dates. The penalty payments had been a severe strain on the company, since they wiped out the profit on each section and a good deal more.

It had become more and more apparent, Strain explained, that the old Morgan-Colbeck disagreement might be behind the trouble. And then Erasmus Morgan, patriarch of the Morgans, had been murdered, and an attempt made to lay the blame on Bill Colbeck. That had brought the Morgan-Colbeck scrap out into the open.

This was the mess into which Doc Savage had ventured. Strain explained that he and Colbeck had not known Doc, nor been aware that the bronze man had been assigned by the federal government to solve the pipeline trouble. This they had not known until night before last, when Doc had called them to his room here at the hotel.

"While he was talking to us," Strain explained, "the Sheriff appeared and arrested him. Savage was accused of killing a fellow named, or called, Preach Jones. They locked Savage up, after he was practically identified as the killer by a girl named Nola Morgan. She had been with Savage when—"

"Wait a minute!" Ham interrupted. "Who was this girl?"

"Nola Morgan. She's one of the leading Morgans, a niece, I think, of the old fellow who was murdered, Erasmus Morgan."

She's more than that, Ham thought. She's apparently the girl who flew back east and got us on the job.

"Do you know the girl?" Strain asked.

"Never met her," Ham said. "Where is Doc right now?"

"In jail. An attempt was made to kill him last night, but it didn't succeed."

Renny stared at Strain with a shocked intensity. "Good Lord, you say that casually!"

"I'm sorry," Strain said. "It's hard to believe such things happen. I didn't feel casual about it, I assure you, although I had met Mr. Savage just once."

"What about this attempted killing?"

"Well, there was mob activity in the street, and someone took a shot at Mr. Savage through the cell window. It missed."

Bill Colbeck snorted, said, "It didn't miss. It was a damned good shot. It was the best shooting I ever heard of. And it didn't miss. It went right smack through a dummy Doc Savage had made of himself out of a piece of wallpaper he'd torn off the wall of his cell. He held this silhouette up in front of the window, and bing! Somebody put a bullet through. Right between the eyes."

Renny asked, "What about this mob?"

"Well, what about it?"

"Did somebody stir it up deliberately so there would be excitement to cover the shooting?"

"Could be," Bill Colbeck said.

Arthur Strain made a quick, unbelieving gesture. "Bill, you're getting a little wild again," he said.

"Wild?" Colbeck wheeled on his general manager. "Look, I've been around trouble before. I know what trouble looks like. And we've got plenty of it right here on this construction job."

"Probably not as much as you think."

Colbeck swore violently. "There's a regular civil war! We're the same as out of business!"

"Take it easy, Bill," Strain soothed.

"Easy, nothing!" Colbeck yelled. "You sat around in a Tulsa bank too much of your life, Art. You may be able to recognize a financial cyclone when you see one. But what you don't know about pipeline troubles would fill six books."

Colbeck's inner tension was bursting out into the open, like a buzzard chick hatching out of a shell. He was scared, and big enough and two-fisted enough to be ashamed of being scared. His excitement was the more stark for that, since a frightened strong man is more disturbing than a scared weak man.

"The job is shut down!" Colbeck shouted. "The men who scare easy are leaving. Hell, I saw a dozen cars headed out of town with men and their families. It'll be weeks before we can get going—but now we'll never get going again."

"What's the trouble?" Renny demanded.

"Money."

Arthur Strain made a slight, embarrassed gesture, saying, "Don't worry about that, Bill. You can count on me to furnish what money you have to have."

Bill Colbeck scowled. He shook his head. Then he grinned sheepishly at Strain. "Thanks, Art," he said.

Renny said, "We didn't come here to pry into your financial problems. What we want to know is what happened to Doc Savage, and what happened to this pipeline construction job."

"Savage is in jail charged with murder," said Colbeck. "The pipeline construction job is blown higher than a kite, nearly."

"Exactly how bad is the construction situation?"

Bill Colbeck hesitated, then spoke quietly, with no exaggeration.

"If we could get the line the rest of the way across the river, we would make it," he said. "We might even beat the forfeit date."

"How far is the line across the river?"

"It's damn near across. Right at the critical point."

"We'll look into that after we talk to Doc," Renny said.

Colbeck grunted, said, "If I can't get that pipeline across the river, you'll play hell doing it."

Renny, Monk and Ham went to the jail. Enroute, Monk said, "Colbeck is worried."

"He is a crude fellow," Ham said. "You notice that last crack he made? If he couldn't build a pipeline across the river, nobody else could."

Renny said, "I sort of liked the guy."

"But he was insulting!"

"Well, he's got things on his mind. He's got reason to be short-tempered, the way it looks to me. I like men to show the way they're feeling. It's these deep foxy guys who hide everything you have to look out for."

"Well, I liked Strain better than Colbeck," Ham said. "Strain didn't have the manners of a goat, at least."

Renny changed the subject saying, "There's the jail."

They had trouble getting to see Doc Savage. The county was holding the bronze man, which meant the sheriff had custody.

Sheriff Tom Scott Morgan examined Renny's special commission cards, laughed and said, "No thanks. They don't carry weight here."

"But—"

"Look," Sheriff Morgan interrupted. "You're going to tell me the unpleasant things that will happen to me if I don't cooperate with you. Save your breath."

The sheriff wasn't being nasty. He was merely stating his position, and making it clear that he felt he knew what he was doing.

"I could promise you some unpleasant things," Renny said.

"No doubt."

"You could be obstructing justice, you know."

Sheriff Morgan nodded. "People been telling you I'm holding this man in jail because he's a Colbeck?"

"We haven't been in town long enough to hear any talk," Renny told him. "And Doc Savage isn't a Colbeck or a Morgan. If you'd call Doc anybody, you'd call him the American people."

The officer considered that for a moment. It made him angry. He jerked a thumb at his own chest. "I'm the American people. They elected me. I take this job seriously. I do what I think is right, and if I'm wrong, I'll take whatever hell is dished out. I'll take it, then go home and sleep, because my heart is pure. But if I do something I don't feel is right, and it turns out bad, I can't sleep, because my heart ain't pure. Get it?"

Renny jumped up wrathfully.

"You're just a lot of words!" he snapped. "You going to let us talk to Doc, or not?"

"I'm not."

Renny demanded, "Is Nola Morgan related to you?"

"Somewhat."

"How much?"

"She's my sister."

"All right, Nola Morgan came to New York and got us on the job," Renny said. "Does that make it any different with you?"

The Sheriff looked him in the eye. "Suppose I was to tell you my sister, Nola Morgan, was right here in town and at home every minute since Doc Savage was locked up? Would that make it any different with *you?*"

Renny's jaw went down. He was silent for a while.

Ham Brooks said, "Sheriff, are you telling us that is the truth?"

"I'm telling you to get out of here," Morgan said. "Now. Right now!"

VIII.

Renny Renwick, Ham Brooks and Monk Mayfair stalked in silence to a restaurant, where they found a table. The waitress came, and they had difficulty thinking of anything to order, half-realizing the hesitancy was due to their depression.

Monk Mayfair, watching the faces of the others, could see that they were having about the same thoughts he was having. His own weren't very pleasant. He had seen enough since arriving to know there was plenty of trouble afoot, and that it was too far along for gentle methods to stop it. It was too far grown to nip in the bud, because it was well out of the bud.

And Monk was convinced that Doc Savage was in very real danger. A murder charge was never something to trifle with, no matter how innocent you were. They executed you for murder, with due process of law, inexorably and frighteningly. The theory was that innocence got its due, but Monk had a hunch that Doc would not be in jail now if he could prove his innocence.

The waitress brought their food. They had ordered eggs because they hadn't eaten since the night before—things had happened too fast in New York to think about food—and so what they wanted was in the nature of breakfast. But the waitress brought no eggs, and apologized, "We usually get them fresh from the country, but now we can't."

"How come?" Monk asked.

"Morgans raise the eggs and they're afraid Colbecks might eat them," the waitress said wryly.

"Which are you, Morgan or Colbeck?"

"I'm an innocent bystander," she said. She glanced

about uneasily. "There's been rumors they would dynamite this place because Bill Colbeck eats here. Do you suppose they would do that?"

"It doesn't sound logical."

"Who said anything about logic?" the waitress retorted.

When she had gone away, Renny muttered, "We had better get organized."

"So I'm thinking," Monk said.

Renny examined his big fists thoughtfully. "How does this sound to you? Monk, you and Ham take the Colbeck and Morgan mess. One of you work on the Colbecks, the other one on the Morgans, and see what you can dig up."

Monk said, "That's a good idea. I'll take the Morgan angle."

Renny added, "I'll go have a look at that pipeline river crossing job. As an engineer, that's probably my best angle. One of our jobs here is going to be to see that the pipeline goes through."

"That's good, too," Monk agreed. "Me on the Morgans. Ham on the Colbecks."

Ham eyed Monk narrowly. "I think we'd better match to see whether you or I take the Morgan angle."

"That's not necessary," Monk said innocently.

"You have any particular preference?" Ham demanded.

"Shucks, no. Makes no difference to me, but I'll take the Morgan angle."

"Because you've heard Nola Morgan is a very pretty girl?"

Renny stared disgustedly at Monk and Ham.

"Holy cow!" he said. He fished a coin out of his pocket and slapped it down on the table. "Call it," he told Monk sourly. "I'm in no mood for this sort of thing now."

Monk eyed Renny's hand sheepishly. "Heads," he muttered.

It was tails.

Ham said, "That's what I get for living right. I think I'll start out by investigating Miss Morgan personally."

* * *

Ham Brooks liked fine living. He was an enthusiast about good food, good clothes, beauty and comfort and existence in the genteel way. When he could, he liked to live that way himself, and he enjoyed seeing others do it. The plantation impressed him.

The white house at the top of the hill road was a conspicuous landmark for miles across the countryside and up and down the river. Ham, turning his rented car into the long sweep of the driveway, examined the place with appreciation.

The mansion had obviously been built before the Civil War days, but it was no seedy relic of the old south. The columns had a fresh majestic sweep, the paint was crisp and white, the lawns manicured, the shrubbery well-cared for. Behind and to the east were the outbuildings, the sheds, the barns, the cribs, the stock pens. There were tractors and combines and fine livestock.

Looking at the place, Ham felt an urge to be a farmer. It was the kind of a place that made you feel that way.

He clattered the brass knocker against the door, half expecting the panel to be swung ajar by a picturesque old darky with white hair and lots of teeth. He was so completely primed to tell an old darky, "Cunnel Brooks to see yoah Mistress, suh," that he was thrown off the track when Nola Morgan herself opened the door.

"Hello," she said.

Ham made foolish noises.

"Come in," Nola Morgan said. "I've been expecting one of you."

"You—uh—know me?" Ham managed to say. He had gotten a good look at the girl by now. Monk'll sure be burned up that he didn't get this part of the job, he thought.

"You are Ham Brooks," she said.

Ham had mentally arranged an orderly sequence of questions, but he was confused, and he asked bluntly, "Was it you who came to New York—you who telephoned me?"

"Of course."

"Why did you leave so quickly?"

"Didn't you get the note I left at the airport? They had men there watching me. I guess they knew I always use that airport when I fly to New York. I should have landed at a different one, but I didn't think of that."

"Your brother," Ham said, "claimed it wasn't you who notified us."

"Did he?" She walked ahead of Ham. "Will you come this way. I want to show you something."

She led the way up a stairway to a large sunny room furnished in wicker and tweedy stuff. Near one of the windows a good surveyor's transit was set up. Nola Morgan went to the instrument. "This is the only thing I could find around the house that would do for a telescope," she said.

She stooped and peered through the transit.

"Take a look," she said. "You may have to adjust the focus."

Through the transit Ham saw a backwater slough, a sloping bank, a man lounging on the bank, and two enormous cane fishing-poles stuck in the mud of the bank.

"Looks innocent, doesn't it," the girl said.

"Yes."

"It isn't," she told him. "Do you know flag code? He's using those poles to send messages to someone."

Ham put an eye to the transit. "He moved the right-hand pole. But it's not semaphore."

"He moves the right pole for a dot, the left for a dash, and both of them for the end of a message. He just reported your arrival."

The man on the bank of the slough, Ham decided, could see about half of the Morgan estate.

The girl, answering a question that popped into his mind before he could word it, said, "There are two more. One on the west side of the place and another one on the north. A rabbit couldn't come or go without them being aware of it."

"Who are they?"

"I don't know."

"Morgans?"

"Certainly not. If they were Morgans, I would know about it."

"Colbecks?"

"I don't know. But I doubt it."

"Then who in the devil are they?"

Nola Morgan shook her head. "Sit down," she said. "I want to talk to you for a minute."

Ham took a chair. He didn't feel like sitting down. It was being more and more impressed on him that something tense and mysterious was happening, and it didn't make him want to sit and talk.

"Listen to me," Nola Morgan said. "Something big, frightening and terrible started happening in this part of the country several weeks ago. It began gradually, so gradually that none of us recognized anything unusual. And I still don't know what is at the bottom of it."

"What about this Colbeck versus Morgan—"

"That's what I'm telling you," she interrupted. "This thing that is happening had to happen behind a smoke-screen. And the smoke-screen that was selected was this Colbeck and Morgan legend."

Ham said, "I just came from town, and what I saw going on wasn't any legend. It was a civil war getting ready to pop."

Nola Morgan said sharply, "Don't tell me my local history! You're an outsider. You don't know anything about it. The Colbeck-Morgan feud was a dead duck twenty years ago. There hadn't been even a fist fight between a Colbeck and a Morgan for ten years. It was just talk. That's all. Talk, like some southerners still talk about the Civil War and damn-yankees. There actually was no Colbeck-Morgan bad feeling three months ago."

"But—"

"Somebody stirred it up. Somebody—a large and very slick organization of somebodies—dug this old feud out of its grave and dressed it up in war paint and feathers and rattled its old bones. Morgans began to hear that Colbecks had said nasty things about them—but the Colbecks hadn't said any such things. Colbecks heard slander which Morgans had supposedly said. Morgans hadn't said it. Lies. Somebody was spreading lies."

"You seem pretty certain," Ham said. He was getting confused, wondering just what was what.

Nola Morgan continued, "Then a Morgan was waylaid and beaten up on a dark road, and his assailants called each other Colbeck names. But we checked into it, and *they weren't Colbecks.* The next week, a Colbeck was stabbed by a man who said he was Finis Morgan. But Finis Morgan was right here in this house at the time of the knifing! We knew that for a fact."

Ham asked, "Who is *we?*"

Nola Morgan's face got a slightly chalky coloring. "Erasmus Morgan," she said. "He was my uncle, and he managed this plantation for me. I don't mean that I employed him. Erasmus Morgan was a very capable and influential man and quite wealthy. He liked this place, and preferred to spend much of his time here. He managed the plantation in order to have an excuse to stay here a lot."

"Erasmus Morgan," Ham said. "Where is he now?"

"Dead," she said grimly.

Ham suddenly wished that he hadn't asked such a blunt question about Erasmus Morgan. The pain in the girl's voice, the tragedy behind her eyes and her manner, made him uncomfortable.

"I'm sorry," he muttered.

Nola Morgan said that Erasmus Morgan had been murdered at night after he had left a meeting of landholders through whose farmland the pipeline was being constructed, a meeting at which the land owners had organized to see that they got fair damages, a meeting that might have been construed as Morgans against the Colbeck Construction Company. But it hadn't been that. It had been only a meeting such as farmers often held when a pipeline was going through their farms.

"He was shot with Bill Colbeck's gun," Nola Morgan said. "The bullet came from the gun, and the gun was traced to Bill Colbeck. But Colbeck didn't do it, any more than Finis Morgan had stabbed a Colbeck a few days before."

She stopped speaking and stared at the floor. Emotion had piled up in her, tightening her throat and holding back her words. She had thought a great deal of Erasmus Morgan, and his murder was a thing about which she could not talk calmly. Ham, wishing for words, could think of none.

Finally, without looking up, she continued, "It was three weeks after the funeral when a man in the state penitentiary, a man named Carl Boordling, gave me a misericord he had made—"

"A what?"

"Misericord. A beautiful, intricate, and yet horrible thing. And I knew, from the strange way Carl Boordling gave me the misericord, that it somehow was a clue, or a solution, to the whole affair. And today, more than ever, I'm sure of it."

"What makes you sure?"

"The efforts that have been made to get the misericord."

"You have it here?"

"No. And I'm not telling anyone where it is."

"But someone wants the misericord?"

"Carl Boordling died suddenly in the penitentiary. I think he was murdered because he gave the misericord to me. A woman came to me. She said, very pitifully, that she was Carl Boordling's mother and she wanted the misericord because it would be a keepsake of her son. I checked on her and found out she was a woman with a police record from Little Rock. Next, I was offered money for the thing. Then I was threatened if I didn't give it up."

"Who is after it?"

"I was never able to find out definitely who it is."

"No suspicions?"

She indicated the man fishing. "He is one of them."

Ham stood up. He said, "This may seem kind of abrupt, but I'm going to go to work on that fisherman right now. What do you say to that?"

"That's what I've been trying to get up nerve to ask you to do," Nola Morgan said.

IX.

When Ham Brooks walked out on the slough bank
beside the fake fisherman, he did so with a casualness
and confidence he certainly didn't feel. Ham now wore
ragged overalls, a straw hat which was a wreck, and
eyebrows considerably darker than normal, thanks to
Nola Morgan's eyebrow pencil.

"Okay, you can go home," he told the fisherman.

The fisherman, a short, dark, full-lipped man, was
eating a sandwich. He was startled. To get time to ex-
amine Ham, he made a business of swallowing half the
sandwich and swabbing out his cheeks with his tongue.

"Says which?" he demanded.

Ham sat down by the fishpoles. "Go home. I'm taking over."

"Yeah? Taking over what?"

Ham laughed. He was proud of how natural the
laugh sounded. "Oh, I'm not a wolf, Junior," he said.
"And you should put some bait on those fishhooks."

Ham calmly picked up one of the poles, made a
series of three movements with it. Then he moved the
other pole, the first one, then the other one. The fisherman watched narrowly, translating the code which
Ham was sending. It was the two letters, OK.

The fisherman grinned. "How come I haven't seen
you around?"

"Maybe I haven't been around," Ham said. "But
don't let that worry you."

"What'm I supposed to do?"

"Go talk to the boss," Ham said.

"Eh?"

"That's right."

The fisherman thought deeply for a while. Ham had

the growing horrible conviction that he had said something to give himself away. But the fisherman complained, "Hell, I'm due for some sleep."

Ham shrugged. "All I do is tell you what I'm told to
say."

The other seemed satisfied. He indicated the white
Morgan house on the hill. "Girl left a while ago. Some
guy with her. They left in a car."

"You pass the word along?"

"Sure."

"Then I should have an easy time of it. Be seeing
you."

The man grunted, and walked away, disappearing
into the bushes.

Ham waited, exhibiting a patience which he was far
from feeling. Knowing he was probably being watched
by whoever was receiver for the messages, he was careful not to do anything suspicious. He sat down and be-
haved as a fisherman would behave. Who was receiving
the fish-pole-transmitted messages, he could not tell,
although his eyes searched the surrounding woods and
fields repeatedly.

Then Nola Morgan's voice called softly, "He's far
enough away."

Ham hurriedly quit the slough bank. His leaving
would alarm the message-receiver, possibly. But he
wanted to follow the fisherman.

The fisherman had walked up a small hill, following
a winding path, and came to a dirt road. He had a car
parked there.

The road was not muddy, but it was soft in the
ditches from recent heavy rains. The man's car nearly
got stuck, and he swore and backed up and lunged
ahead, and finally got going. By that time, Ham and
Nola Morgan had reached their own cars.

Ham was driving the car he'd rented, and Nola Morgan had borrowed a machine, a coupe. It was Ham's
theory that their quarry would be easier to follow with
two cars.

Their system was for first one to follow the quarry,
then turn off into a side road before the fisherman's

suspicions were aroused, and the other take up the trail.

They went north on a highway, west on a blacktop road that was nothing extra, and on gravel again to the blufflands which overlooked the river and the long sweep of the building pipeline.

The fisherman pulled his car into a filling station which somehow, without there being anything definite to justify the impression, had the air of a black market layout. As Ham drove past, he saw the fisherman walking toward a tourist cabin. Ham didn't pay too much attention, being afraid to turn his head lest he be recognized. He had pulled his hair down over his eyes, put on a different hat, and made himself a trick moustache out of a folded shoestring, but he didn't have much confidence in the disguise.

Around the next turn, there was a long hill, and he found that Nola Morgan, who was ahead of him, had pulled off into a lane. He stopped beside her car.

She said, "That's Whitey's back there—a logical place for him to stop."

"Logical?"

"Whitey runs a tough joint."

"Is he a Colbeck?"

She grimaced. "No. I hope you haven't the idea that this country is populated exclusively by Colbecks and Morgans?"

"I was beginning to wonder."

"Well, that's a long way from being a fact," she said. "Come on. Let's see what we can find out."

Ham had his own ideas about a woman's place, particularly when trouble was around. He touched her arm, and said flatly, "You stay here. Get in the brush and keep out of sight. I'll look around."

She looked at him steadily. "I suppose you can see that I'm scared," she said. "But I'm not too scared to help."

"That isn't the point. This sort of thing is man's work."

"I hope you're not disgusted with me?"

"Quite the contrary, believe me," Ham assured her.

He left her in what he believed was sufficient concealment. It was a brush thicket, and if their cars were discovered from the road, she would have a chance to slip into a gully and get away. Or, if shooting started at the filling station-tourist camp, she was close enough to the cars to get to one of them and escape.

"Remember, stay right here," Ham warned. "And if there is trouble, get help. Don't try any heroics."

"I will." She was noticeably pale.

Ham left her. He went toward the filling station. Because he was not sure whether there were guards in the neighborhood, he moved as cautiously as possible.

The filling station-tourist camp layout was larger than he had thought. There was a small lake behind, evidently a slough arm of the river, with a dock and floating boathouses. The place had a sullen, seedy look, and nothing had been built with any consideration for beauty.

Ham picked the spots where brush grew, where the weeds were tallest. He should, he decided, not have much trouble crawling from one cabin to another until he found the one where his quarry had gone. He worked forward.

He didn't get far.

Sound, a stirring in the bushes close by, made him tighten out flat on the ground. The next instant there was a hard, unpleasant object against his back.

"Lay still, bud," a voice advised. "This thing in your back is a twelve-gauge shotgun."

Ham lay still.

The voice called, "Okay, Pack. This him?"

Ham lifted his head. He saw a compact man come out of the bushes. The look on the man's face put a coldness all through Ham, for it was the expression of a man who had no feelings about life or death, one way or the other.

There were other men, two of them, armed. But they were just other men at the moment, other men with normal emotions of fright and nerves and nausea. The nausea and the coldness leaped frighteningly through Ham. He was quite convinced that they were going to kill him.

The man Pack stooped and looked at Ham, examined Ham's face. He smiled a little, completely without feeling.

"That's the one Nola described to us," he said. He straightened. He lifted his voice. "It's okay, Miss Morgan," he called.

What a child I was in her hands, Ham thought sickly. And then, because his rage was like a scalding bath, he said what he thought, not considering that there was a lady present.

X.

Renny Renwick encountered Monk Mayfair in the middle of the afternoon on the pipeline construction job. Renny was looking over the river-crossing, and he found Monk working. Monk was swamping for a welder.

"What you doing out here?" Renny demanded. "You're supposed to be digging up information."

"That's what I'm doing," Monk assured him. "I met a welder named Dave somebody-or-other in town, and we're getting to be thick friends. This Dave was a little tight, and he let slip some stuff about being on the inside. I think he really is. Dave's swamper had quit, and so I talked him into letting me take the vacant job myself."

"The idea being to try to pump this Dave?"

"That's it."

"Have you learned anything yet?"

"Nothing except that this thing is serious. What have you found out?"

"Not much we didn't know already. When are you and Dave off work?"

"About an hour," Monk said. "You might stick

around and sort of follow us. Maybe something will turn up."

Renny nodded. He continued on his job of surveying the construction work.

Renny had told Monk that he'd learned nothing they didn't already know, but this was an understatement. He'd turned up much that was important, and indeed it might even be as vital as anything. He didn't have his fingers on any villains yet, but he had a hunch he could grab them where the hair was short and make it hurt.

He walked back along the line. Colbeck Construction had good equipment. Very good. Not flossy stuff, but real working outfits, and Renny had a hunch that there was no better equipment anywhere—which made it doubly mysterious that Colbeck Construction was having so much trouble.

He walked around a big ditching machine, a special job constructed for this big pipe. Good outfit, and it had cost plenty.

He went on, thoughtfully, to the river bank. The pipe was in the ditch up to the river section, and the papering machines were wrapping it before the winches lifted the pipe so the skids could be removed and the pipe lowered into the ditch. After that would come the backfiller, and the fencing crews, and the job would be done.

The pipe was being jointed together on shore for the river crossing. The joints, forty-foot river-weight steel, would be butted on the bank and the line-up clamps put in place, then tack-welded. After the stringer beads had been run by the main welder, the pipe would be worked, an inch at a time, farther out into the river.

It was supported on barges, which were carefully moored and snubbed. On the barges, the big barrel-shaped river-clamps were put on the pipe. These weighed almost a ton a section, two tons per clamp, and their purpose was to hold the pipe on the river bottom.

It sounds simple, Renny thought, just stringing a pipe across a river. But with a river like this, it's about as simple, in many respects, as building another Golden Gate bridge.

He could see—anyone could see—that the work was practically at a standstill.

Renny discovered Bill Colbeck. The owner of Colbeck Construction was on the river barges, working his way along the catwalks toward the shore. He paused to go aboard a dredge, but did not remain there long. He came ashore and approached Renny. The man had the facial expression of a whipped animal.

"How's it going?" Renny asked.

"Fierce," Colbeck muttered. He seemed inclined to talk now, a change from his attitude at the hotel. "I've got sanding-in trouble now. This river is a devil."

He meant, of course, that the ditch they had dredged in the river bed for the big pipe was filling with sand faster than it was supposed to.

Colbeck glanced at Renny sheepishly. "I think I'd better apologize for my attitude."

"Eh?"

"It didn't quite dawn on me who you were, Renwick," Colbeck said. "After you left, it hit me, and I dug up some back copies of engineering journals with your articles in them. It made me feel foolish. You seem to be about twenty times the engineer I'll ever be."

Renny grinned slightly and said, "Don't believe all you read." He indicated the pipeline river-crossing. "If you could get the line across this river, you would feel better, eh?"

"Feel better, my God!" Colbeck said. "It would bring the thing down to my size. It would save my neck."

"How long is it going to take you?"

Colbeck's mouth corners sagged. "I know you're engineer enough to see the truth. I doubt if Colbeck Construction will ever be able to put that pipeline across."

Renny turned to look back at the river crossing. It was, he reflected, a tough job. And it was a job that would have to be pushed to a quick completion, if the big pipeline was to go into operation.

Renny had been on the telephone to Washington earlier in the afternoon, and he had received a blunt statement about just how imperative the pipeline was to the war progress. The beginning of the line, the hundreds of miles from here back into the mid-continent oil fields, was already being filled with oil. The sections on east were complete, and almost entirely water-pressure tested. In brief, the whole line was ready to go except this vital link.

The ugly part of the situation was this: No one but Colbeck Construction could finish this link of the line within, at best, several months or a year. The reason for this was the special machinery necessary.

Building a 24-inch pipeline was something new. A long line of that diameter had never been attempted before. For this river crossing, Colbeck Construction had started a year and a half ago designing and ordering the special machinery for the river crossing part of the job. The machinery was here. It was all right here on the river bank, on the water, on the barges. That machinery had to be used. Without it, there would be a delay of months or a year until similar machinery could be constructed.

Renny scowled at the sullen, nasty looking river with its squirming expanse of muddy water. It was a big river. It was treacherous, the kind of a river that would crush the soul of an engineer.

Renny turned to Colbeck.

"What would you say to my lending a hand?" he asked.

The emotion, relief and hope, that lunged through Colbeck for a moment made the man speechless. "You—you mean that?" he asked, at last.

"Sure."

Colbeck put out his hand. "Brother, you've got a job," he said. Then, because his voice was so hoarse with emotion, he cleared his throat.

They rode back to the hotel which was Colbeck Construction headquarters. Renny asked, "How much sleep did you get last night, Colbeck?"

"A couple of hours. Which was more than I got the night before."

Renny said, "You pile into bed right away. Get some sleep, so you'll be worth something."

Colbeck grinned. "I believe I might. I'll take you in to Art and explain the situation."

Arthur Strain was sitting in the office behind a pile of telephone books. He indicated the telephone wearily. "I've run up a thousand dollars in telephone tolls," he complained. "We haven't got a chance of hiring experienced pipeliners to replace our men who are quitting. We're licked. Ordinarily, we could use green help. But this river job demands experienced men."

Colbeck looked uneasily at Renny Renwick. "What do you say to that?"

"We may whip it," Renny told him.

Arthur Strain, somewhat startled, asked, "What's this? You two were about to chop each other's heads off when you first met."

"Renwick is going to take over the job of putting that pipe across the river," Colbeck said.

"What?" Strain gasped, and his mouth remained open.

"That's right," Colbeck said.

"Good Lord!" Strain said softly.

"Look, you don't need to be so astonished," Bill Colbeck told his general manager. "Renwick is more engineer than I ever thought Colbeck Construction would ever have working for it. I'm damned glad to get him. You should be, too, considering how much money you've sunk into the concern."

Arthur Strain whistled shrilly. He fumbled for a cigarette and lit it, all the while staring from Bill Colbeck to Renny Renwick. Speaking over and through his amazement, he said, "I'm bowled over. But Bill is right. This is a damned fine break."

"Renwick has some plans," Colbeck said.

Renny asked, "Skilled manpower your principal difficulty right now?"

"That's right," Arthur Strain agreed. "We have lost, for one reason or another, our foundation of skilled and experienced men. Some of them have been hurt— and Colbeck will tell you that he's believed some of the accidents that injured them were rather strange—and some of them have quit us because of this Colbeck-Morgan feud."

Renny said, "All right. First, get hold of all the experienced men you've got left. Jerk them off whatever jobs they're on now. Get them here on this river job. Every man who has experience."

Colbeck grunted pleasantly. He reached for a telephone. "Some of them I can get by telephone. We use short-wave radio to keep in touch with our other line crews, so we can get others that way."

"You're supposed to get some sleep," Renny reminded him.

"I'll sleep fine," Colbeck said, "after I know the men you want are on their way."

Arthur Strain said, "Renwick—even with all our men, you won't have enough. I know. I had this same idea, and I checked our experienced-man lists."

"Get them here," Renny directed. "We'll use what we can get, and short-cut the job."

"That'll mean taking chances, gambling. That river crossing is a devil. Lose an inch, and you've lost it all."

"That's what we'll do."

Arthur Strain shook his head slowly. "That'll be like walking a tight-rope across Niagara Falls. Either the rope holds you, or you're a gone goose."

"That's about it."

"I'm afraid I'll have to be on record as opposing your idea," Arthur Strain said.

"Want to help us, or want to quit now?"

"Oh, don't get me wrong," Strain said. "I'll help with every lick I can hit. After all, I've got something like four million dollars of my own money sunk into this job. If we whip that river, I might salvage that."

"Good."

"I hope you know what you're doing," Strain said grimly.

"I know what I'm doing," Renny told him.

It was dark, nearly midnight, when Renny left the hotel where Colbeck Construction had its headquarters. Bill Colbeck had gone to bed, and so had Arthur Strain.

They had managed to locate a skeleton crew of men

with river experience, divers, dredge men, men who knew pipe and a river.

Knowing pipe and a river was the thing. They had to have such men. It was a specialized knowledge, like being able to use a bombsight to put a bomb through a factory roof from twenty thousand feet, or being able to take a barrel of crude oil and get a lump of synthetic rubber out of it. Except that bombardiers and synthetic rubber chemists were a lot more plentiful than men who knew how to get twenty-four-inch pipe across a devil of a river.

Renny jumped when a, "Ps-s-s-t!" came out of the darkness. It was Monk.

"Thought we were going to get together after work," Monk said.

"I got too busy," Renny told him. "You got something?"

"I sure have." Monk beckoned. "Better get out of sight. I don't think anybody suspects me yet, but I want to avoid taking chances."

Renny joined Monk in the murk between two buildings. Monk explained quickly, "That welder I was swamping for, that Dave bird, is mixed up in it, all right. He's going to some kind of a meeting, and he's going to put in a word for me with his boss."

"You must have really put the pressure on him," Renny said.

"Yeah. The point is, we might trail this Dave to the meeting, and do ourselves some good."

"Let's go," Renny said grimly.

"I wish we could get hold of Doc."

"Any word from Doc?"

"I was over to the jail a minute ago. The Sheriff threw me out again. He wouldn't even listen to me."

Renny said, "That Sheriff throws us out a little too promptly."

"Eh?"

"You know something?"

"What do you mean?"

"I have a hunch this jail thing is a rig. Don't ask me why, because I haven't any proof. But that Sheriff isn't a fool, and he's been acting like one. And when intelligent people begin doing fool things, and Doc is in the neighborhood, you can generally bet a fuse has been lighted somewhere."

"But what could be going on?"

"Don't ask me," Renny muttered. "Let's start shagging around after this Dave individual."

The man called Dave had a room in a green bungalow on Wisteria Street. The light in the room went out ten minutes after midnight, and shortly a figure came out of the house.

"That's Dave," Monk whispered to Renny. They were sitting under a low pine tree in a yard across Wisteria.

Dave went north. Monk and Renny followed, moving through yards, avoiding the sidewalks and streetlights. Dave headed for the center of town, the business section, which was largely in darkness.

A block west of the town square, which was the usual park containing the county courthouse, Dave turned into a vacant lot used for parking. He climbed into a large truck with a van body, and backed it out.

"Holy cow!" Renny rumbled. "We'll be lucky if we don't lose him now!"

To their relief, Dave pulled into a filling station on the next corner. The attendant began filling the gas tank.

"Come on!" Monk said. "I think we can climb into the back of that truck without him seeing us."

Renny thought so, too. They kept close to the fronts of stores, doubled in behind the filling-station building, watched their chance. While the attendant was accepting payment from Dave, they were able to move silently to the open rear of the truck van, lift themselves up on the tailboard, and inside.

They sat there, in intense darkness, pleased with themselves.

The truck got moving. It lurched out into the street, and turned south.

Several bulky objects in the front of the truck body which Monk and Renny had taken to be freight of some sort now stirred and became men who had been concealed under a tarpaulin.

Glare from flashlights abruptly filled the truck.

Renny's shocked, "Holy cow!" did not get out of his throat. It seemed to stick there. There were, as nearly as his blinded eyes could discern, seven men besides themselves in the truck. He wondered, foolishly, how so many men and guns could have been hidden there without Monk and himself realizing it in time.

One of the men pulled the van doors shut, after stepping carefully past them, to say, "You with the big fists—we'll search you first."

The truck drove, as nearly as Renny and Monk could estimate, about seventy miles, most of the distance on concrete. During the long ride, at least two hours, all seven of the men spoke a combined total of not more than ten words. They hardly took their eyes off Monk and Renny, kept the flashlights on, and kept their guns—mostly shotguns—on cock.

Then, for about a mile, the truck jounced over rough road, the last quarter-mile steeply downhill. Renny smelled river just before they stopped.

Some of the men unloaded, and spoke in low voices to other men outside.

"Out," Renny and Monk were ordered.

They were taken aboard a houseboat, a lubberly vessel consisting of a ponderous barge with a square unlovely house structure built upon it.

One of the men hauled open a floor trapdoor.

"Down," he said.

Renny and Monk climbed down into the hold of the barge. The bilge stink in the place made them both cough. There was about an inch of slime underfoot, and where the barge was down at the stern, probably a foot of dirty river water. There were two electric lanterns which gave quite a bright light.

"Ham!" Monk exploded.

Ham Brooks was sitting in a kitchen chair, with both arms extended out from his sides and held in this position by half-inch rope tied to his wrists and to either side of the barge hull.

Behind Ham, also on a chair with her wrists similarly secured, was a girl.

Monk, looking past Ham at the girl, decided she must be Nola Morgan.

The man Dave said to someone in the deckhouse above, "Toss two more chairs down here."

Monk and Renny were put in the chairs, told, "Hold out your arms!" Dave did the knotting of the ropes to their wrists, using sailor knots and tying them as tightly as he possibly could. Renny, clenching his teeth with pain, saw that the girl's hands, and Monk's, were purple and useless from the constriction of the ropes which held them.

Monk, when he could get his mind off the pain of his wrists, asked, "Are you Nola Morgan?"

"Yes," she said.

Ham said, "They caught us this afternoon. I thought for a minute Miss Morgan had led me into a trap, because right after the men grabbed me, one of them asked another if I was the man the girl had described. I took that to mean Miss Morgan had decoyed me into an ambush. I yelled something about it—and that tipped them off Miss Morgan was near. That was what they were trying to find out. It was a trick. They caught her."

Ham's voice was bitter with self-condemnation. He had been responsible for the girl getting caught. He was sick about that.

Nola Morgan spoke, evenly enough.

"There's a chance for us," she said. "They want the misericord."

"Misericord?" Renny said.

Nola Morgan said, "If I give the misericord to them, they promise to turn us loose. Mr. Brooks thinks they won't."

Ham said, "They won't. You can look at them and know that."

"We'll have to take the chance."

"No."

The girl told Renny and Monk, "I'll have to give them the misericord. If I don't, they will leave us here in the houseboat when they drift it against the dam."

Renny stared at her unbelievingly. "What are they going to do? Blow open the dam in the river above where we're putting the pipeline across?"

"That's right. They're going to load the houseboat with dynamite, drift it against the dam and set it off. They'll knock out the dam watchman so that he can't give an alarm or stop it."

Renny felt his mouth getting dry from fear. He thought of the surly yellow river, already near flood, and he thought of the pipeline machinery on the lowlands at the spot where they were trying to put the line across the river.

Blowing the dam might not cause any great flood, and probably it wouldn't drown anyone. But it would sweep away the barges and wreck the special machinery for handling the twenty-four-inch pipe. It would certainly do that. For six months, a year maybe, there would be no line across the river. Not until that special machinery was replaced.

With that conviction in his mind, he had another thought, a wry one, to wit: It was odd that he should be worrying about the pipeline, whereas his own life and the lives of the others was equally at stake. That way of thinking was a soldier's way of thinking. Because actually a great deal more in the way of blood and tears and human values depended on the completion of the pipeline than hinged on whether or not Nola Morgan and Monk and Ham and himself continued to live. This pipeline was a vital weapon against the monster of war; without it, the monster would certainly flourish, live longer and more horribly.

Renny shivered.

XI.

The office had no windows, but it did have a large skylight through which all the scattered spark-like stars in the night sky were visible. The office was long, narrow, with a very high ceiling. Once, it had been a hall in the center of the building, which accounted for the absence of windows. It was an ancient worn place, but regal, too.

Tom Scott Morgan, sheriff of the county, found himself stepping softly when he came into the room. He grinned at himself, thinking that it was funny how another man could impress you until you even walked lightly in his presence.

The Sheriff put down the tray he was carrying, placing it on the table. "I figured you might use something to eat," he said.

Doc Savage had been pacing the room, around and around with a steady, restless, intense stride. He paused, and said, "Thank you." And in the same breath, asked, "Has the man from Little Rock gotten here yet?"

"Not yet," the Sheriff said. "The train will be twenty minutes late. I just called."

The bronze man made a move to resume pacing, just enough of a move to hint that he was on edge and wild with impatience. Then, with outward calm that was unruffled, he sat at a table and took one of the sandwiches.

"Any trace of the truck?" he asked.

The Sheriff was uncomfortable. "No. The last report we've been able to dig up is that it was heading north on the river highway. There's a dozen roads it could have turned off."

"Your men are still sure that Monk and Renny climbed into the truck?"

"Yes."

"What about Ham and your sister? Any trace of them?"

"No, not a sign," the Sheriff said.

Sheriff Tom Scott Morgan spoke heavily, and now it became his turn to feel the stomach-hollowing rage of impatience, of futility. Because he was a careful, taciturn man who never liked to show his feelings, he deliberately sat on the corner of a desk and dangled a foot. This waiting was agony for him.

He knew it was a waste of time for him to think about the situation. He'd already beaten his brains until they ached, helplessly. His helplessness made more complete his trust in Doc Savage; he was like a man who couldn't swim hanging on to one who could.

However, he had trusted Doc Savage from the beginning. The first thing he had done after arresting Savage was to get in touch with Washington by telephone, and with the Governor of the state. Their instructions had been to work with Doc Savage, and that was his inclination, anyway. He had explained this to his sister, Nola, and she had surprised him by agreeing immediately. She had not, at first, realized Savage's standing.

As Doc Savage had made succeeding moves, the Sheriff had become more puzzled. He had understood Doc's motive in sending for his aides in New York—but why had the bronze man despatched Nola on that mission? They had talked over the summoning of Monk, Ham and Renny here in this office—Bill Colbeck and Arthur Strain had been present · at the time—and it had struck the Sheriff that it would be much easier and more sensible to telephone Monk and the others. But Doc had not agreed. He had insisted on a personal messenger, and Nola was a logical one, because she had a good private plane.

Very carefully, though, Doc Savage had explained to Nola that she might be followed or waylaid and she must be careful. There had been only Nola and her brother present when Doc explained this. The bronze man had, the Sheriff knew, been reluctant to let Nola do the job. But she had, and she had come back safely, and she had been followed as Doc Savage predicted she would be.

The bronze man, the Sheriff realized, had known almost certainly that the girl would be followed. This had surprised the Sheriff, and given him the conviction that Doc knew exactly what he was doing.

Why Monk and Ham and Renny hadn't been told that Doc Savage was really not under arrest, the Sheriff didn't know. He suspected it was a case of not having too many cooks. As far as the Sheriff knew, only he and his sister were aware that Savage was not a prisoner.

Savage's instructions had been to allow everything to proceed normally, as it would if he were in jail.

The exception was the misericord. They had sent for that.

Doc Savage lifted his head abruptly, listening to a train-whistle in the distance. He glanced at the Sheriff, and the officer nodded. "He'll be on that train," he said.

"The misericord will be brought directly here?" Doc Savage asked.

"Yes."

The misericord had been in the safety deposit box in the Little Rock bank where the Morgans kept an account. Nola Morgan had taken it there, as soon as she learned that it was important, and that it was desired by others who were willing to take violent measures to get it.

Two deputies had gone to the Little Rock bank to get the misericord. They had left yesterday, and the delay was due to a misunderstanding with the bank officials, necessitating considerable telephoning for the purpose of identification.

But the misericord should be on that train which had just whistled. Doc Savage wanted to see it. In a few minutes, it would be in his hands.

Doc asked the Sheriff, "Any more threats?"

The Sheriff shook his head. Rage made him

compress his lips until they were as tight as the hard lips of a catfish.

There had been only the one telephone call, anonymous. Turn over the misericord, or Nola Morgan would be killed. This communication had been their first proof that Nola Morgan was in trouble, and ever since the Sheriff had been fighting a sickness inside.

Footsteps sounded outside. A voice called, "Tom?"

"They're here," Sheriff Tom Scott Morgan said swiftly. He opened the door. "You got it?" he demanded.

The two deputies who had gone to Little Rock came inside. One of them said, "Sure. Here it is."

The misericord was a large one, about sixteen inches long. A true misericord was a thing with a thin needle-like blade, its purpose being to slip between the joints of a suit of armor in order to finish off the occupant. This one was large for that, although the blade was thin enough, and wicked.

Doc Savage turned the misericord in his hands. It was hand-made, and exquisitely so. The workmanship was careful, painstaking. He held the weapon by the blade and swished the handle up and down, and the blade was flexible.

"The handle been taken apart?" he asked.

Sheriff Tom Scott Morgan nodded. "Taken apart. The whole thing X-rayed, and gone over with a microscope for signs of engraving. Nothing to be found."

Doc pulled the blade thoughtfully across a finger, testing it.

"This was made by Carl Boordling in the State Penitentiary," he asked. "And it was given to Nola Morgan with the inference that it was the clue to who murdered Erasmus Morgan?"

"That's right."

The bronze man examined the blade intently, and moved a fingernail over its edge. He seemed totally preoccupied in the cutting edge of the knife, as if it held the truth about the knife.

"What about this Carl Boordling," the bronze man said suddenly. "Who was he?"

Tom Scott Morgan had much information about

Boordling on the tip of his tongue. "The man was educated, a college product, an engineer, who went to the dogs. He came here from the east. I think his family was killed in an automobile accident when he was driving the car, and this put him on the downgrade. He was here in town about two years, and hung out with a tough crowd.

"Several months ago, Boordling was suspected of a black-market business in gasoline tickets. He would do anything for money. Later he was arrested—"

"After Erasmus Morgan was killed?"

"Yes. But he was never suspected of any connection with the death of Erasmus Morgan. Boordling was arrested for black-marketing gasoline, and convicted and got a quick trip to the penitentiary. Somehow or other he wound up in the state pen, not the federal, because the state handled the prosecution. Anyway, he was in State when he gave my sister that misericord. And a few days later he died, ostensibly from poison he had secured from the penitentiary photographic darkroom chemical supply, and taken deliberately. Suicide. My sister thinks he was murdered."

Doc said, "Will you bring me this Boordling's record?"

The Sheriff stood up quickly. "Sure." He went away, and was back shortly with the galley card.

Doc looked over Carl Boordling's record. It was not particularly vicious; it was just distasteful and unpleasant. It was the story of the fall of a man from a respected and skilled position. The wreck of a career.

Abruptly Doc Savage picked up a pencil and ringed a part of Carl Boordling's record.

"Employed five years with the King Novelty Company, during which he was credited with four inventions." The bronze man leaned back; for a while he looked at the ceiling fixedly, thoughtfully. "I think I remember some of the products of the King Novelty Company," he said.

Suddenly he fished through the papers on his desk. Not finding what he wished, he asked the Sheriff, "Do you have one of your business cards with you?"

The Sheriff shook his head, then admitted sheepishly, "I got an old campaign card of mine in my billfold. That do?"

"Let's see it."

Sheriff Morgan was baffled by what the bronze man did with the card. Doc merely held the edge of the card against the blade of the misericord and—holding misericord and business card close to his face—slowly cut into the edge of the card with a single long stroke.

That was all. But from the bronze man's facial expression, the Sheriff knew that something important had happened.

Doc got to his feet.

He wrapped the knife very carefully in paper, tied it with string, and handed it to Morgan. "Hang on to this," he said. "It's going to hang a man."

"Damn me!" Morgan said. "I don't get it."

Doc said, "Keep your deputies on call here. I'm going out to see a man. If things go right, I will be able to wind this thing up quickly by myself. If not, I'll need help, and plenty of help."

Morgan indicated the knife. "What'll I do with this?"

"Keep it safe."

"But if something would happen, how would I know—"

"Get the King Novelty Company on the telephone and ask them what Carl Boordling invented for them," Doc said. He moved toward the door.

"Wait a minute!" Morgan said sharply. "What's the idea of not telling me what this misericord means?"

"Our bird is a very bold bird, but if it was to get around that we know what the knife means, the bird wouldn't be bold. The bird would take wings, and might get away. Or is that childish?"

Morgan scratched his head. "I'll think about it and let you know."

Doc Savage moved rapidly when he reached the street, heading for the business district. It was very dark, the hour not far from dawn, and the streets deserted.

He walked rapidly, then slackened his pace. He had

been determined on a course when he left the jail, but now indecision had taken hold of him. He was not sure.

He stopped finally, in the murk of a doorway, and gave more thought to what he should do. His first intent had been to act directly, to confront the man he suspected, to charge the man, arrest him. He had enough proof. Until tonight, he had had suspicion, enough suspicion to make certainty in his mind. He had known quite surely who had killed old Erasmus Morgan, and who had caused all the trouble for Colbeck Construction, and he had known why. But the proof he had was circumstantial, a putting of two and two together to get four. It was not direct proof. And direct proof he had to have. The knife, the misericord, had given him that. He had more than an opinion, a guess, now.

But now he was thinking of Monk, Ham, Renny and Nola Morgan, and he wasn't quite sure direct action was the thing. Standing there in the darkness, his uncertainty increased until he decided to do it differently.

He resumed walking until he came to an all-night garage with a lunch stand adjacent. In the lunchroom there was no one but a sleepy counterman.

"Use your phone?" the bronze man asked.

"Go ahead. It's a pay phone," the counterman said indifferently.

Doc Savage picked up the receiver. But he did not make a call; instead, he put the receiver back on the hook, and went outside.

Walking slowly in the darkness, he began practicing Pack's voice, as nearly as he remembered it. He went back, with his mind, to the minutes three days ago when he had been hidden in the rope sling under the pipe-truck and had listened to Pack talk to his men. He concentrated on bringing out of his memory Pack's tone, his inflection, all of Pack's character that was in Pack's speech. He tried Pack's voice again and again, using it to rehearse the simple speech he intended to make over the telephone.

He went back to the lunchroom telephone and called the number he wanted.

"I guess you know who this is," he said into the telephone mouthpiece. "I wouldn't call you like this, but there's a bad break. We can get the misericord if you'll come out here where we're holding them."

That was his speech. That was all he intended to say. He held his breath, waiting.

Low frightened profanity came over the wire for a moment, then, "I'll be there right away!" The receiver went down on the other end of the wire.

The bronze man breathed inward deeply, held the breath, let it out with a rush of relief. His shirt was wet with the perspiration that tension had brought.

XII.

The highway was a damp ribbon through the pre-dawn fog. It was no longer dark, but the sun was not visible because the fog that came from the river, where the cold sullen muddy water was condensing the moisture in the warmer air, was crossing the highway in slow rolling masses.

The fog, or possibly dampness coming up through the concrete during the night, had put a wet film over the highway on which showed to some extent the tracks of the car which Doc Savage was following.

By keeping a close watch on the pavement, he could guess how far the other car was ahead, and measure his speed accordingly. He was going fast. For thirty miles he had not been under fifty. For a while he had been able to watch the car without difficulty, because the driver had kept his yellow fog lights on, but now that it was lighter, the fog lights were off, and it was something of a blind-man's buff.

When Doc suddenly discovered the fresh car tracks were no longer on the wet pavement, it was a biting shock. He slowed the car, a little at a time, decreasing the engine speed so that it would sound as if it had gone on. He pulled over to the side of the road, shut off the motor, got out and went back, running.

The car could not have turned off far back, probably within the last half or three-quarters of a mile. He kept to the side of the road, on the shoulder, watching and listening as he went.

He found a side road, gravel. It did not show the tracks nearly as plainly, but there were pebbles which had been turned over freshly, small signs, difficult to locate. The car had turned off on the gravel.

He did not go back for his own machine. This road would not extend far. It led down toward the river, and there were no bridges here, nowhere for the road to go but to the river bank.

He followed it half a mile, then heard men running in front of him, coming toward him. He left the gravel road in a hurry, taking cover.

The running men appeared out of the fog, two of them, Dave and another. They were breathing heavily.

Dave stopped, told the other man loudly, "This is far enough for you. You stay here. If you hear my signal, pass it back quick."

"You'll whistle three times if cops come, twice if somebody comes and you're not sure whether it's cops, and once if it's somebody who is okay?"

"That's it," Dave said.

Dave ran on up the road. The man he had left got off the road, taking shelter in bushes, and remained there.

Satisfied the pair were lookouts only, Doc Savage went on, keeping off the road, moving through the brush parallel to it as silently as he could.

He came shortly to a house, a ramshackle place that had no panes in the windows and no doors on the frames. Nearby were two sheds obviously used as garages. Beyond was the river, a floating dock, a houseboat tied to the dock.

In front of one of the garage sheds stood the car which Doc Savage had followed here. Three men waited beside it, impatiently, glancing often at the houseboat.

Shortly a man came running from the houseboat carrying a man's coat, hat, trousers and necktie. The garments, Doc saw, were those that had been worn by the man he had trailed.

One of the waiting men started a hurried exchanging of the clothes for his own. He got into the car when he had finished the job.

He asked anxiously, "Think I look enough like him to fool anybody who happened to be trailing him into following me away from here?"

"Keep your face down, and you'll get by."

"What if I'm picked up?"

"You don't know anything. Stick to that."

The man drove away. He was frightened.

The others watched him go, and one muttered, "I wish to hell that dynamite was here, and this thing was over with."

"What I don't get," his companion complained, "is who made that telephone call, if Pack didn't?"

"Damned if I know."

"Well, it's sure queer."

"Just so they don't catch that truckload of dynamite on its way here. That would be a hard thing to explain." The man nodded toward the river dam about a mile downstream. "They would sure as blazes guess it was going to be used on the dam."

That was all Doc Savage was able to get of their conversation, because the pair moved into small bushes and crouched down there in hiding. Doc had not been able to hear all their words, but by watching their lips closely, he had a general idea of what they had said.

A truck and dynamite and the dam—these were words that had clattered heavily on his ears. He frowned at the brown ugly river, visible between the bushes, wishing he didn't have to face the conviction that these men intended to dynamite the dam and send an increased volume of water down to ruin the Colbeck Construction river pipeline crossing job.

Suddenly Doc wished he had brought along help. It

would be no spectacular flood if they broke the dam, because it was not a high dam. It was not even likely that much farmland would be flooded. But the pipeline-crossing would be wiped out. All the barges, the machinery that was specially designed for work with twenty-four-inch pipe, would be torn loose, smashed, lost in the river.

He decided, abruptly, to get to a telephone and summon help. There should be houses along the highway from which he could telephone.

He was moving away through the undergrowth when he heard a truck in the distance. Then a whistle, and the whistle was relayed. A single whistle. That, he remembered, was to mean that whoever was coming was known. And he could tell that the truck was on the gravel road.

He halted, weighing possibilities, and in the end decided he dared not take the time to go call help.

He went back, this time to the river bank. In the bushes there, he stripped off shoes and coat and shirt and necktie, concealing these carefully in the weeds. He rolled his trouser legs as high as they would go, so they wouldn't bag full of water and impede swimming too much.

The truck arrived. It was not a large one, and the back was open. It contained possibly a dozen metal kegs of the type used to pack blasting powder.

"Hey, I thought it was supposed to be dynamite," someone complained.

The driver said, "I was lucky to get this. It'll do the job."

It would do the job all right. It would do it as well as dynamite, probably.

Doc Savage decided that now was as good a time as any to try to reach the houseboat. He couldn't wait much longer, because the fog was beginning to thin over the river.

He eased quietly into the river. Because this was backwater from a dam, and the river was high and tormented anyway, enough bushes overhung the water to conceal him.

The water was cold; not a clean bite, but a nasty, clammy, lifeless chilling sensation. He sank very deep, and took his time.

It was not too difficult, if he had no mishaps. The greatest distance he would have to cover without showing himself—which meant swimming under-water—was not more than fifty feet. There was nothing to keep him from making that, nothing whatever. But at the end of it, if he put his head out of the water in the wrong place, he would probably be shot instantly. It was not an easy swim.

He breathed very deeply and rapidly to get an extra charge of oxygen, then took a normal breath, sank and swam. He allowed for the slight current, swam with long strokes on his back under the water, so that he could tell if he came too near the surface.

There was plenty of air in his lungs when he bumped into the houseboat. He worked around to the stern. The slime seemed to be half an inch thick on the timbers.

He raised to the surface and got air into his lungs and nothing unexpected happened.

He was on the river-ward side of the boat. By lifting an arm, he could touch the edge of the hull, the rail. He closed both hands over this, lifted silently on to the deck.

He could not stay there. He could hear voices in the superstructure, one of them the voice of the man he had followed here. They were excited, uneasy.

Near the bronze man's feet was a crude hatch, a square affair, that might admit him to the innards of the houseboat hull. He sank beside the hatch, found it had a heavy set of hinges, a hasp, with a bolt thrust through the hasp. He managed to unscrew the nut on the end of the bolt with his fingers.

The hatch made a small rusty grunting as he opened it. Out of the hole came the smell of disuse, of river slime.

He went down quickly, pulling the hatch shut behind him to block off the light. He crouched there. There had not been much light outside, but this was dark by comparison.

At the far end of the cavernous, low-ceilinged barge hull, a single electric hand-lantern, hung from the ceiling. Its battery was low, the light from it reddish and inadequate.

He distinguished four figures tied to chairs—Monk, Ham, Renny and Nola Morgan.

He became tight with anxiety lest they had not recognized him. Then he heard Monk, his voice so grated by pain that it seemed to come from a sand-filled throat, say, "Quiet! For God's sake, be quiet!" Monk had recognized him.

The four, Doc saw, were not tied to the chairs, but to either side of the hull instead. Their arms were stretched out tightly, and their congested hands were not pleasant to look at.

There were no guards in the hull. Doc went forward quickly. He had his pocket knife out when he reached Renny, and he sliced through the rope.

Renny's arms, when they came loose from the rope, seemed to take on enormous weight, a force that pulled Renny forward and down, all but out of the chair. And they wouldn't bend.

In the midst of his trouble with his arms, Renny tried to point upward. He was afraid to speak. He was trying to signal.

He meant that there was a hatch overhead. Open. It led into the cabin.

Doc nodded that he understood. He went on, cut loose Nola Morgan next, then Ham and Monk. All of them had the same difficulty with their hands and arms. Their arms had been stretched out by the ropes so long that now they were of no use.

Doc watched them closely. There would be a few moments now when they could do nothing. When, moreover, there would be awful stinging agony as circulation resumed in their tortured hands. He watched them fighting the pain. He went to each of them silently, doing what he could to restore use of their arms.

* * *

Overhead, there was scuffling, and a heavy bump as a burden was slammed down on the cabin floor. Someone cursed the slammer of the burden, ending by asking what he was trying to do, blow them all to kingdom come.

The other laughed sourly. "Black powder won't explode from shock."

"Well, take it easy anyway," the first man snapped. "How many more of those kegs are there?"

"Eleven more. Twelve altogether."

"Is it enough?"

"If it's set off right, it is."

"Well, how'll we set it off?"

They got into an argument then about how to set off the powder, one school of opinion maintaining that if it was just exploded in the cabin, or even in the hull, most of the force would be expended upward, and the dam wouldn't be blown out even if the barge was smack against the dam at the time.

Doc beckoned at Nola Morgan, Monk and the others. He indicated the stern hatch where he had entered. His plan was to get all of them outside and into the river. And then, if they were very lucky, they could swim underwater as far as the shore.

"Can you swim fifty feet or so under water?" he whispered to Nola Morgan.

She nodded.

They were under the hatch, and Doc had his hands against the underside of the hatch, ready to shove, when he heard footsteps on the deck. One man.

The man walked to the riverward end of the houseboat. He stopped, standing directly overhead. Doc stood there tensely, imagining the man looking around, searching for signs of trouble.

"What the hell!" the man overhead said explosively. He stooped, and Doc heard the bolt rattle against the hasp. The man had discovered the bolt out of the hasp, was replacing it. They were locked in.

But the man didn't go away. He stood there, and his curiosity must have climbed, because suddenly he yanked the bolt out and hauled open the hatch. Then he made a fool mistake, putting his head down the hole to see if anything was wrong.

Doc got him by the throat.

XIII.

The ideal result would be to get the man silenced instantly. Doc tried very hard to do it. He failed. It seemed to him that the victim could not possibly have made more noise. The fellow kicked his feet frantically, on the deck, beat the deck with his hands. Moreover, he made an assortment of squawks by squeezing air out past the bronze man's fingers around his throat.

Doc got one hand loose, hit the man an uppercut, as hard as he could manage. That silenced the fellow. But it was too late. They were yelling in the cabin. The man had a revolver. It dropped down into the hull. Monk got it. His hands were so stiff that he had to hold the weapon with both of them.

"Out!" Doc said. "Fast!"

He went out of the hole himself. Their position was bad. They were outnumbered. The others were in no condition for really effective fighting.

Men were coming down the narrow deck from the deckhouse door, shouting questions.

Ham Brooks, with tardy presence of mind, shouted, "It's all right. I tripped."

The men kept coming.

Doc Savage reached up, got the overhang of the deckhouse roof, and chinned himself, hooked his elbows over the edge, and climbed on top. The roof was tar-papered, and the covering was sun-cracked.

There were two stovepipes protruding from the roof. Doc kicked them violently as he went past, hoping the commotion in the cabin would add to the confusion.

One of the stovepipes broke off, bounced ahead of him, and he scooped it up.

He discovered a man standing on the floating dock, holding a powder drum in his arms, staring foolishly. Doc threw the stovepipe at the man, and it hit him squarely across the face. The man did not drop the drum, did not move, did not do anything but stare. He had a revolver stuck into his belt.

Doc decided to try to get the gun. He made a short running jump for the man. The spectacular method would have been to jump and hit the man with both feet, an impact that would kill or badly injure the fellow. It was tempting. But if something went wrong, it could readily mean a broken leg. Doc jumped for the dock beside the man.

He landed heavily, letting momentum throw him against the man. The fellow staggered, flailed his arms, the powder drum falling. Doc tried to grab him, but the man—gun still in his belt—somersaulted off the dock backward into the river.

The powder drum was rolling slowly. Doc got it before it went off the dock edge, and with it, jumped back aboard the houseboat.

Two men, just coming out of the door, saw him and retreated. They backed into the cabin. There were four others in the cabin at least, judging from the sounds.

Doc, close against the dockhouse wall to one side of the door, struck the powder drum against the edge of the door. The lid, a push-in affair similar to those on most tin cans, popped off, letting the black powder flow out.

Doc heaved loose powder through the cabin door as if he was shoveling wheat. The powder scattered in the cabin about like black wheat. When he had the drum nearly empty, he heaved that inside, too.

"If you shoot," he shouted, "you'll explode the powder!"

This wasn't exactly true. Unless the gun flame actually touched the powder grains, it wouldn't catch. And if it did, it would burn, not explode. But it would burn very briskly.

*   *   *

At the stern, there was scuffling. Doc hadn't noticed how many had run aft. But now a shot banged out at the stern; a man said something sick and horrified before he stumbled backward into view. He sat down on the deck, holding his upper chest.

Monk came into view, holding a gun with both hands, aiming at the shot man's head. But Monk changed his mind—to Doc Savage's unbounded relief—and kicked the wounded man's jaw somewhat out of shape, instead of shooting him again.

Monk shouted at Doc, "Only two came back here! Renny got the other one!"

"Throw me your gun!" Doc said.

On shore, a man galloped into view and bellowed, "What the hell's going on there?"

Monk decided to shoot him.

"Throw me that gun!" Doc said again.

Monk got it this time. He started to toss the weapon toward Doc, became afraid it would fall overboard, and stumbled down the deck a few yards before he tossed it.

Doc caught the weapon.

He put the muzzle close to the powder he had spilled and pulled the trigger. The muzzle flame fired the spilled powder.

The amount of fire and smoke was entirely satisfactory. Doc lost his eyebrows, and as much of his bronze-colored hair as wasn't too damp to singe.

Inside the cabin, there was a whoosh! Smoke. Fire. Screams.

Doc had stumbled back and fallen in a sitting position on the deck, thinking he was burned worse than he was. Organizing himself, he rolled over and aimed carefully at the man on shore, who was still bellowing demands about what the hell was wrong.

Doc shot at the man three times. Three shells were all that were left in the gun. Unscathed, his target galloped off into the brush, yelling violent personal opinions.

Doc stared the the gun. The barrel, he noticed for the first time, had a noticeable bend.

Monk shouted, "Don't shoot that gun! I hit at the

guy Renny got and missed—struck the deckhouse and bent the barrel."

"You picked a nice time to tell me," Doc said.

A man came out of the cabin door. He came out in a flying leap, smoke streaming from his clothes, apparently blinded. He tripped over the deck rail and slammed down flat on the dock in a fall that was awful, but probably not fatal.

Ham Brooks—he was up on the cabin top— shouted, "The whole boat's going to blow up!" This was for the effect, because it wasn't going to do anything of the kind. But it was good propaganda for the men in the cabin. They began coming out.

Three appeared, one of them temporarily blinded, the other two confused but with good eyesight. Monk and Ham and Renny jumped down on the float and cooperated in a reception committee. They couldn't do much more than club with their benumbed arms, but they did that with enthusiasm.

Another man dashed out of the cabin. Nola Morgan said, "I'll try my luck on this one." She had picked up the heavy short bolt which had been through the lock hasp of the stern hatch, and she held it tightly clenched in her fist for weight and authority.

She hit the man's jaw. He dropped as if killed. Nola let fall the bolt, and clamped both palms against her cheeks.

"Oh!" She was horrified. "I didn't intend to hit him so hard! I killed him!"

She hadn't. The man rolled over, got up, and fell into the river, came to the surface, clutched the edge of the dock and hung on, screaming that he couldn't swim and how nice he'd be if they only wouldn't let him drown.

Monk looked at the deckhouse. "The big stink himself hasn't come out!" he said.

Doc listened to a man moaning and shrieking in terror inside the cabin. He decided the fellow was probably harmless, and went in. The place was full of smoke and the formidable odor and bite of much burned powder.

With a little groping, Doc got hold of Arthur Strain and hauled him out.

About that time, they heard a truck motor start, and heard the truck leave rapidly.

"There goes the rest of them," Renny said disgustedly.

Doc said, "I'll see if there's a phone at the dam."

The bronze man went ashore, and ran toward the dam. He exhausted his wind before he reached the dam, and arrived puffing for air.

He found a fat, amiable, white-haired man serving as dam watchman. The watchman was disgruntled.

"What the devil's going on?" he demanded. "My pal Bill, who was playing checkers with me, lit out a minute ago like he was afire."

"Who is your pal Bill?" Doc asked.

"Fellow who lives on that houseboat where the rumpus was."

"Your pal Bill," Doc explained, "was probably going to crack you over the head in a few minutes. Then they were going to float the houseboat against the dam with a load of powder aboard, and blow out a section of the dam."

The old man said something appropriate, and added, "I better get my shotgun."

"Where's your telephone?"

"In the shed. Blow out the dam? Who'd want to do that?"

"A man named Arthur Strain," Doc told him. He went to the telephone.

Late that afternoon, Sheriff Tom Scott Morgan came into his office grinning. He told Doc Savage, "Strain is arguing with the Prosecuting Attorney, offering to plead guilty of trying to squeeze Bill Colbeck out of Colbeck Construction. All Strain wants in return is not to be charged with murdering Erasmus Morgan."

"That would be a good trade," Doc said.

"Wouldn't it! Fat chance Strain has got."

Monk and Ham and Nola Morgan had been waiting

in the office. Nola asked, "Tom, have you got that misericord? I want to see it work."

"Oh, sure." The sheriff went to the desk around which they were sitting, opened a drawer and produced the misericord. "It was right here all the time. I thought you knew that. No, I guess I forgot to mention it."

Doc Savage demonstrated with the long-bladed misericord and a stiff business card.

"Carl Boordling, the man who made this knife, was evidently a party to the murder of Erasmus Morgan, or at least he knew that Strain did it," Doc explained.

He indicated the misericord's blade edge.

"Carl Boordling," he said, "was once with a novelty manufacturing concern which marketed one of those dime-store gadgets you probably have all seen. The gadget consists of a round piece of cardboard with a metal or plastic ribbon attached to the center. You hold the cardboard in one hand and draw the ribbon between the thumbnail and finger of your other hand. There is a sound-track, small ridges and depressions just as in the cut of a phonograph record, on the ribbon. When your thumbnail is drawn over it the novelty gadget will say something like, 'Hello, sweetheart,' or, 'Happy birthday, dear.'"

"When Carl Boordling was sent to the penitentiary on another charge, he must have been afraid Arthur Strain would kill him because of what he knew. So he made this misericord by hand, and he put a sound-track on the blade. It must have been very painstaking work, but Boordling was an expert at that sort of thing, so he managed very nicely."

Doc drew one edge of the knife across the card edge.

It said: "Arthur Strain killed—"

He drew the other edge over the card and got: "Erasmus Morgan."

"That," Doc Savage explained, "is why Arthur Strain was so anxious to get the misericord. It was probably the only real evidence against him."

Renny Renwick and Bill Colbeck arrived shortly afterward. Colbeck was excited. "I hear Strain's trying to make a deal. Confess he was throwing the hooks into me if they'll not charge him with murder!"

"Not a chance of such a deal," Doc assured him.

"I hope not!" Colbeck said indignantly. "He's got a nerve!"

Renny volunteered, "Doc, we're going to lick that river crossing. We've got enough experienced men. I think we'll have the line across the river in another two days. Anyway, we're sure to get it across."

Monk asked Colbeck, "You'll lose your time-forfeit anyway, won't you?"

"I suppose so," Colbeck admitted.

"Will it break you?"

"It'll sure give me a hell of a bend." Bill Colbeck grinned. "I like the way it's turning out, though. My God, it would have been awful if Art Strain had boosted me out of the company and taken control."

"Would Strain have managed that?"

"He sure would have. I was all set to take another loan off him, and I couldn't pay it back if this river-crossing had flopped—which he was going to see that it did. And I'd have given him enough more company stock to give him iron-bound control. Yeah, he'd have stolen the outfit."

Nola Morgan shuddered. "It doesn't seem possible there could have been murder and such conniving for control of just one business concern."

Bill Colbeck snorted. "Listen, I've got a fifteen million dollar outfit. I work all over the midwest. And you don't build twenty-four-inch pipelines with peanuts."

Monk looked admiringly at Bill Colbeck, thinking that Colbeck didn't look or act like a guy with fifteen million. Monk liked to hear somebody talking about that much money. It restored a guy's faith in himself. Monk's bank-account was currently slightly below zero, so his faith needed restoring.

He made a mental note to put the bite on Bill Colbeck for a small loan. He'd probably get it.

On the strength of the idea he made sheep's eyes at Nola Morgan. He'd ask her for a date, he decided.

It was discouraging to have Doc Savage stand up at

this point and say, "Miss Morgan and I are going out tonight and see what we can do about forgetting this mess."

Most unsatisfactory.

CARGO UNKNOWN

I.

Renny Renwick had felt uneasy all day. He had narrowed it down in his own mind to one of two possible causes. The first was the London fog. He disliked fogs unreasonably. Today's was a stinker; it made you feel as if eels were crawling all over you.

The second probability, which Renny Renwick thought was more likely, was that he was being followed. However, he hadn't been able to prove this to himself. He hadn't caught anybody hanging around on his trail—exactly.

He was worrying about it, wondering if it was possible that he was merely a nervous old fuddyduddy, when he got a telephone call.

"This is Commander Giesen," said the caller. "Could I see you immediately?"

"What about?"

"I'd rather not say over the telephone."

"Come on over," Renny said. He was mystified.

But a little thought while he was waiting for the man's arrival convinced him that he had heard of Commander Giesen. The Commander was someone important attached to, or in charge of, the staff of one of the liaison departments set up to smooth the working-together of English and Americans. This was all Renny knew about him. It was just a fragment of fact that stuck in Renny's mind. It might not even be the same Commander Giesen.

Only it was. He identified himself.

"Can we talk here?" Commander Giesen asked.

"Sure," Renny said.

The Commander was a tall middle-aged man with a rather stony presence and no little dignity. He was not a man you would like as a boon companion, not a fellow you would invite out for a drink with the expectation of having a roistering evening. But he was a man you would instinctively trust.

"This may strike you as unnecessary," the Commander told Renny. Then he went to the door, and spoke to three men who were outside.

The three men proceeded to go over Renny's hotel room as if hunting diamonds. They gave particular attention to the windows, pictures, openings, but omitted nothing.

"No microphones or eavesdroppers, sir," one of them reported. And the three left.

Renny wondered if he looked as startled as he actually was.

The Commander said, "What I have to say needs a preliminary speech which will go something like this: You are Colonel John Renwick, an engineer by profession, and you are also associated with Doc Savage. You have been in England as a consultant on industrial conversion back to peace production. Your work is finished. You have been complimented by the government office, banqueted by the factory men, decorated by the queen, and now you're ready to go back to New York."

Renny waited. He wondered what was coming.

The Commander leaned forward. "I am not flattering you, but instead am pointing out that you are a man of considerable ability and consequence, and that we are fully aware of it."

"I'm not such a big shot," Renny said modestly.

"Big enough to awe us somewhat," said the Commander. "And additionally you have a reputation of being quite frequently interested in the unusual, the mysterious."

Renny frowned. "Mysterious and unusual—what do you mean?"

"You are," said the Commander, "supposed to be a man who likes adventure."

"It sounds rather corny when you put it that way," Renny said. "But it's probably true. Anyway, I've heard other people say that about me. I guess it applies to all five of us. There are five of us associated with Doc Savage, you know."

"I know," agreed Commander Giesen, nodding. "Your prestige as a Doc Savage associate influenced us quite a lot in deciding to ask you to do this rather unusual job."

Renny examined the other. "You came here to ask me to do something?"

"Righto."

"What is it?"

"I understand you have some submarine experience," said Commander Giesen.

"That's right."

"What sort of experience, may I ask?"

"I've designed them," Renny said. "I've built them and I've test-dived them. I've done every kind of creative engineering job there is to do around a submarine."

Commander Giesen looked relieved. "This isn't an engineering job."

"Well, what kind of a job is it?"

"We want you to go back to America aboard a submarine," the Commander said.

"Ride back to the United States on a sub? That what you mean?"

"Yes."

"Look, I'm not so hot about the idea," Renny said immediately. "I've been over here quite a while, working my tail off, and now I'm done and I want to get back to God's country. I've got passage wangled on a plane. I can be in New York in twenty-four hours or so. A submarine trip would be fast if it took less than two weeks. And submarines aren't built for comfort. No, thanks."

"What if I insisted?" asked Commander Giesen.

"You'd have to insist pretty loud."

"You don't want to go?"

"You bet I don't."

"Then I won't insist."

"That's fine," Renny said. "I won't have to hurt anybody's feelings by refusing."

Commander Giesen smiled thinly. "Will you give me five minutes of your time?"

"What for?"

"To convince you that you really want to go to America on this submarine," said the Commander.

Renny hesitated. "Five minutes," he grumbled. "Go ahead."

Commander Giesen gestured at the door. "You saw those three men come in here and search the place before I began talking to you?"

Renny showed sharp interest.

"That's right," he said. "What was the idea?"

"A precaution," said the Commander, "against our being overheard,"

"Overheard by whom?"

"I wish I knew!"

"Don't you?"

"No." Commander Giesen leaned forward earnestly. "There is the damnedest mystery connected with this submarine trip."

"Eh?"

"What we want you to do," said the Commander, "is go aboard the *Pilotfish*. The *Pilotfish* is the name of the submarine. After you get aboard, and immediately after sailing, you will be handed a sealed envelope containing an explanation of the mystery, or as much of it as we know the answer to."

Renny frowned. "You want me to sail on this sub without knowing a damned thing about why?"

"The sealed documents will tell you why."

"After I sail?"

"Yes."

"Why not now?"

"You mean, why can't we tell you what we know of the mystery now?"

"Yes. Why not?"

"Because," said the Commander, "it is too risky. There is a chance that you might be forced, much against your will, to divulge the information."

Renny's frown changed to a grin.

"You're quite a psychologist, Commander," Renny said.

"I had no intention—"

Renny interrupted with a snort. "How much more can you tell me about this thing?"

"Nothing more," said Commander Giesen. "Except the name of the submarine commander, the location of the craft, and the time of sailing."

"That," said Renny, "is what I meant by psychology." And he began laughing.

Commander Giesen was disturbed by Renny's mirth. "I am not trying to be funny, I assure you," he said stiffly.

Renny hammered his knee delightedly.

"I'm laughing at myself, not at you," Renny explained. "You have heard of the fire-horse who snorts and prances when he hears the firebell? Well, that's the way your talk about mystery and danger affects me. It's as funny as anything."

Commander Giesen looked confused.

"You couldn't keep me from sailing on that submarine now if you wanted to," Renny told him. "I'm like the old fire-horse. You've told me just enough to fascinate me. Just enough for me to smell smoke and hear the firebell."

"That pleases me very much," said Commander Giesen.

"It doesn't please me!" Renny rumbled. "A man of my age shouldn't let a smell of excitement stampede his common sense. It makes me wonder when I'm going to grow up."

"I won't go," Renny said, "unless Doc Savage okays it."

Commander Giesen showed anxiety. "But how long will it take to find out about that?"

"Not long. We'll try the trans-Atlantic phone."

Renny fretted as he waited. He was not certain that Doc Savage was in New York, and if so, whether he could be located at once. Doc had a great many interests, aside from his avocation of chasing excitement, so it was possible Doc wouldn't be around their headquarters hangout on the top floor of a midtown New York skyscraper. Doc might not even be in the States. Now that the war was winding up, Doc was giving most of his attention to getting his industrial holdings back into peace-time production, and Renny knew it was proving to be a headache of proportions.

Renny asked Commander Giesen, "How much of what you've told me can I tell over the telephone?"

"All of it," said the Commander. "However, I wish you could code it somehow."

A moment later, the operator reported Doc Savage on the wire in New York.

Renny said, "Doc? . . . Renny . . . How are things going? . . . Yes, I've finished and I'm ready to come back. It's about that I want to talk to you. I'm going to say it in Mayan, so listen."

Mayan was one of several languages Renny spoke, the particular one which he figured was least likely to be understood by an eavesdropper. The lingo, which had a preponderance of grunts and cluckings, was one which Renny and Doc and the others of their group had picked up a long time ago on a hair-raising venture they had taken into Central America. As far as Renny knew, he and Doc and the other four of their group were the only ones in so-called civilization who spoke it. There might be others, but they weren't likely to be hanging around London or New York telephone offices.

"Did you understand all that, Doc? I'm pretty rusty with the language," Renny said when he had finished explaining about the mysterious submarine trip to New York which he was being asked to take.

Doc said he had gotten it.

"Any objections to my going?" Renny asked.

Doc said he hadn't any. His only objection was that he wasn't there, so he couldn't go along. He sounded intrigued by the thing. "Go ahead, and good luck," he said.

"By the way," Doc said, "did you know Monk and Ham are in London?"

"Holy cow! I didn't know that!"

Monk and Ham were two other members of their group.

Doc explained, "They are at the Strand Palace. I

just got a cable from them giving their address, and saying they were on the way home."

Renny was delighted. "Hey, I'm going to call them and see if they'd care to make this sub trip with me."

"That's up to you," Doc said. "You're sure you gave me all the dope you have about this matter?"

"All I know."

"It sounds extremely queer," Doc said.

"As queer as a goose riding a bicycle," Renny admitted.

"Good luck."

Commander Giesen clapped his cap on his head and extended his hand. "The *Pilotfish* is waiting for you at Pier B, Southampton. Her skipper is Commander Tomkins Wickart. Goodbye and good luck."

Renny said, "Wait a minute, I'm taking along two friends, Monk Mayfair and Ham Brooks, if they'll go."

"So I gathered."

"Is it okay?"

"Better than okay. Goodbye."

"Hey, when do I get that envelope with the sealed orders?"

"Not sealed orders, old chap. Information. That is, information to the best of our knowledge."

"What's your rush?" Renny asked.

The Commander smiled. "No rush at all, really. I can stay all afternoon, if you wish. But there is nothing more to be said. I supposed you wouldn't want me around bothering you. I can't tell you another thing."

"One thing before you go," Renny said thoughtfully. "Yes?"

"At different times today," Renny said, "I've had a feeling someone was following me." He stared at Commander Giesen intently. "Hey, what's the matter?"

The look on Commander Giesen's face startled Renny. It was a sick expression. The man moistened his lips uneasily.

"Could you," he asked, "be mistaken?"

"I might."

"Did you actually see anyone?"

"No. That's why I'm admitting I could have been having an attack of imagination.

"I hope," said Commander Giesen grimly, "that you were. Because if you were actually being followed, you may be in for something."

"What do you figure I would be in for?"

Commander Giesen didn't sound cheerful when he answered.

"Hell," he said.

"Oh, come now—"

"Hell!" said Commander Giesen. "Purgatory, I mean. A very purgatory of excitement and terror. I do hope you're wrong about being trailed. I do hope you are."

II.

Monk and Ham were glad to see Renny Renwick. They called Renny a big-fisted bum and wrestled him down on to the floor, all in delight.

Monk's full title was Lieutenant Colonel Andrew Blodgett Mayfair. He was a chemist. The peculiar thing was that he was an actual genius of a chemist.

Monk was a short, wide, hairy, homely, apish fellow with approximately an inch of forehead and a squeaky tin can voice. He looked like a fellow who would have barely enough gumption to dress himself. His manners were as direct and tactless as a St. Bernard puppy's. He had an endless supply of practical jokes and wise-cracks with which he haunted his pal, Ham Brooks, and innocent bystanders, alike.

Ham Brooks also had a large title and reputation. But Ham at least looked the part.

Ham was Brigadier General Theodore Marley Brooks. He was a lawyer. He was a wide-shouldered, flat-bellied man with the large voice of an orator. He always dressed, or overdressed, to dandified extremes, and affected a Harvard accent so thick you wanted to scrape it off him. He was a good guy. The clothes and accent were affected largely because they irritated Monk.

Renny asked, "Have you two got anything special on your mind?"

They said they had no plans. Except that they were returning to New York, of course. They had been in France on some kind of a commission, one of the Allied special advisory committees which were currently flitting all over the world telling nations how to run their business.

Renny was pleased.

"You're going back to New York by submarine with me," he said.

No hats were thrown into the air.

"Not me, brother," Monk said firmly. "I've been on a submarine. And I made a little discovery to the effect that a submarine is one thing that scares hell out of me. I don't like 'em."

Ham also had his opinions.

"No, thanks," he said. "I'll just crawl in a barrel, pour cylinder oil over myself, and practice hitting myself on the head with a gaspipe. Same thing, exactly."

Renny hid a grin. He'd had about the same reaction himself. He wondered how Monk and Ham would respond when they heard the rest.

"That's too bad," Renny said. "There is something very mysterious about the sub trip. On top of that, I think someone has been trailing me around all day. I was hoping you fellows would come along for the ride, and I've been assured it may be a hair-raising ride. However, if you're not interested—"

Monk grinned at him. "Baiting us, eh?"

Ham demanded. "What's this about a mystery?"

Renny told them all he knew about it. Before he was halfway through the story, he saw that he had them hooked.

He could only keep a straight face until Monk and

Ham had said they guessed they'd better go along. Then he burst out laughing.

Monk asked, "What are you cackling at, anyhow?"

"I'm just beginning to realize," Renny told him, "how much alike we are."

They caught the three-ten train which put them in Southampton before dark. They boarded the train separately, and Monk and Ham snooped and prowled, trying to find out whether anyone was really trailing Renny. They had no luck, and tried to blame Renny for the absence of excitement.

"Listen, you two," Renny snarled at them. "I don't *know* that anything at all is going to happen. Get that through your heads."

They found one of the scarce cabs at Southampton, and rode it to the pier, where they found the *Pilotfish* was not lying at dock, but had her hook down in the bay. The sub's launch took them out after they identified themselves.

They stepped out on the low deck and climbed over the rail.

A square, amiable looking man came on deck. Obviously he had dashed below to put on his black necktie and uniform blouse.

"I'm Commander Tomkins Wickart," he said.

The skipper of the *Pilotfish* did not look at all excited, Renny noticed. Wickart was either unaware of any mystery, or else he was an excellent actor.

Renny said, "You may think this is a bit unusual, Commander. We haven't any orders in writing. However, we were told to sail with you."

"That's been straightened out," Commander Wickart told him. "You'd better show me some personal identification, though."

He checked over their personal papers and was quickly satisfied.

"You won't find the ship the most comfortable in the world, but we'll do our best to take care of you," he said. He called a mess boy to show them below.

The utter placidity of the man moved Monk to speak. There was supposed to be something cooking, but the skipper was giving no sign of it. Monk was puzzled.

"What's going on, Commander?" Monk asked.

Wickart placidly stuffed tobacco into his pipe. "Why, nothing much. I'm afraid you're in for a dull trip," he said. "However, you should be able to get enough routine color."

"Color?" Monk exploded. "Who wants color?"

"You do, don't you?" Wickart asked idly. "You three are war correspondents, aren't you? At least I was told you were."

Monk opened his mouth, but caught Renny's eye and didn't say what he was planning to say. Instead, he remarked, "So you're not figuring on any excitement?"

"Very little chance of anything, I'm afraid," Wickart told him.

"When do we sail?"

"Midnight."

They were guided below. They found they were to bunk separately, Monk and Ham in the forward torpedo room and Renny doubling with the skipper.

"I don't get this," Monk told Renny. "You suppose the skipper doesn't know anything about what's going on? Or is the guy stringing us?"

They discussed it and decided they couldn't tell. Ham joined them and complained, "War correspondents! Who told him we were war correspondents?"

"Maybe this sealed envelope I'm suppose to get will straighten it out," Renny suggested.

The messenger carrying the sealed envelope was at that time getting out of the plane which had brought him from London. He had the envelope strapped to his left thigh with adhesive tape, and he carried a leather satchel handcuffed to his wrist as a dummy. There was another envelope in the satchel, the contents a meaningless gibberish that anyone not in the know would think was a code.

The operations officer at the field explained, "There's a jeep waiting to take you wherever you're going."

The jeep contained a corporal and a private, and

they had what appeared to be the proper documents. The messenger made certain about the documents before he rode with them. The two in the jeep explained that they didn't know where they were to take him.

The messenger told them the waterfront.

The sun was now down. It was fairly dark. The private at the wheel of the jeep drove rather recklessly, and on a lonely stretch of street, he hit the curbing. It was a glancing blow, but the jeep rolled to a stop.

"What the hell's wrong?" demanded the corporal.

"It won't go," the private explained. "The motor runs, but nothing happens."

"Get out and see what's wrong, dammit," the corporal shouted.

The private alighted and walked around to the back of the jeep. He had a wrench in his hand.

The messenger must have been somewhat suspicious, because he turned alertly, endeavoring to watch the private, and at the same time keep an eye on the corporal. He failed. It was the corporal who brained him.

The messenger made a gurgling sound after he was hit. He sprawled back with his head hanging down, his nostrils, mouth and split skull leaking blood.

"Damn you, you sure made a mess of him," the private said sickly.

"Push him back in. You better hold him. Let's get where we're going," the corporal said.

They drove only a few blocks, then turned into a small garage, the doors of which opened to take them inside.

There were several men waiting there.

It was quite dark, and the corporal peered around blindly, then demanded, "Clark here?"

"Yes."

"Here he is," the corporal said.

"Close the doors. Then let's have a light," Clark ordered.

As soon as the doors were closed and the lights on, the corporal and the private went to the back of the garage. They began exchanging their army uniforms for sailor outfits with the insignia of the submarine service.

Clark was a thin man with the single quarter-inch stripe of a warrant officer, and the sparks of a radio electrician. He had soft, brown calf-like eyes, and they were completely tender and gentle as he examined the dead messenger.

"Too bad he bled like that. We can't use his uniform," Clark said quietly. "But get that bag loose from him, empty his pockets, and strip him."

Nobody moved, and Clark looked at them. He cursed them mildly.

"What the hell's wrong with you?" he asked them. "Get busy."

He sounded completely mild and harmless, which had the effect of sickening and startling his men. But the men went to work on the body efficiently enough.

The lock on the satchel balked them. Clark said, "Cut it open. We'll find another bag that will serve."

They swore at the unreadable contents of the envelope after they got it out of the bag. Then they found the other envelope, the genuine one, which was taped to the deceased messenger's leg.

Clark read the contents. He began reading with a pale face and the expression of a cowboy who is suddenly wondering if a rattlesnake has crawled into bed with him during the night. He looked more satisfied with himself after he finished.

It apparently occurred to him, as he folded the document, that he had forgotten to control the expression of his face, because he frowned slightly, and then was looking gentle and mild again.

"There ain't been any hitches?" one of the men asked him anxiously.

"No hitches," Clark said, using a sweet, boyish voice.

He examined the envelope seal, which he had not broken, having removed the documents by slitting the envelope end. "This is a standard seal," he said. "It won't give us any trouble."

He went to a handbag in the back, and returned

bearing another envelope, which he compared with the first one.

"See, there's no difference anybody would notice between the genuine one and this dummy I had already fixed up."

He was pleased about this.

He gave an order. "Fall in! Full gear, and fall in!"

He watched his men as they fell in. He lost some of his smug satisfaction. Two of them had not done a very snappy job of the simple maneuver. He cursed them. "I thought I told you so-and-sos to get the fundamentals of drill into your heads!"

The two, who had obviously never been in a navy, showed alarm. They had been working on it, they protested.

Clark snorted. "It's a damned good thing there isn't much formality on a submarine, or you two would fall on your faces at the first inspection." He scowled at the group. "Attention!" he rapped. "Open ranks, march! . . . Right face! . . . Forward march! . . . By the right flank, march!"

He worked them for a few moments, his purpose being to get their attention, to impress on their minds his position of command. Then he stopped them and made a speech.

Clark said, "All but one of you will go aboard the submarine. You will have the regulation papers installing you as replacements for certain members of the submarine crew. By the time you get there, Commander Wickart of the sub will have received, through what he will think is official channels, information of the change. In other words, six of you will go aboard the submarine and take the places of six men of the regular crew who will receive leaves of absence and orders to report later to another division."

He smiled at them gently, confidently.

"There is no reason for you to be scared," he told them. "I can assure you that every official order necessary to this trick has been counterfeited with complete accuracy. In every case possible genuine official forms have been stolen and used.

"Of course, you are going to be afraid anyway. But when you are scared, the thing to remember is that the only man who does not get scared is the one who hasn't any brains to get scared with."

He made an emphatic gesture. "This is going to work. You all know me, and you know my reputation for careful planning." He smiled again. "Most of you know me from Chicago in the old days. And you know that I've never been in the penitentiary myself, and no man who has worked for me has ever been in the penitentiary as a result of doing anything in which he followed my orders. Now, this is all the speech I'm going to make. We've been over this before, and all of you know what you're going to do when we get on the submarine. Remember your instructions. Follow them. Don't get squeamish. Don't pick the wrong time to get a conscience. And you might as well keep in mind this point: any man who, through losing his nerve or failing to follow orders, endangers the rest of us or our plan, will have to be disposed of. We naturally hope that won't be necessary."

They got this point.

Clark turned to the former corporal who had helped waylay and murder the messenger.

"Gross," Clark said, "you are the only man we are leaving behind. You are the guy who is going to deliver the envelope containing the explanations, or what purports to be, to the sub."

Gross nodded. He wore now the appropriate uniform and insignia for his part. He was a wide man of about thirty with loose cheeks and an effect of perpetual dampness about the eyes.

He picked up the phony envelope.

"I deliver this, get it signed for, and clear out," he said.

"That's right. And don't be afraid something will go wrong."

"I'm not expecting anything to crop up," Gross assured him,

Clark nodded. "After you do that, get the hell busy trying to get back to New York. You should be able to make it. You've got war correspondent's credentials and plenty of money."

"I'll do my best."

"When you get to New York, start preparing things to complete the job from that end. You know what men to contact, and what you'll probably need in the way of equipment."

Clark gave them his benign smile.

"Let's get going," he said tenderly.

III.

Renny Renwick, Ham Brooks and Monk Mayfair had mess with Commander Wickart and some of the other officers including Lieutenant Gifford, the navigator, and an engineering officer called Speck. They never did learn Speck's last name. There was also Gallyhan, an assistant engineer; Kovic, electrical officer, and Clark, who was communications officer.

Commander Wickart had the idea he was going to raise turkeys after the war, and he was very hot about it. The early part of dinner was sprinkled with turkey talk. Later Clark, the communcations man, said that he had been ashore almost the whole afternoon trying to raise some 6L6 tubes for the sound apparatus. He told about finding a quart of Scotch whiskey in a little shop, marked way under the current high price, apparently because the proprietor had no idea what it was. Clark had bought the Scotch, and he produced the bottle to prove it. Monk thought Clark was going to offer everybody a drink, but instead of that, Clark contributed the Scotch to the medical locker.

When they were on deck, Monk said. "I wonder if that Clark guy has been an actor?"

"What makes you think that?" Renny asked him.

"That sort of deliberate way he has of talking, and of giving everything he has just the right emphasis."

"Probably an ex-radio announcer," Renny said. "He sounded more like a radio announcer to me."

Their discussion ended, because they heard one of the deck force reporting to the petty officer of the watch. "A launch standing this way, sir."

"I hope that's our sealed envelope," Monk said. "I'm beginning to itch to know what this is all about."

The launch warped up to the port sea ladder, and a petty officer bounded aboard, slipped on the damp deck, and would have fallen if a deckhand hadn't grabbed his arm. The man swore, and produced some papers.

A few minutes later, Commander Wickart popped out of the torpedo room hatch and sailed past them. They heard him saying, "—the damn, pin-headed navy, never satisfied to let something alone!" He said more that contained more feeling.

Renny, nervous, jumped up and asked, "Anything wrong, skipper?"

Wickart thumbed his own chest indignantly. "Twenty years I've been in the navy," he said. "You'd think I had seen all the jackass tricks they can pull on a man. By God, what do they do now? They furlough part of my crew and send replacements who, for all I know, may never have seen a submarine!"

He went over and beat his pipe angrily against the conning tower.

"Just before sailing, too!" he snarled. "Lord, will I be glad to get on that turkey ranch!"

He went away and Ham Brooks chuckled and said, "Give you two to one he never goes near a turkey ranch until they ease him out of the navy in a wheel chair."

"No sealed envelope," Monk grumbled.

For a while they listened to confusion in the forward torpedo room. The leave party was going ashore, and the newcomers moving in to take their place. The talk was the talk you would expect, with profanity and laughter. The men who were being relieved were glad to get ashore.

Renny drew one conjecture from what he heard.

"Evidently the sub has been at sea quite a while, and just in port a little time," he said. "Otherwise those sailors wouldn't be so anxious for shore leave."

Monk listened to the pleased talk of the shore party. "That speaks for the accommodations on this pigboat, doesn't it?" he said gloomily.

About ten o'clock, Commander Wickart confronted them nervously. "You fellows really were supposed to get a sealed envelope, weren't you?" he demanded.

"So I was told," Renny said.

"We're scheduled to sail at midnight," Wickart said anxiously. "It should be getting here."

Ham told him, "Here comes a small craft. Maybe this is it."

It was. The messenger came aboard, saluted, and asked for Colonel John Renwick. Renny identified himself. He signed the receipt for the envelope, and fingerprinted it by request for further indentification.

It was a standard navy department envelope, and the contents did not have much bulk. The wax seals made big warts on every seam. Renny suddenly stared at it, then looked at the others.

"Holy cow!" he wailed.

"Now what?" Monk asked.

"It's marked to be opened twelve hours after sailing," Renny yelled. "What the hades do you think of that!"

The uproar brought Commander Wickart back to find out what was wrong. He puffed his pipe placidly, not much impressed by the news.

"Sealed orders aren't unusual in the navy," he said. "I have it happen to me frequently."

Renny was indignant. "Orders! This is supposed to be information!"

The skipper shrugged. "We're going to sail now," he said.

Lieutenant Gifford, the navigator, came on deck with the small wooden box that contained the stadimeter. The engines began to pound. There was a rumbling forward as the anchor came up. The bos'n reported, "Anchor secure, sir."

The *Pilotfish* picked its way toward the breakwater with stadimeter and pelorus. Renny glanced at his watch and found it was twenty past eleven. The night was dark, no moon and not too much starlight. A battle wagon, anchored to port, was a large grim lump of deeper night. They dropped some headway, worked through the net, and the sub began to roll a little with the feel of the open sea.

Renny stood with the skipper in the conning tower. "Rig for diving," Wickart said into the voice tube.

"Will you tell me why we have to run submerged today?" Renny demanded.

"We don't."

"I shouldn't think so, with the war so nearly polished off as it is."

Wickart poked his thumb down in his pipe bowl, burnt it and swore softly. "Orders are to run under battle conditions, which means ready to dive any time."

Reports came in. "Rigged forward," from the electrical officer. "Rigged aft," from an assistant engineer somewhere. The voices had a soothing routine sound. "Main induction open, main ballast flood valves closed. Rigged for diving."

The skipper said, "Station the submerged cruising section, but hull and battery vented outboard. Take over, Lieutenant." Wickart turned to Renny and the others. "How about a spot of coffee below?"

Renny thought they'd probably have to listen to more talk about turkey farming, but it turned out they were spared the turkey farm.

Commander Wickart waited until the mess boy who brought the coffee had gone. The air-conditioning whispered softly. It was comfortably cool, but the air already had the characteristic oily smell.

"I gather they didn't tell you much," Wickart said unexpectedly.

"Much!" Renny laughed sourly.

"They haven't told me much, either."

Renny looked at the skipper speculatively. "Do you feel free to tell us anything that might be interesting?"

"I don't know how interesting it will be. But I can tell you what little I know."

"By golly, do that!" Renny exclaimed.

The skipper of the *Pilotfish* began talking so matter of factly that it was not immediately evident that what he was saying was important. Or at least interesting and mystifying.

The preliminary part of his recital, the normal-sounding portion, filled about five minutes. The *Pilotfish* had left an unnamed port, French not English, a week ago. The sailing had been under sealed orders, and the orders, opened after they were at sea, had directed the *Pilotfish* to proceed to the German coast, to Nordstrand, which was a neck of water on the west coast of Schleswig Holstein, between the North Frisian and East Frisian Islands. The place was really a part of Heligoland Bay.

"I wasn't too happy," Wickart related. "The Fritzes had sowed mines around there thicker than fleas on an African dog. To make it more interesting, we were to travel submerged, as much as possible, which didn't make much sense. But the funny thing was that we were supplied with exact course bearings to take us through the mine fields. I saw the series of bearings, the original document, not a copy, and they were in German. The German language."

Renny said, "The Germans had furnished you with a course through the mine field, you mean?"

"They had furnished somebody with it. Somebody higher up. Maybe Commander Giesen."

"Was Giesen aboard?"

"Yes."

"Giesen," Renny explained, "is the guy who roped us into the affair."

"I surmised he had. He's the big cheese for our side, I'm fairly sure."

Eventually the *Pilotfish* had come to anchor offshore from a small north German town named Husum. Not close in, but out far enough to have deep water.

"Then there was funny business," the skipper said abruptly, and stopped talking for a while.

It developed that the entire crew of the *Pilotfish* had been herded into the forward one-third of the submarine and locked up there for three hours.

"Except me," said Wickart.

He grinned at them slyly.

"But I haven't the least idea what they brought aboard," he said. "I was kept in the conning tower, and they used the torpedo room hatch."

"Who used it?"

"I don't know who. I don't know whether they were Fritzes or not, because I heard both English and Fritz language talked, and American, too. Like I say, I was asked to remain in the tower. It was as dark as a witch cave, and no lights were shown."

"Commander Giesen had charge of this?"

"That's right."

"Something was brought out of Germany and put aboard your vessel?"

"That's right."

"You don't know what it is?"

"No idea."

"Is it still aboard?"

"Yes."

"Where?"

"In what was my cabin."

"Is there any reason," Renny asked thoughtfully, "why we shouldn't take a look and see what was brought aboard?"

Wickart smiled slightly. "I have been tempted myself, although I have strict orders not to attempt to enter the cabin, nor to permit anyone else to do so."

"No chance of sneaking a look, eh?"

"It's hardly feasible."

"Sealed, eh?"

Wickart nodded. "Welded shut."

"Welded!"

Wickart said, "There are four spot-welds along the edge of the door, and these are sealed with documentary-type wax."

IV.

The *Pilotfish* ran at three quarters speed throughout the night. An hour before dawn they dived, and stayed down until the sun was twenty degrees up in the sky in order to escape the dangerous twilight time. They surfaced again.

Renny and Monk and Ham learned they were not expected to stand the regular four-hour watches. Renny, knowing about the monotony of the long voyage ahead of them, advised that they take the same four-hour watches as everyone except the skipper. Renny took the bridge watch with the navigator.

They had sailed at midnight. At least midnight was the official time, which meant that it would be noon before Renny could open the envelope. It was now nine. He felt uneasy, consumed by curiosity.

With Monk and Ham, he visited the skipper's cabin, which was the one room aboard the submarine which had no dual purpose. It was a captain's cabin, solely. They didn't get inside the cabin, of course, since the door was welded shut, as Wickart had said.

While they were standing in front of the door, Renny began laughing.

"What's so funny?" Monk wanted to know.

"Us." Renny said. "Us, standing here looking at the door like a bunch of awestruck kids."

The *Pilotfish* continued to charge ahead at sixteen knots. Gifford, the navigator, got his sun shots, and Renny checked them with him, getting about the same position on the chart.

Renny was off watch at twelve. Monk and Ham had been watching him like eager owls for the past half hour. He nodded at them, and produced the envelope.

They held the official opening of the envelope in the maneuvering room, which was at the moment deserted. Renny inserted his pocket knife blade and slit the flap. There were four sheets of paper inside, and he unfolded them one at a time, and examined them each from top to bottom.

Renny's long face had the queerest of expressions when he had finished his examination.

"Holy cow!" he said.

"What's it say?" Monk demanded.

Renny said, "This'll surprise you, anyway."

He showed them the sheets of paper.

The four sheets were quite blank.

The ship was running through a slight sun-kissed sea, rolling comfortably. They found Commander Wickart on deck. Renny told him about the envelope contents.

The skipper of the *Pilotfish* gave them a blank look, for the words had been startled out of him. He fell back on the solace of filling and lighting his pipe, then finally he said, "Unusual."

"I call it damned queer," Renny rumbled. "What the blazes was blank paper doing in that envelope? You know something? I wonder if that envelope could have been tampered with."

Wickart contemplated them. "Just what do you know about this?"

"Just what we've told you—nothing," Renny growled. "Why? Have you got some more information?"

Wickart shook his head. "Except this. I rather think I was to take orders from you fellows. However, I got the idea that Doc Savage was going to be aboard."

"Doc Savage is in New York," Renny told him.

"I guess that's why he isn't aboard then."

"What gave you that idea about Doc?"

"Giesen said something, He said that Doc Savage would probably be aboard for the trip from England to America. He just said that once, then didn't mention it again."

Renny said, "We work with Doc Savage."

"I know that," Wickart told him. "Quite a man, I've heard." The skipper smoked silently for a few moments. "But you fellows work with Savage, so you're supposed to be on the extraordinary side. If you have any suggestions, let's hear them."

"You've got a radio?"

"Of course. But I'm supposed to keep radio silence."

"I think," said Renny, "that we had better break radio silence, get hold of Giesen, and find out if that envelope was supposed to be full of blank paper."

"Will you give me a written order to that effect?" the skipper asked.

"If you want to be in the clear, yes."

They found Clark, the communications man, routing him out of his bunk. Clark's responsibility was the radio, and he had the key.

A moment after he opened the radio cabin door, Clark swore wildly. "Dammit, look!" he cried.

Renny knew radio. He fingered around over the equipment, picking up shattered parts. The radio wouldn't function. They could neither transmit nor receive.

The skipper's temper split, and he suddenly had Clark by the jacket lapels. "Who smashed the radio?" he yelled. Clark looked sick. He mumbled that he didn't know.

"By God, we'll find out who smashed it!" Wickart shouted.

The outburst caused Renny to do some thinking. It seemed to him that the skipper was unduly excited, unless there was more than the smashed radio to cause it. It seemed to him that Wickart had already been worried.

The skipper did not take them into his confidence until the following morning.

"It's the replacements," Wickart told Renny. "I'm beginning to wonder if they've ever been on a submarine before."

"You're talking about the men who came aboard at the last minute before we sailed?" Renny demanded.

"They're the ones."

"How many?"

"Eight."

"And you mean they've never been on a sub?"

Wickart scowled. "By God, I don't know. They know some of the stuff they should know, but there are other things they should know and don't. They act like rookies, and the ones that don't act like rookies seem to be working like hell to show the others the ropes."

"Let's talk to them one at a time," Renny said.

"I think we'd better."

The interviewing occupied a full day and was generally not very satisfactory. The eight sailors had papers which were in order, and they answered most of the questions as they should be answered. But as a whole, they did not give complete satisfaction, although there was nothing directly suspicious. Nothing to warrant taking action.

The next surprising thing was the complete placidity of the following days. Life settled into a humdrum routine of watches, of eating and sleeping and working. Clark spent his off time fiddling with parts from the radio, endeavoring to rig emergency equipment. He finally had to report that he was not able to make even a receiver that would work.

Finally there came a night when Gifford's star observation showed them in Long Island sound, the outer end.

Wickart was pleased. His relief showed when he said, "Well, we've practically made it, and we're still a happy family."

He gave orders to stand in toward New London. Their destination was the New London submarine base. They ran on the surface, chugging along peacefully. The stars were out and the night air was balmy. Renny noticed Clark, the communications man, at the navigator's table. Apparently Clark was looking at their last position figures, which were written on a pad. Renny's suspicions were not aroused, which was an oversight he forever regretted.

When it came, it was sudden. The diving alarm sounded. "Get her down! Crash dive!" a voice screamed into the tubes. The engines choked to a stop.

Everyone on the bridge tumbled below, through the conning-tower hatch. No one knew as yet what had happened. Then the whole ship jerked, wrenched, belched with the sound of an explosion.

Renny was near the gun access hatch when the blast came. The ship was still on the surface. Renny's first idea was to get on deck, and quick. He clawed a life preserver out of a rack and was shoving his arms through it as he made for the ladder.

Someone was climbing ahead of him. It was Clark, Renny saw. And when Renny reached the top of the ladder, Clark turned and kicked him in the face. A hard kick. It knocked Renny loose from the ladder, and he fell to the floor plates with an agonizing impact. He was stunned, for a few moments unable to move.

The gun access hatch slammed. They had closed it from the outside.

The second explosion came. Another nasty belch and jolt. The lights went out.

Renny fought his helplessness, fought with a brain that seemed to have lost all of its connections with his body. For the moment, he couldn't make any of his muscles function.

The *Pilotfish* was sinking by the nose. The floor took more and more of a tilt until it would have been impossible to stand. A few loose objects clattered across the floor, then Renny felt himself sliding. He stopped against a bulkhead.

There were voices. The voices were men screaming, but they were beyond the bulkheads somewhere and very small. Louder was the noise of another explosion, after which the shrieking of high-pressure air escaping drowned out all small sounds. There was the smell of burned insulation and ozone as the water got into batteries and shorted them.

Feeling came back to Renny's hands. He could move them. When he could bend his arms, he fastened his life preserver.

There was a banshee squealing somewhere close. It was high-pressure air bleeding into the compartment, probably from a ruptured line. The pressure was building up. Renny began swallowing hard and pumping at his ears with his palms to equalize the pressure.

The hatch! If the pressure blew open the hatch, the sea would come in. He shoved himself along the bulkhead and managed to reach the ladder. Climbing laboriously, he reached the hatch and dogged it tight. He climbed down laboriously. A few more loose objects clattered along the floor plates.

When the ship hit bottom, it was with a heavy shock. There was a shotgun explosion and colored sparks as wires burned out at the other end of the compartment, a small version of hell that lasted a split part of a second. After that the high-pressure air squealed like a pig for a while, then gradually died. There came a few more sounds, nasty ones, as the whole died.

They were resting almost horizontal on the bottom.

Renny rubbed a hand across his nose, then examined it foolishly. His nose was bleeding. That would be the pressure.

He crawled to a bulkhead and put his face to the small round dead-light, trying to see into the next compartment. He failed, then remembered he had a pocket flashlight, and used that. There was nothing but foul ink-black water on the other side. The compartment was flooded.

The sickness that gripped him at the discovery made him lose his grip, and he skidded and fell to the slippery floor, bruising himself.

Submarine lung! The thought beat into his mind. Lungs should be in a locker in this compartment. Some of them, at least. The fourth locker he investigated held one, a single lung. There should have been a regular quota. There wasn't. Just a single lung.

He examined the lung wildly, afraid that it was defective. It didn't seem to be, and he lay down weakly. Relief hadn't made him sick again. It was the awful pressure. The compartment was charged with high-pressure air. There must be ninety pounds to the square inch.

*   *   *

Stillness had come. A grisly quiet.

Forcing himself, fighting down the hysteria that would come too easily, Renny got a hammer he had seen in one of the lockers. He began beating on the deck, using code.

At first he got no answering tapping. Then a return signal came, audible enough. Renny began to tap laboriously, wishing bitterly that he was better with his code.

"H-o-w m-a-n-y a-l-i-v-e," he pounded laboriously.

"Twenty-seven," came the answer.

Monk and Ham were among them, Renny learned next. The news was wildly good, so good that he sobbed. Monk was doing the sending from the other end.

"Can you see the escape hatch?" Renny asked.

"Jammed. Everything is jammed," Monk said.

"They did it?"

"Yes. To plan. They intended to kill everyone."

"Can you get out?"

"No."

Renny shuddered. The situation was bad. It could not be worse. He asked them about escape lungs.

"No lungs," Monk said. "We're trapped. How about you?"

"I can't do a thing," Renny reported.

"Can you get out?"

"Maybe."

"We can't," Monk hammered slowly. "We can't use the hatch if it would open. No high-pressure air."

Directly opposite of his own trouble, Renny thought. There was too much high-pressure air in his compartment. The high-pressure tanks were probably empty, and no doubt a lot of their contents had bled off into this compartment.

"Estimate how long you can hold out," he transmitted.

The answer did not come for a frighteningly long time.

"Twelve hours," Monk sent finally.

"Maximum?"

"Twelve hours absolute maximum," Monk said.

"Who says so?"

"Wickart."

That was enough. If Wickart said it was twelve hours, it would be twelve hours. Renny reached his decision, the only one he could reach.

"I'll try to get out," he said. "Can you stream the marker buoy?" The marker buoy was a balsa wood float at the end of a line that would mark the submarine's position.

"They jammed that, too," Monk reported.

"I'll try to get out," Renny said.

"Good luck."

"Same to you fellows." It was such an inane thing to say in parting under such circumstances.

The business of getting the hatch open was a hair-lifting one. The pressure inside was much greater than the outer water pressure. When the hatch was loosened, it would pop open like the cork coming out of a champagne bottle, and the high-pressure air inside would blow out with the violence of a charge leaving a gun. It would have to be done carefully, if he was to escape being killed.

There was the matter of an ascent line, too. Renny believed they were down at least a hundred and fifty feet. If he just popped to the surface, he would die shortly with the bends. He had to ascend slowly, decompressing as he went.

The only line he could find was a manila one of about a hundred feet. It would have to do. He considered himself lucky at finding even that.

He studied the hatch for a while, and finally worked out a method of rigging the rope so as to enable him to stand at the far end of the compartment, where he could cling to pipes, and undog the hatch by hauling on the rope. He got the system ready, and went to the pipes to which he intended to cling, holding the rope.

He charged the lung with pure oxygen, shut off the charging chuck, and adjusted the nose clip, put the mouthpiece between his teeth. He inhaled and exhaled, testing. It seemed to be all right.

He hauled on the rope. The hatch blew open. The

outrush of air first jerked him. Then water poured in, a round solid snake of it that hit the floor plates and dashed itself all over the compartment. He had, while the compartment filled, the most frightening few moments of his life.

He worked his way to the hatch, made the rope fast by its end after undoing it from the dogs. Going up, the lung gave him plenty of buoyancy.

Being unsure of the depth, he decided at least six minutes would be needed for the ascent. That would give him a margin of safety, time for decompression, the flutter-valve in the lung taking care of pressure equalizing between his body and the sea.

An experienced submarine man would have had less trouble than he was having, because ascents with the lung were part of their training.

He reached the end of the line. The line was no longer. He had no means of knowing how far the surface was above him. He would have to give himself time to decompress fully, then take a chance and let go. He counted off the minutes, then released his grip.

He shot upward for a long enough interval to frighten him intensely. Then he was on the surface, tearing the lung from his face.

He heard someone say, "Hell, here's one of them!"

Someone grabbed at him, got the mask. He let go the mask when he saw an arm swinging a clubbed oar against the starry heavens. The mask was torn from his face.

The oar came down on his head.

There were shots, three of them he believed. He didn't know whether they hit him. The oar had already bashed out his comprehension of what was happening. It was just that unconsciousness was a little slow coming. He was under the water, and it was very black, before he stopped knowing anything.

V.

Blackness changed to two things, blackness and sound. The sound finally became predominant over the blackness. It was a monotonous sound of *wham*-chug-chug-*wham*-*wham*-chug-chug-chug-wham-chug. An engine. Renny realized that it must be an engine, and it followed when he got the smell of fresh fish that it must be the engine in a fishing boat. A one-lung motor in a fishing boat. Renny opened his eyes, to a dome of stars and the irregular silhouettes of a small boat and at least three fishermen.

Renny's lungs felt scorched, and he knew that salt water must have been in them. His skull, to feel as it did, surely had holes in it, and his ribs ached intolerably. A little thought gave him the probable reason for his ribs aching. Artificial respiration. He must have been hauled partly drowned from the sea and brought out of it.

Two round balls, a little one and a big one attached together, appeared above him. This was a very round fat man who said, "How you feel, bub?"

Tension flowed out of Renny and relief flowed in. This man hadn't been on the submarine.

"Okay," Renny muttered.

"I bet," the man said. "Yeah, I bet."

"Who're you?" Renny asked.

"Name's Nick. Nick Padolfus."

"This your boat?"

"Mine and the finance company's, yeah." The fat man grinned.

"Fisherman, eh?" Renny said slowly.

"Yeah."

There were two other men in the boat. One of them
141

was steering. The other was sitting on a box over the one-lung motor, and he splashed a flashlight on Renny. Renny gasped painfully, for the light felt as if it was going to destroy his aching eyes.

The fat man spoke suddenly. "Listen, bub, we ain't gonna get in trouble, are we?"

"How you mean?"

Nick was silent a while. "Was that shooting we heard?"

"Eh?"

"Noise like shots, and flashes of fire," Nick explained. "We saw them as we were coming down the Sound. We could hear the shots. Three shots. Signal of distress, like in Boy Scouts."

He paused and rubbed his fat round face with a palm. "Only boat run away. It was no distress signal, huh?"

"A boat ran away, eh?" Renny said.

"Uh-huh."

"What kind of a boat?"

"Cabin cruiser. Pretty good one, about fifty feet, with big motor. She sound like airplane, that boat."

"And you picked me up?"

"Yep."

"Pick up anybody else?"

"Nobody else around."

"Thanks," Renny said. "Let me rest a minute."

He didn't need rest, but he wanted to get his thoughts into something resembling order. The disaster to the submarine had rattled him, or at least he was rattled now that it was over.

"Nick," Renny said tensely.

"Yah?"

"Take me back to where you picked me up," Renny said grimly. "You've got to mark the place with a buoy."

Nick considered this for a while. "No," he said.

Anxiety gripped Renny. "Why not?"

"Two hours since I pick you up," Nick said readily. "Too far back. Look. Almost in port."

Renny raised up and looked. He had been in New London before, and it wasn't New London. It was, he decided, the little town of Noank, not far from New London. The submarine had actually gone down in Block Island Sound, instead of Long Island Sound proper.

But where, exactly, had the sub gone down?

He asked Nick. "Nick," he said, "get your chart and mark the exact spot where you picked me up."

Nick laughed. "Charts, I never use him." And then, probably because of the way Renny gasped in alarm, Nick added, "Me, I don't read."

"Can't read?"

"No read, that's right. I don't tell everybody that."

Nick had a cottage in Noank, and so did the other two men, who were his brothers-in-law. They lived on the same street, the same block. Nick Padolfus block, it was called, Nick explained cheerfully.

Desperation must have been helping to drive Renny into recovery. He was not back to normal, but he could get around unaided and think fairly straight.

Twenty-seven men trapped in the *Pilotfish*, in a sweating steel tomb between one hundred fifty and two hundred feet below the surface. Twelve hours, Monk had said. They could hold out twelve hours. At least three of the twelve hours were already gone.

Nick was sure he could find the spot where he had picked up Renny. "Sure I find him," Nick insisted. "Not on chart, though."

One hundred and fifty or two hundred feet. That was deep. You would need more than shoal water stuff to get down that deep. You needed the best equipment and needed it fast.

"Where's a telephone?" Renny asked.

Nick didn't have a telephone. But one of his brothers-in-law, whose first name was Jake, had one.

Renny called Doc Savage from Jake's. He got Doc immediately at headquarters, although it was past midnight. Doc slept at headquarters more often than not when he was in the city. Doc Savage had no sort of family life.

Renny said, "I'm in a jam, Doc," and told the story. In the telling, he started with being approached by

Giesen in England, the envelope containing the blank paper, the new men who had come aboard the *Pilotfish* at the last minute, the Atlantic crossing, and what had happened tonight.

"Clark, the communications officer, was one of the gang, maybe the ringleader," Renny said. "The eight sailors who came aboard just before we sailed pulled the job. Why they sank the sub I don't know, but I can guess that it's connected with the sealed compartment."

"What sealed compartment?" Doc asked.

"Holy cow, I left that out." Renny explained about the submarine getting something off the German mainland in the dead of night, something mysterious that was sealed in a compartment aboard.

"This is enough talk," Doc said. "I'll start getting salvage equipment together."

"What do you want me to do?"

"You can come to New York if you can get hold of a plane. But be sure this Nick Padolfus is where we can pick him up at any time."

Nick said sure, he would be home any time they wanted him. He hadn't heard the story Renny had told over the telephone. The brothers-in-law hadn't heard it either. They were puzzled, but did not seem alarmed. Renny had been afraid they would get scared and that the fear would make them hard to handle.

"Just call on me," Nick said. "I be here. Me and my brothers will get some sleep. Wake us up any time."

"This is important," Renny said.

"Sure, sure," Nick agreed. He did not seem particularly impressed.

The lummox may think nothing of it and go off on a fishing trip, or a visit somewhere, Renny thought uneasily.

"Look, Nick, there's a thousand dollars in it for you if you can find the spot where you picked me up," Renny said. "Another thousand apiece for your brothers-in-law."

Nick's eyes popped. He was sufficiently impressed now.

Renny went back to the telephone. Twelve hours.

Nine hours now. Eight hours and forty-five minutes, as a matter of fact.

He started telephoning for a plane. A light plane, a charter ship, anything. Anything that would fly. He finally found one, a T-craft, at Foster field. Foster was close. He telephoned for a taxicab.

He made two more calls, one to the State Police of Connecticut, the other to the navy. For the State Police he merely identified himself as a Doc Savage associate, and described, as nearly as he could, Clark and the other eight sailors. He asked that they be picked up on sight, and received assurance that they would be.

The navy call was to Washington. He tried to get hold of the officer who was Commander Giesen's department superior. This call was a flop. The officer was not available, but the operators would try to find him. Renny left instructions that the call be completed, if it could be completed, to Doc Savage in New York City.

The taxi was outside now.

"We be here," Nick assured him. "You come back any time."

The taxi driver, for an extra ten-dollar bill, broke every speed regulation ever dreamed of by the ODT and the state of Connecticut.

At Foster, they had called the Hartford CAA weather station for the winds aloft. He ran his eyes over the report, reading surface wind eighteen miles, forty-four miles at two thousand, forty-eight miles at three thousand, fifty-one at four thousand, all from sixty degrees. There was luck. A spanking tail wind, fifty-one miles an hour at four thousand.

The T-craft was a BL with a sixty-five-horse power motor. It was one of the fastest of the light ships. But he needed that extra fifty-one miles on the tail.

He flew without a chart. New London was his first check point, and he got an estimated ground speed of a hundred and thirty. That was about right. He'd been climbing some. It was a hundred and thirteen miles to La Guardia Field.

He ignored the traffic pattern when he came into La Guardia to save time. There was plenty of runway, so he set down downwind, then didn't wait for his green light. He'd been getting nothing but red lights anyway. He'd broken every rule in the book. He cut the switch and locked the hand brake and piled out and ran for the administration building.

Someone yelled at him. Someone in a uniform. Somebody who wanted to raise hell about that landing, he knew. He went on. The CAA would probably jerk his license for this, but a license was a small thing now.

He got a break at the taxi stand. There was a police prowl car there, two officers inside. He ran to the machine.

"I'm Renwick," he said. "I work with Doc Savage. Can you get me to his place in a hell of a hurry?"

The two policemen examined him. Apparently they knew him. The one on the right opened the door and got out. "Take my seat," he said.

The prowl car ran through the night, chasing its headlights and pursued by the whimper of its siren. The driver asked no questions. He just drove.

Renny's ankles were cramped from riding the rudder pedals of the light-plane. He ached all over, and his lungs still burned from the salt water that had been in them, making him cough almost continuously. But he leaned back, and for the first time since disaster had hit the *Pilotfish,* he began to entertain something like hope.

The name of Doc Savage was magic. Particularly was it magic with the New York police, because Savage had worked for and with the department over a length of time. Doc had lectured frequently at the police academy, and at special meetings, so almost all the cops knew him by sight and by reputation.

Magic. A good example was the way this prowl car was rushing him into town, no argument and no questions.

He was fortunate to be able to put this in hands as capable as Doc Savage's. He knew this. And the knowing it put a tight, eager constriction in his throat.

VI.

Renny's destination was one of the most prominent midtown skyscrapers. He scrambled out of the police car, and for a moment he glanced up at the building. It was a thundering giant in the darkness, and it was a good thing to see that men could create such things.

Renny went inside, wondering just why the building had comforted him. That was a goofy idea. What he had felt, more likely, was the comfort of being home, because the building was probably as much home as he had. It was more accurate to consider it the home of Doc's group. They were all in pretty much the same boat in their aloneness as far as having family ties was concerned.

That, Renny thought, must be why we're so close. Why we feel that trouble for one of us is trouble for all. We have no close relatives. Life has cheated us that way. They made up for it by the closeness of their association, Doc Savage and the five others. A psychologist would probably explain it that way.

Their aloneness might account for their liking for adventure, too. Renny had never thought of it that way. But it might be.

Doc Savage himself, for example, had no family, and only one relative, a cousin named Patricia Savage, who lived in New York and was a bit remarkable herself.

The strangeness of Doc's upbringing, Renny was quite certain, accounted for Doc Savage's being unusual. It was surprising that he wasn't more extraordinary than he was. Doc had been placed, when he was a baby, in the custody of the first of an endless succession of scientists, philosophers, thinkers, who had been charged with the job of educating him and training him. There was no publicity. The scientists, thinkers—now and then a quack, too—had been paid for their work. The elder Savage paid them. Doc had never known his mother; she had died when he was less than a year old. The elder Savage had died about the time Doc's unusual training had been finished.

Renny had never heard Doc talk much about his youth. Doc preferred not to do so. There was, Renny knew, a mystery. A mystery about the motive of Doc's father in giving Doc such a queer upbringing. The elder Savage had been a sane man, even if his handling of the boy hadn't indicated it. During the twenty years of Doc's strange training, the father had been driven by some grim, unwavering purpose. He had died, through misfortune, before he had been able to tell Doc the real reason for the strange training. Why? Doc didn't know. The mystery had remained to plague him.

The weirdness of Doc's early life was a path which had led him naturally into the profession he followed now. If it could be called a profession. It was hard to define. The newspapers sometimes said that he was an extraordinary man who was devoting his life to righting wrongs and punishing evildoers who were outside the law. But Renny didn't quite agree with that. It was true as far as it went, though.

The newspapers also called Doc a mental wizard, a scientific genius and a muscular marvel. This was the kind of copy newspapers liked, but it was also partly true. Not that Doc was anything abnormal. He wasn't. He was just a man with enough ability to overawe you, and enough in his early life to make his actions unaccountable.

Doc liked the unusual. The unusual in all things, mechanical as well as mental. A sample of the mechanical was the special high speed elevator which operated to his eighty-sixth floor suite in the building. Renny gritted his teeth now as he rode the elevator upward. The damned thing always scared him.

"I'm glad you came," Doc said. "I need your help getting stuff together."

Doc Savage was a physical giant whose skin had

been semi-permanently bronzed by tropical suns. His features weren't regular, but it was a handsome face, and the remarkable thing was how few marks it bore from the exciting, dangerous life he had lived.

Renny said, "I'm not going to tell you how scared I am. We haven't got much more than six hours to get down to that submarine. I'm scared stiff. I don't think we've got a chance."

And then suddenly he was in a chair, shaking uncontrollably. Suddenly he wanted to blubber, and he couldn't keep back the tears. He put his face in his hands and cursed his fright, his weakness, which wasn't weakness at all, but exhaustion plus the awful fear that they weren't going to be able to save those in the *Pilotfish*.

Doc looked at him. "You've had a rough go," he said. He went into the other room. There were three rooms in the eighty-six floor suite, this reception room, the library and the laboratory. Doc came back with something in a glass. "Swig this."

Renny took the glass. "It won't make me sleep?"

"No. It'll let your nerves down a little, is all."

Renny drank the stuff. He leaned back in the chair. He began coughing. He was still coughing almost continually, because of the effects of the water that had been in his lungs.

He listened to Doc Savage making telephone calls. It dawned on him finally that Doc was trying to locate a rescue chamber. No rescue chamber? The thought hit him hard. He hadn't dreamed they wouldn't be able to get a chamber.

"My God, what's wrong with the salvage boat station at New London?" Renny asked hoarsely.

"Not available," Doc told him.

"But they keep it stationed there all the time."

"That's right. Only just now it is off the New Jersey shore. A school sub got into trouble down there yesterday and they sent the salvage boat out to stand by."

Renny did some mental calculation. "It couldn't get to the *Pilotfish* in time."

"Not a chance."

"We've got to find another chamber."

"We've got to try."

A rescue chamber was the best method of reaching a helpless submarine lying as deep as the *Pilotfish* was. It was a big can of a thing with no bottom and it could be lowered and attached to the undersea boat with fittings there for that purpose. Actually it was more complicated than that, but that was fundementally what it was.

A diver, of course, could reach the *Pilotfish*. The depth wasn't prohibitive. But there was a limit to what a diver could do. The rescue chamber was the answer. If they could find one.

They weren't going to find one, it became certain.

It was agonizing for Renny to sit there and listen to Doc's futile telephoning. Renny knew submarines. The horror of what must be happening in the *Pilotfish* became clear in his mind whenever he gave it a chance.

By now the carbon-dioxide percentage would be climbing. The men would be getting listless as the poison got into their bodies. But their bodies would be in better condition than their minds.

The certainty of death, the most ghastly of the things that can torment a man's mind, would have been working on them for nearly six hours now. Of the twenty-seven men, all would be affected. Some worse than others. The strain would snap minds in some cases.

Renny had never been through such a thing, but he had heard the talk of men who had. It didn't make good listening.

He said hoarsely, "Doc, is our own equipment—"

"What we have is ready to go," Doc said.

Renny nodded. He understood that with their own equipment, it was a gamble. They had diving stuff, but it was not designed for anything like this. Doc did not want to take a chance with it, Renny realized.

He looked at his watch, then wished he hadn't when he saw how time was flowing. The urge to be moving, doing something, was overpowering. Yet there was nothing to do, nothing better than what Doc Savage was doing. If they could find an escape chamber, if by God's luck they could locate one, these minutes they were gambling in the search would pay off with the lives of twenty-seven men.

Doc Savage was trying factories now. Plants which might be manufacturing escape chambers, which might have one on hand. He was getting no results.

Tormented by the certainty that they wouldn't be able to get a rescue chamber, Renny jumped to his feet. He paced, out of habit, to the window. The windows offered a breathless view of the city. The view would fit almost any thoughts that happened to be in an onlooker's mind, Renny had long ago learned.

He stood looking out, clenching and unclenching his teeth, trying to stop coughing. Trying to make his mind pull a miracle out of thin air. His head ached and his skin was dry and he hurt when he moved, and now, when something stung his face in two or three places, he didn't immediately realize what it was. There had been a noise, too, a *whap!* of a sound.

He thought Doc had dropped something, and half-turned to see what it was—when Doc Savage slammed into him. They went down below the window.

"Don't you know when you're being shot at?" Doc asked.

Shot at? Renny flattened out instinctively. And suddenly he could think clearly and normally. It was as if danger had put a solid path under the frightened feet of his thoughts.

He looked up. The hole in the big window was round, with small cracks radiating from it. What had hit his face had been bits of glass.

Another bullet came through, making another hole, and cracking the window more extensively. Now a piece of the heavy plate glass toppled out and landed, jangling as it shattered, on the floor.

Doc Savage looked intently, first at the perforations in the window, then at the wall where the bullet had hit. He was calculating angles, deciding where the bullet probably had come from.

He crawled to the telephone. He dialed the police. "The Mercator Automotive Building," he told the police. "Someone is shooting at us from there. Probably from one of the top floors."

He made another call, this one to the night superintendent of the Mercator Building. He got the number from the directory.

"Pull the master switch that supplies current to your elevators," he said. "This is the police." He listened for a while, said, "I know it's unusual. Pull that switch. The police will be there in a minute. We're trying to trap a man on one of your upper floors."

He hung up then, and reached for his hat. "Come on," he told Renny. "The Mercator Building is the only one where the shot could have come from. And it had to be fired from somewhere above the twenty-fifth floor of the Mercator, because you can't see this window from any floor lower. Too many high buildings in between. Come on."

They ran into the corridor, entered the elevator. As they rode down, Doc explained. "We can't waste much time on this. But the Mercator Building can be on our route to the warehouse."

The warehouse was their supply station. It was more in the nature of a seaplane hangar on the Hudson river waterfront. They called it the warehouse, but the only fact that justified the name was that they kept their equipment there.

Doc took the elevator past the lobby to the basement level. He had a small private garage in the basement, where he kept a car, and Renny had another, and Monk also. Monk's machine was gaudy enough to satisfy a Balkan dictator. The machine Doc selected was Renny's. Renny was an engineer, and he liked fine automotive machinery.

The door had an automatic opener; the panel swung up of its own accord in time to let them out. They pulled into traffic.

The Mercator Automotive Building was three blocks over and a short drive north. They were turning north when Doc heard the shots. Three shots, as nearly as he could tell.

There were four policemen outside the Mercator when they arrived, and a sprouting crowd. Inside, in the lobby, a plain clothes detective and a uniformed policeman were bending over a man dying on the modernistic dappled brown and gray floor, beside a trombone case.

The plain clothes man still had his service revolver in his hand.

"Doctor'll be here in a minute," he told the dying man, his voice holding no special feeling.

The dying man had the look of a man of seventy and his years were probably nearer fifty. He was a man whose past was on his face. A man who had through his early life been a glutton in all things, and had gradually become without pride, morals, money or the ability to think logically. He was an old and ugly animal dying there.

The detective had shot him expertly in the chest.

The detective glanced up at Doc Savage.

"Like that." The detective snapped his fingers. "The janitor shut the electricity off the elevators. This fellow was in one of them. We turned on the current, and he brought the elevator down and came out waving this." He took a revolver out of his coat pocket and showed it. "There wasn't much I could do but let him have one where it would stop him quick."

The uniformed patrolman said, "He was carrying this, too."

He opened the slide-horn case. It held a hunting rifle, calibre .270, with a scope sight. The rifle was apart and lying in cotton in the case.

"Barrel is still slightly warm from the shots, believe it or not," the patrolman said.

Renny said, "He's probably the one who shot at me." And resumed coughing.

The dying man made a series of bubbling noises. His eyes were widely open.

"Hear me all right?" the detective asked him.

The man moved his eyes enough to show that he heard.

"Here's the doctor," the detective told him. Then the detective glanced up at Doc. "If you want to treat him, that is."

Doc nodded. Kneeling beside the man, he asked, "Know me?"

The man did. The sickness in his eyes, greater than the fear of death, showed that he knew.

He was going to die. Doc knew that after his examination had been in progress a few moments. No medical skill could save him.

Doc glanced at Renny. "The nearest drugstore." He told Renny what to get. "I haven't a prescription blank. Better take a policeman along so you will get it."

Renny went away. He was back remarkably soon with the prescription. It was a drug, a stimulant that would work quickly. Doc hoped it would enable the man to talk a little.

He gave the stuff time to start working after he administered it.

"Why did you shoot at us?" he asked the man.

The fellow showed his teeth unpleasantly. He wasn't going to talk. But the fear was a filth back in his eyes, in the looseness of his cheeks.

"You want to die?" Doc asked coldly. Scaring a dying man was a job that sickened him. But it had to be done.

The dying man rolled his lips inward and his eyelids outward as terror took hold of him. Probably his body was not suffering much. He apparently did not know he was going to die.

The man said firmly, "I was hired." His voice was low and pushed out against a bubbling, but it was understandable.

"Who hired you?" Doc demanded.

The man was scared now, and he had no hesitation about ratting.

"Diver," he said. "Diver Edwards."

Doc glanced at Renny, who shook his head. Neither of them had heard of anyone named Diver Edwards.

"Where is Diver Edwards now?" Doc asked.

The bubbling and words got unintelligible, but Doc decided the man was saying he didn't know. "Telephone," the man said, then more that was not understandable, and "called two hours ago."

"He hired you by telephone?" Doc asked.

"Yes," the man said distinctly.

"Where does he hang out?"

The dying man made a difficult business of saying something about the navy. Renny didn't get it, and asked, "What did he say?"

"I think he means this Edwards is in the navy."

Renny said, "Holy cow!" explosively. He got down beside the man and began describing Clark, the communications man of the *Pilotfish*. He described Clark because he suspected Clark and because Clark was easy to describe. "That sound like the guy?" he finished.

"No, that's Merry John," the dying man said.

Surprise hit the detective hard and he swore. He grabbed the dying man and yelled, "Merry John? You mean Merry John Thomas?"

The dying man made a particularly loud bubbling which trailed slowly into death.

The detective said, "Hey, has he—" He stood up slowly. He looked sick. "Do you suppose I killed him when I grabbed him that way?"

Doc said, "No, of course not." This was not true. The detective had killed the man, although the man would have died anyway. But what was done was done and the detective had meant no wrong, so there was no use telling him something that would haunt him.

Doc added, "Merry John? Who is he?"

"A smart operator in the old days." The detective got out a handkerchief to mop his face. "Merry John Thomas, the gentleman of Sutton Place. I guess he was before your time, Mr. Savage."

"What became of him?" Doc asked.

"He disappeared. It was a good thing he did, too, because we finally had the goods on him. And he was a tough one to build a case against, because of the way he operated. He was an organizer. That was back in the days when we had gangsters running wild. He was sort of a first-class mobster who free-lanced his services. I guess you would call him an efficiency expert. Anyway, he was plenty slick, and as cold-blooded as a frozen fish. He engineered more than one mass killing back in the wild days."

"How old would he be?"

"Under forty, I think. Probably about thirty-eight."

Renny said, "That would about catch Clark's age."

What happened next stunned Doc Savage, made him doubt that he had any intelligence at all.

The detective shoved out his jaw aggressively and said. "I'd like to find this Mystic where Merry Johnny is at."

Doc stared at him. "Mystic? Nothing was said about Mystic."

"I thought there was," the detective said. "The guy said something about the telephone call, the one that hired him, being made from Mystic, wherever that is."

Doc felt as if he had been hit a blow. "You—you think he said that?"

The detective nodded. He said apologetically, "Maybe I understood him better than you did because I've got a kid who is tongue-tied, and got an impediment in his throat which makes him talk a little like that fellow was talking to you. I mean, I'm used to understanding my kid, and so I probably got it better than you would."

Renny was staring at Doc.

"Mystic!" Renny croaked. "My God, do you suppose they've found that fisherman, Nick? He's the only one who knows where the *Pilotfish* is lying!"

VII.

Renny's car, which Doc Savage was driving, had a standard police siren under the hood and a pair of fog lights with red lenses. Doc switched the siren on, and its demanding wail got them through traffic at about fifty miles an hour; the red lights reassuring any dubious officers and making them easy for motorists to spot. He drove toward the warehouse.

The warehouse was an ancient brick structure, not as large as others in the neighborhood and certainly less prosperous looking. The legend, *Hidalgo Trading Company,* was hardly legible on the front.

Doc liked gadgets. Before the war, when he'd had spare time, he amused himself by devising screwball ideas in the way of gadgets. Trick guns, anaesthetic gases, little grenades which did unexpected things, and chemical mixtures which would do an assortment of things ranging from turning a man's skin green to making sharks afraid of him.

The warehouse door was equipped with a gadget. A radio opener. You pushed a button in Renny's car, and the door opened. It was a fairly simple contraption, and lots of people had taken to putting similar devices on their garage doors.

The air was hazy, the odor of the harbor a heaviness, and the water out beyond the warehouse greasy and lead-covered. The gulls were flying with quick nervous darts and sailings, and there were more of them than was normal. Weather signs! Renny shuddered, and looked at the sky.

There were high cumulo-nimbus clouds here and there, particularly in the east. Renny moistened his lips nervously. Weather. A cold front. That was what that hard tailwind he'd had from Connecticut meant.

Weather, he thought, is all we need to add to our troubles.

Doc had pressed the button which actuated the little transmitter of the door-opener. Renny watched the door begin rising, lifted by the motors inside which had been turned on by the signal.

Renny noticed the small panel truck parked at the curbing near the door. The truck did not belong to them, but there was no reason to be suspicious of it because the waterfront streets were busy these days. But at least he noticed the panel truck a moment before it became a sheet of boisterous flame.

The whole panel truck seemed to explode. The blast gave the car in which Doc and Renny rode a violent kick which turned it half around, then heaved it over on its side.

There was just the one whistling blast. Then silence.

"Stay in the car," Doc warned.

Renny mumbled, "There might be more guys with rifles around. I know." He remained still.

Doc moved his head until he could see out through the rear window of the car.

Where the panel truck had been, there was nothing. There was some smoke above where it had been, and below the brick street paving had been scooped away and the concrete curbing shattered.

Glass toppled out of a window half a block away and hit jangling on the sidewalk. Windows all over the neighborhood were broken.

Doc looked at the warehouse door. His stomach grew hard and seemed to crawl.

Whoever had laid the blast in the truck had tried to kill him, and had known something about explosive engineering. There had been more than TNT in the truck. There had been shrapnel, and the shrapnel had been so placed that it would blow back against the door. Bolts, fragments of iron, were embedded in the door where it was not torn and shattered.

Doc said, "The explosive charge in the panel truck was wired to the door. When the door opened, it went off."

Renny nodded. "Holy cow, if we had been opening the door by hand, there wouldn't have been a grease spot left."

"The trick wasn't too dumb."

"You suppose it was the same guy who shot at us? I mean, were both attempts engineered by the same bird?"

"About all we can do is make a guess," Doc said grimly. "I am going to make a run for the warehouse. Have you got a gun?"

Renny brought out a long-barreled pistol.

"Good," Doc said. "If anyone shoots at me, shoot back at them."

Doc made a quick dashing run for the warehouse. Nothing happened. He called, "It seems clear!" and Renny joined him pistol in hand.

The explosion had attracted a normal amount of at-

tention. A crowd was beginning to gather, largely steve-
dores and waterfront hangers-on.

Doc, on the theory that the police might find something if all the clues in the neighborhood were not
trampled out, yelled, "Stay back! Call the police!" He
shouted this at the spectators, sounding as alarmed as
he could. "Get back! Call the police!"

Renny demanded, "Are we going to stick around
until the cops come?"

"We haven't the time," Doc told him.

They flew the amphibian. It was not a big plane by
modern standards; it would be small alongside a B29,
and even beside a Mitchell. But it had two motors and
fair speed and plenty of iron in its soul. The sweetest
part of all was the way it was at home on land or
water, and its sturdiness.

They worked for a while, frantically, loading diving
equipment aboard. Renny saw that Doc had already
been at the warehouse and had prepared diving stuff.
Gotten together as much diving equipment as they had,
which was far from adequate for a deepwater job the
size of this one.

"When you were here earlier," Renny said, "was
that panel truck parked outside?"

"I didn't notice," Doc confessed.

The other end of the warehouse was closed by huge
doors which rolled on a track and were operated by
motors. They held their breath when they had to open
these, afraid there would be another explosion. But the
heavy panels rumbled open without incident.

Doc rolled the amphibian down the ramp. There
was a clever gadget for maneuvering, a shaft which
turned a small steerable propeller underwater. It was
as efficient as having an outboard motor attached for
maneuvering, and much simpler. Doc taxied the amphibian slowly out into the river with this device. He
touched the wheel-up button and the wheels disappeared into the wells, drawing their streamlined covers
after them.

Doc got out of the cockpit.

"You get her in the air," he said. "I am going to

start using the radio, in hopes that we may finally find a submarine salvage boat that can reach the *Pilotfish* in time."

Renny nodded. He went through the check-off list mechanically, worked the primer pumps engaged the electric inertia starters. The engines caught, and he went through the warm up routine. Oil pressure, fuel pressure, open the manifold-pressure gauge vent line, check cylinder temps, props in low pitch, shutters open. The hatful of things a man had to watch.

Finally he put the ship in the air. Climbing into the east, he saw there was weather ahead.

The sky had a hot, bold look. The cumulo-nimbus were standing up like monsters, some of them ten thousand feet high, anvil-topped. They were boiling, changing shape continually, some of them with undersides as black as polecats.

The amphibian climbed slowly, for the air was rotten, had no real lift. And it was rough, too. The ship bounced on thermals, lunging upward and sinking and hiking up on first one wing then another.

Renny looked at the cumulo-nimbus clouds and cursed them in a low, awed tone. He was afraid of such clouds. He had a lot of flying time to his credit, but only once had he flown into a really bad looking cumulo-nimbus, and he wouldn't have done that except that he had been flying along on instruments, and bored into the thing without seeing it. If a gigantic dog had seized the plane and tried to shake it to death, the effect could not have been more hair-raising. Finally clear, and thoroughly terrified, he had climbed above the overcast and looked back to see what he had flown through. The cumulo-nimbus had been standing there, a tall black monster of a cloud. He hadn't forgotten it soon.

If there was a cold front, and a bad one, there might be terrible weather over Long Island Sound for hours. Weather could easily prevent them reaching the *Pilotfish*.

Even now, things would be getting desperate on the *Pilotfish*.

For hours now, they would have been sitting there knowing death had its grip locked around them. They would have been sitting there in the utter silence of the deep sea. Listening to their own hearts hammer, to the slow leaking of water through the glands where the electric cables and pipes passed through the bulkheads.

Renny could visualize, far too clearly, their plight.

The carbon-dioxide content would be going up. At the depth at which the *Pilotfish* was lying, the effects of the carbon-dioxide percentage rise would be increased. Six percent or thereabouts was supposed to be fatal. Down more than a hundred and fifty feet, they would have to keep it below six percent. Probably below three per cent.

I hope, Renny thought, that they've got soda lime. The soda lime was absorbent. With the chemical, they could combat for a time the carbon-dioxide rise. But it would only push back death for the moment. Monk undoubtedly had figured all the chances when he gave his twelve-hour estimate.

I don't see how we can make it, Renny thought wildly. And his mind seized the horrors of death by carbon-dioxide and ran crazy with it.

Death by asphyxia. Giddiness, headache, vomiting, a dull helpless drowsiness, a loss of the ability to move, a general weakness. The heat of the body gradually lost. Face getting livid, breathing loud, and the heart at first rapid, then losing its pace and finally stopping.

He had seen carbon-dioxide death cases. Their post-mortem appearance was one of swollen faces and purplish coloration. The limbs frequently rigid. More rarely, the countenances were calm and pale after death. But always the right cavities of the heart, the lungs and the larger veins would be found gorged with venous blood after death.

Suddenly he was aware that Doc Savage's hand was on his shoulder, shaking him.

"What's wrong?" Doc demanded.

The horror of what he had been thinking, Renny realized, must have been on his face. His lungs ached as if he had been having trouble with his breathing.

He said, "Nothing." He cleared his throat. The plane was skidding. He straightened it out.

Doc wasn't fooled. "You were in that submarine mentally, weren't you?"

"That's right," Renny admitted it in a low voice.

"You are not doing anyone any good. Better stop it."

Renny shuddered. "I know." Then emotion crowded his voice upward and he said, "I don't see why the hell I am running around up here while Monk and Ham are in the *Pilotfish!* Why did it have to happen to them? Why not me instead? I got them into the mess in the first place."

"Cut it out," Doc said.

Renny, louder and more violent, said, "In England, I talked them into going! They didn't want to—"

Doc got a hard hold on his shoulder and showed him a square bronze block of a fist. In a voice that took the wildness out of Renny the way a rasp would take tarnish off brass, Doc said, "You want to cut that out? Or do you prefer a little knuckle anesthetic?"

Shortly Renny glanced up at the bronze man. "Okay," he muttered.

VIII.

An updraft got under a wing of the plane, gave it a mighty kick. The motors seemed to sob, and Renny grabbed instinctively for something to hold on to.

Doc Savage glanced out of the cabin windows. He tried not to look discouraged. He knew Renny had turned his head to watch him.

Weather they were going to have. A fine witch's tempest of it.

The cumulo-nimbus was standing up for miles

ahead of them. Anvil-tops, the clouds were called. Thunderheads. Inside them lightning crawled and the awful thermal winds roared. No one really knew how fast the winds blew in the bigger cumulo-nimbus clouds. There were reliable estimates of winds above four hundred miles an hour, which were hardly believable. The Caribbean hurricanes were rarely checked in excess of a hundred miles an hour.

No one, Doc reflected, who hadn't flown near those clouds in a plane, or hadn't studied meteorology, would realize the astounding danger and force they represented.

Far ahead, the cumulo-nimbus were black, somber. The blackness meant hail, and hail would chew their plane to a battered wreck and spit it toward the earth. Hail was bad stuff in a plane. It was almost the ground equivalent of driving your automobile into a brick wall.

The strange thing was that, to the average guy on the ground, it just looked like a cloudy day. "Getting ready to rain," was probably the casual remark being passed. It would be hot. Probably still. On the ground the weather wouldn't have the reality that it had here in the sky.

Not that it would keep them from reaching Mystic. It wouldn't. In fact, they were almost at Mystic now. Renny was turning his head, asking. "You want me to put her down?"

"You make the landing," Doc said. "But first, circle over Mystic and show me where this Nick lives."

Renny banked the ship slowly, and just over the thousand-feet legal limit for flying over populated places, pointed out the house of Nick Padolfus. "The green house," he said. "In the block southwest from that vacant lot by the large building with the red roof."

"The one with the garden?"

"That's it."

"Gray roof?"

"Yes."

"Where do the brothers-in-law live?"

Renny showed him. He described the houses. Then the plane was out over the bay. He set the flaps and low-pitched the prop, full-riched the mixture, checked his carburetor heat, set his stabilizer.

There was plenty of room and the sea was calm. None of the turbulence in the sky showed on the water. But it would later. The storm might strike before long.

Doc glanced sourly at the sky, at the harbor. He said, "This is no place to be caught in a blow." He indicated the shore. "And that gang may have something cooked up for us. Better take her in the air, after you put me ashore. I'll have the walkie-talkie with me, so keep the wavelength tuned in."

Renny asked, "'That sand bar be all right?"

"Yes."

Renny silently swung the ship into the downwind leg, the base leg, the final approach. He did a good job and there was not much splash and very little roughness. He used the little hull propeller gadget to send the plane cautiously toward the sand spit which was exposed—it was low tide—and solid. He watched the water depth closely, and finally said, "I guess you'll have to get your feet wet after all."

Doc said, "It doesn't matter." He had the walkie-talkie slung over his shoulder. It was a standard army outfit.

"Make this quick!" Renny urged.

Doc nodded. He jumped for the shore. The water was about knee deep, the bottom solid.

Renny kicked the plane out into clear water, put it on step and took it into the air immediately.

Several people had appeared on the beach. They stared at Doc Savage curiously. Someone, a small boy, yelled a question, wanting to know what kind of a plane that was. Doc told him and kept walking.

Doc Savage moved alertly, watching the people, keeping himself from being stationary long enough to be a target. He wasn't sure he was in immediate danger. He was just being careful.

The men off the submarine were, or had been in Mystic. He was sure. The mumbling of the dying man in New York had proved that. So they were in Mystic when the telephone call was made.

Whether they knew about Nick Padolfus was another matter. He didn't want to think they did.

But it was a frightening possibility. Mystic was a small place, and in such a place the news that three fishermen had picked up a mysterious man in the sea would travel fast. Everyone in town knew it by now, no doubt. Everyone, at least, who was a native resident and belonged to the local gossip circles.

Renny had probably told Nick Padolfus and his brothers-in-law to keep it quiet. That was asking a lot. Nick and his relatives didn't know Renny, and there had been enough strangeness about the affair to make them want to talk. So they'd talk. Human nature was human nature.

Doc turned into an alley. The moment he was out of sight, he ran. He ran until he came to a sort of a park, brush-tangled, where he could travel more slowly and remain out of sight.

He was scared.

Suddenly, now that he was alone, he was realizing how frightened he actually was. Before, he had been busy enough to keep from thinking about it. Now it crowded in and seized his mind.

They had a few hours—four or five, by stretching it—to find a submarine lying under at least a hundred and fifty feet of water and save what was left of the crew.

They had, to be practical about it, no idea whatever where the submarine was lying. The only one who knew that was Nick, the fisherman.

Nick, the fisherman, who lived in a green house with a gray roof in a yard with a little garden.

He was coming to the house now. Because he was afraid, without knowing for sure that there was reason for fear, he did not march straight up to the door. He slipped into the garden.

The garden had high rows of grape vines, a fine arbor of wine grapes. There was sweet corn, with concealing rows which he could follow toward the house.

He came close to the house. Thunder whooped suddenly overhead, a great gobbling uproar that ran back and forth across the heavens. There was no lightning. Just a great crackle of thunder, and after that a stillness that was almost complete. Almost complete, except for something strange in the way of sound that was coming from the house.

He stood very still and listened to the sound, at first thinking it was something cooking on a stove in the house, something boiling and bubbling. It was such a sound. Except that it began and stopped at intervals, at about the intervals at which a person would breathe, if the breathing was done laboriously.

He went into the house hurriedly.

IX.

It was a youngish man with a large mouth and eyes like boiled eggs lying on his back breathing noisily because of two knife holes in his chest. He should have been dead.

Doc Savage went down beside him and said, "Don't talk now." He did what could be done quickly. There was no telephone, Renny had said. He'd have to send someone for a doctor to finish the treatment.

Condition of the wound, the progress of the clotting, indicated the man had been stabbed probably more than half an hour ago. So it was probably safe to step outdoors. Doc ran to the nearest house.

"Get hold of an ambulance and a doctor. Then call the state police," he said. "Have them all come to Nick's house."

The woman he told it to was fat and dark-eyed. But she nodded competently. "I have a telephone," she said. "Okay to use that?"

"By all means."

Doc went back to Nick Padolfus' small green house.

He examined the man on the floor again. He said, "The ambulance is coming. So are the police." Both bits of information seemed to cheer the knife victim.

Doc added, "Don't try to talk yet." He went through the man's pockets, finding some paper money, a pair of dice, a sailor's palm, a part of a ball of Italian marlin, a billfold containing some one-dollar bills and a membership card in a fishermen's association.

"Nick's brother-in-law?" Doc asked.

The man nodded slightly.

Doc said, "Some men came here hunting Nick? That what happened?"

The other nodded again.

Doc said, "If you can write, nod."

The man could write.

Doc got out pencil and paper. He said, "If you talk, you're likely to start a hemorrhage and have all kinds of trouble. So write it out."

The man was more sickly faint than weak. He wrote large letters in a thoroughly legible schoolboy-like hand.

Four men. More outside. They hunt Nick. I tell them go to hell and they stab me. He paused for a while, thinking.

Doc demanded, "Did they ask you where you picked up the man at sea last night?"

The man wrote. *Yes.*

"What did you tell them?"

Said didn't know.

"Was that the truth?" Doc asked.

Yes.

"You were on the boat when Nick picked Renwick out of the water," Doc said. "How come you don't know the location?"

We were asleep. Tired.

Doc frowned, then demanded, "You'd had a hard day fishing, and you were asleep, resting. You say we. Does that mean you and Nick's other brother-in-law were both asleep?"

Both of us.

"Does either of you know where Renwick was picked up?"

Only Nick knows. We wake up after Nick pick up Renwick. Not before.

The fat woman had aroused the neighborhood. Faces were appearing at the windows. Doc could hear voices, questions, someone saying the doctor would be here soon, someone else demanding if it was Nick who was hurt.

"Where is Nick?" Doc asked.

The man wrote. *Nick and Jake at Nick's boat. They go clean up boat.*

Premonition took hold of Doc Savage like a chilling fever. He straightened. He demanded of the faces at a window, "Where is the doctor? Isn't he ever going to come?"

The faces stared at him with an assortment of puzzlement, suspicion and fright. One finally said, "The doc's out here now."

"What's he waiting on? Send him in!" Doc said violently.

At length the doctor did come in. He was a round little man with spectacles and a diffident uneasiness. He said, "I didn't come in because I understood you had stabbed this man and I felt the police—" He went silent, looking at Doc Savage. His eyes got roundly surprised. "Bless my soul! Aren't you Clark Savage?"

Doc said, "That's right, Doctor. This man has two stab wounds, one of which probably has damaged the hyparterial bronchi, while the other is lower in the lung and probably more serious. Keep him from talking. The police will want to question him, but do not allow him to speak. He can write out answers, however."

The physician looked uncomfortable. "I didn't know, or I wouldn't have waited—"

"No harm done," Doc said.

A lie, that. No harm done? It had lost three or four minutes, and minutes gone were great strides taken by death. In the *Pilotfish* by now, minutes were probably very long, dark and frightening.

In the yard, Doc collared the first man who was obviously a native. "Where does Nick keep his boat?"

The man stared at Doc, wet his lips, finally croaked,

"A block to your right, then straight ahead." He was scared.

I must be beginning to look as wild as I feel, Doc thought. He headed for the dock, running easily, with long strides.

The walkie-talkie, slung over his shoulder, beat against his ribs as he ran. He slipped the sling over his head, switched the little radio on and gave Renny a call.

"Renny," he said, skipping the formalities ruled necessary in radio communication. "Make a pass out over the Sound. Fly over the region where you think the submarine may be. Look for an oil slick."

He tried to keep his voice normal, but strangeness got into it. Enough strangeness to alarm Renny.

"What's gone wrong?" Renny demanded.

Doc told him. He used no more than twenty words to do it.

"Holy cow! Clark's men are trying to wipe out Nick and his two brothers-in-law."

"That's the way it looks," Doc agreed.

"But why? Why would they do that?"

"Somehow they must have learned that you don't know where you were picked up, but that Nick can find the spot," Doc said.

"How would they find that out?"

Doc said, "From Nick, maybe."

Horror must have silenced Renny, because he said nothing.

Doc repeated, "Fly out and see if there is any oil seepage to mark the location of the *Pilotfish*."

After a while, Renny said hoarsely, "You know what those devils probably did?"

"We can both guess," Doc told him. "When you came to the surface last night after you got out of the submarine, they tried to kill you. Their shooting at you—three shots which Nick mistook for a distress signal—caused Nick to come and investigate. They saw his boat, and it scared them away."

"Nick thought they'd left—"

"They didn't, obviously. They hung around, then followed Nick's boat to Mystic. That would be simple.

They could run without lights. Nick's boat was showing running lights as required by law, wasn't it?"

Renny suddenly began cursing. Profanity was not natural to him, so that as he used it now it had a stilted, frenzied, inarticulate helplessness.

Doc interrupted, "That kind of language will lose you your radio license so quick—"

"Damn the license to hell—"

"Stop that!"

Renny went silent.

"See if there is an oil slick," Doc said wearily.

The fishing boat was easy to find. The name across the stern was *Nick's Baby*, which made it simple enough. She was probably thirty-five feet on the waterline, not as large as some lifeboats on liners. She was high-hulled, solid-looking, with a plumb bow, some tumblehome amidships and a double-ender stern. A good sea boat. But the double-ender stern probably detracted from her qualities as a fish boat.

Lobster traps were stacked high on the wharf. Doc moved behind those, stood watching and listening for a while. The wooden lobster traps, like chicken crates, hid him.

Nick's Baby had the customary large working cockpit, the mast and net gaffs, the swordfishing lookout seat atop the mast and a platform for spearing swordfish stuck out from the bow. She was decked over forward, and there was an ungainly pilothouse.

She was no yacht.

Doc lifted his voice.

He called, "The police will be here before long. I want to talk to you before they get here."

His reply was silence. The boat bobbed a little with the waves. He could hear the small waves clicking against the hull, against the wharf piling under him.

He tried it again.

"Before the police get here, maybe we can make a deal!" he called. He made it loud enough that he was sure it could be heard aboard *Nick's Baby*.

No answer.

He watched, listened, until his eyes ached and his

ears got to ringing softly and his apprehensions slowly made him ill.

Another big clap of thunder ran across the sky. It sounded like a big bowling ball on a tin roof. Again there was no lightning. Just the brobdingnagian chuckle of thunder.

Doc ran, jumped aboard *Nick's Baby*. There was a rope fender on the cabin top and he grabbed it and sailed it at the cockpit, bouncing it along the cabin top so it might sound as if he was running to the stern. He himself went forward and jammed his head and shoulders down the forward hatch.

He hung there with his head and upper body inside the hatch. Slowly, the rest of him disappeared into the cabin. In a couple of minutes he came out again, much more slowly, and leaned against the stub of a mast. His facial expression was considerably more ill than it had been when he went below.

After a while, he sat down, sinking slowly and resting crosslegged. He sat there contemplating nothing with the grimmest sort of intentness.

It thundered again, weakly and far off. Half a dozen gulls whipped down like loose gray leaves swirled by a wind that didn't exist. At first the gulls were silent, then suddenly they began chorusing their forlorn cries, and continued making them as they fled. The smell of fish, and particularly the unlovely odor of menhaden, was a heavy presence in the still air.

He unslung the walkie-talkie again.

"Renny," he said.

There was no response.

He tried it again and again, saying, "Renny," anxiously, and changing it to, "From Savage to Renwick. Come in. Come in, please." He got no answer.

He lifted his eyes to the sky. But the sky was empty of everything except the crawling black cumulo-nimbus clouds that were lowering and threatful. No plane. No sound of a plane. No hope, almost.

Hope, he thought grimly, is as necessary as air for breathing. Without it, things ended before there was an end and purpose was not purpose nor was it anything else.

He grimaced. The devil with vagueness. To pot with philosophy. The simple fact was that they were up against a blank wall.

They had four or five hours left to locate the *Pilot-fish* and they had no more idea than rabbits where the submarine was.

Unless, of course, Renny located it from the plane. He was out there now, seeking traces of oil that might have bled from the fuel tanks.

Doc eyed the sky bitterly. The heavens were full of smouldering violence, and shortly there would be wind and rain, so that it would be almost impossible to locate anything like an oil streak on the surface. It was impossible right now, probably. Because the clouds and the lightning and the brewing storm would give the sea a strangeness.

He shivered.

Time was a poison. Time was death. Given forty-eight or even twenty-four hours and the *Pilotfish* could be found. The Navy had plenty of sonic locators for just such jobs, and the general location of the *Pilotfish* was known. Her whereabouts was certainly known within a radius of, say, ten miles. The sound bouncers would make duck soup of that. But it would take time.

Was there a chance of the men in the *Pilotfish* lasting more than twelve hours? If what Monk had tapped out to Renny about the high-pressure air, about the high-pressure tanks having bled themselves, it didn't look like even twelve hours.

They probably had plenty of pure oxygen. They must have a little high-pressure air, too. And if they were lucky, they'd have plenty of soda lime which would help absorb the deadly carbon-dioxide. Twelve hours was a long time under such conditions.

Soon Doc got Renny on the walkie-talkie. The walker was not designed for much distance and the sky, gorged with the turbulence of the oncoming cold front, was crackling with atmospherics. Renny had been out of range of the little outfit. But now he was coming back.

"Nothing doing," Renny reported.

He sounded as if he had aged a decade.

"No oil slick?" Doc asked.

"No oil slick."

"Would the weather keep you from seeing one?"

"It would help keep me from it," Renny muttered. "And the weather is getting worse."

Doc asked, "Did you try the radio?"

Renny said he had. He had guarded the band the *Pilotfish* would use for a radio distress call. There had been nothing.

"Do you think there is much chance they could get a radio signal out?"

"None at all," Renny said. "Remember, I told you that the radio apparatus was smashed shortly after we sailed. Clark, the communications man, must have done that. He denied it at the time, naturally. But now we know Clark is mixed up in this thing, so he probably did it."

Doc said quietly, "Come on in."

He told Renny the location of the little wharf where *Nick's Baby* was lying. He gave Renny the wind direction and probable velocity.

"Taxi up to the boat after you land," he said.

The plane, noisy and frightened in the storm-charged sky, came straight in on the crosswind leg, did a ninety-degree turn and sat down. The landing was somewhat ragged, bad enough to make Doc realize that Renny was probably in no shape for flying. Renny, as a matter of fact, should be in a hospital after what he had gone through.

There were several dinghies tied to the wharf. Doc got into one, sculled out to the plane, and got aboard. He shoved the dink away with his foot. It would drift up on the beach, because the wind, when it came, was going to be onshore.

Renny's eyes were beginning to get a flat lifelessness. He asked hoarsely, "Nick?"

Doc indicated *Nick's Baby*.

"Nick and the brother-in-law named Jake are in the cabin," Doc said. "Both have been stabbed to death."

X.

Renny stared unseeingly at the instrument panel. He doubled a fist as if his control had slipped and he had to smash something. The fist was enormous, almost an abnormality. It was cut, bruised and still dark with the oil stains which it had picked up aboard the submarine. Renny looked at the lifted fist. He lowered it.

"You'd better fly this thing from now on," he said. "My wheels are about to fly off."

He spoke heavily, then got out of the cockpit, moving as if he was stiff and old. He went back to one of the cabin seats and sank into it.

The motors were still turning over. Doc opened the throttle bank slightly, used rudder, and taxied out into the harbor.

He was going out into the harbor because the plane cabin was no safe place if they were shot at. And there was a possibility that they might be shot at. If Clark or his men were still in Mystic.

"Renny," he said.

"Yes?"

"What do you figure their chances for lasting more than twelve hours on the *Pilotfish?*" Doc asked quietly.

Renny answered immediately, in a way that showed he had been thinking about it, had been giving it all the thought that he could.

He said, "Monk has had submarine experience, He had quite a bit before this thing came up. And Wickart, the skipper, was alive in there with them. Wickart is a good sub man. I don't think those two would be fooled."

"They had time to form a judgment? Time to look

over the damage, the air supply, the oxygen, the soda lime, and all the rest?"

"They'd had time."

"Then it's twelve hours?"

Renny glanced at the clock on the instrument panel. "It's less than four hours now," he said.

Doc Savage was watching the bay. It was very slick looking in places, and riffled with small waves in other places. Little gusts of wind were beginning to move about.

Off to the west, he saw a fish jump, or make some kind of a violent flip with its tail. He didn't see the fish, but the splash was considerable. . . . He became rigid. He watched the bay. Two more "fish" jumped, this time about a hundred yards apart.

Not fish, of course, but ricocheting rifle bullets. They were being fired upon. He hadn't heard the bullet sound, because the motors were running.

He swung around slowly.

"Renny," he said. "Renny, we have one chance."

Renny stared at him. "Eh?"

"We are being shot at."

Renny shook his head, not understanding. He said. "What do you mean, chance? What chance? I see we're being shot at. It's coming from the headland, isn't it?"

Doc studied the spot where the bullets had ricocheted. The headland was probably right. It was brush-grown, and he remembered that a road swung out around the point, but that there were no houses. He'd noticed that much from the air.

The reason the snipers had picked the point, however, was more obvious. Their take-off route, the into-the-wind line the plane would logically follow in taking off, lay directly over the point. The snipers, no doubt, had planned to pump bullets into the plane as it went overhead.

They must have become impatient.

Doc Savage said, "Let's see what we can do toward holding them there until one of us can get on their trail."

In a moment, Renny's hands were fastened to Doc's

shoulder. "Doc, if we can catch them!" he yelled. "They must know where the sub is lying! If we can get one of them!"

"That's probably our one chance," Doc agreed.

He fed the engine's throttle, just enough to make the ship gather speed. He kicked rudder, sending the plane in a circle back toward the other side of the bay. His idea was to make the snipers think that he was preparing to take off.

Renny was talking wildly, elatedly, saying. "You know what's behind this? That room! That compartment in the *Pilotfish,* welded shut. It's what's in that compartment that they're after. It's got to be. They're sticking around to be sure we don't know where the sub is. But they know, because they must plan to go back!" He said all this with seemingly one breath, and then fell to coughing nervously.

"Renny!" Doc shouted. "Renny, something to make smoke."

The engineer looked up vacantly.

"Something to make smoke," Doc repeated.

Renny pulled himself together. He went back to the equipment cases which were clamped to the solid framework of the fuselage. He dug around in the cases until he found smoke grenades. The smoke grenades were part of a more or less standardized assortment of weapons which they carried.

These were "scare" grenades. A few police departments had them. They would make a surprising amount of extremely black smoke, and the smoke would have an acrid, choking quality and a distinct odor of mustard. It almost exactly imitated mustard gas, and would scare the devil out of anyone who knew what mustard gas was.

Renny passed them to Doc Savage.

"One is enough," Doc said. "Here is what I am going to try: We'll put the plane in position for a take-off, then fake a fire, using the grenade to release a cloud of smoke. There is enough breeze to drift the smoke toward shore. I think I can swim fast enough to stay ahead of the smoke, so that the snipers cannot see me. In other words, I want cover to reach shore."

Renny nodded. "What do I do?"

"Tease them into thinking you're going to take off and they can get a shot at you.".

The plane was fairly close to the far shore now. About as close as it was safe to sail. Doc kicked the nose around into the wind. He opened the throttle smoothly to the fullest, as he would for a take-off.

Renny had the cabin windows open. Doc dropped the smoke grenade on the floor, pin pulled. Instantly it disgorged black smoke in enormous quantities which the draft whirled out of the open windows.

"It's all yours, Renny," Doc said.

He closed the throttles, slid back in the cabin, wrenched open the door, waited until plenty of smoke had boiled out around him, and dived. Enough smoke was swirling out of the cabin door that he was sure they couldn't see him from the other side of the bay. It was more than a mile from here to where the snipers must be hidden.

He came up and swam rapidly for the shore. It was about a hundred yards. The smoke, heavy, hung to the surface of the water. Shortly beach mud was underfoot. He slogged ashore.

There were spectators by now. Several persons near the shore had been watching the plane, and seen the smoke appear. They had raced to the beach.

Some of them saw Doc.

He heard his name. Someone had recognized him.

He went on, keeping ahead of the wind-carried smoke, until he reached the cover of trees. As he ran, he searched for a car.

Back on the shore, they were shouting at the plane. Did the plane need help? No, it didn't, Renny bellowed. There had just been a little fire. It hadn't hurt anything. Renny's bellowing voice sounded remarkably robust, healthy, fresh. His big voice would probably be the last part of him that would collapse.

Now there'll be silly stuff in the newspapers, Doc thought sourly. Something goofy about him coming ashore from the plane in a cloud of smoke, only some reporter would be sure to dress it up with wild feathers. He scowled, embarrassed by the prospects.

Publicity of the wild sort always embarrassed him. The newspapers invariably picked out something spectacular, which usually meant something silly, and played it up. There was nothing particularly goofy about using the smoke grenade. It was an accepted military practice to cover maneuvers with smoke screens. But when this got in print, it would make him red-eared to read it.

The car he found was a taxi. It was a marvelous place to find a taxi. Pure luck. But the driver wasn't hot about getting a fare. "I want to see that plane burning," he said.

"The plane isn't burning," Doc told him. "If you want to make about a dollar a minute for the next half hour, let's get going." He shoved a bill into the man's hand. "Here's twenty minutes in advance."

The man looked at the bill with appropriate respect. He folded it and stuck it in the defroster guard so that he would have it under his eyes.

"What's the catch?" he asked.

Doc described the point of land where he wanted to go. "How quick can you make it?"

"That's about four miles," the driver said. "Say about two minutes."

"Don't overdo it," Doc said.

As a mater of fact, they took only a little more than five minutes for the trip.

"Cut off your engine and kick the clutch out," Doc said. "Let's do the last half mile without undue uproar."

The curves in the road were gentle and the going slightly downhill. They raced along in what would have been a satisfactory silence if the springs had not squeaked like hungry mice.

When the spot where the snipers were probably located was about a quarter of a mile ahead, Doc indicated a place where cars had been leaving the road. Where picnickers had been pulling off to park. "See how quietly you can put it in there."

The old car rolled off the road and behind the bushes as quietly as could be desired.

"Now you wait here," Doc said. "Better stay in the car. If you're asked questions, say you're watching the plane."

The driver stared at him. "How legal is this?"

Doc hesitated. Minutes, the way things were going, were worth more than diamonds. But he didn't want the driver getting dubious and leaving.

Doc showed the man a folder. It was an impressive folder complete with picture and fingerprints, and it identified Doc as a special agent, civilian section, the United States Navy. The commission was a survival of some earlier work he had done for the Navy.

The driver nodded.

"There's a double-barreled shotgun in the trunk, with some number fours," he said. "You have any use for it?"

"I hope not," Doc said.

"It's there if you want it."

"Thanks," Doc told him. "Just so you're here when I want you."

"I will be."

Doc went toward the tip of the neck of land.

He could hear the plane out on the bay. The motors were whooping alternately, then settling down to idling speed. Through an opening in the brush, he saw the ship. Renny was out on a wing at the moment, pretending to tinker with one of the motors. The amphibian was far enough away that it was not likely to be shot at.

The distant noise of the plane, Doc hoped, had covered any sound the taxi had made. If his luck held, it had.

His luck was good enough. He found their car first. It was parked carefully in a lane, turned toward the road ready for a hurried departure.

He moved very carefully then. He wished he'd brought the walkie-talkie, but he hadn't. He'd been afraid the set wouldn't stand the wetting when he swam ashore. With the set now, he could have suggested that Renny create a diversion, draw the fire of the snipers.

The snipers would, he assumed, be near the beach.

Probably lying in the tall salt water grass which grew near the shore. He operated on that theory, and searched the sand for footprints. He didn't find any tracks. He heard the voices first.

The initial voice was uneasy, demanding, "By God, how much longer we going to stay here?"

The second voice was gleeful with ridicule. "What's the matter, Joney?"

Joney cursed. He had a slight Irish accent. He said what half-smart so-and-sos he thought they were. "That plane is messing around out there for some reason," he said.

"Sure it is," the other agreed. "One of us put a bullet into the works somewhere, and they're trying to figure out what happened."

"There's no more smoke."

"Sure. They got the fire out."

Joney said, "You damned guys don't seem to get it through your heads you're dealing with Doc Savage."

"Scared, Joney?"

Joney said damned right he was scared.

Where's the third man, Doc Savage wondered. They were talking as if there were more than two. There might be more than three, too.

"I wish to hell I had a telescope sight," Joney said. "I bet I could pick off that guy the next time he comes out on the wing. And listen, why is it the same guy on the wing every time? You know what? I think there's only one of them on that plane."

They didn't laugh at that. It gave them something to think about.

Doc had been working forward cautiously. Now he found where they were hiding. They were sitting behind a thin bush, two of them together. They had Garand rifles, standard issue types. Looking at the rifles, Doc wondered if they had brought the weapons from the submarine. If so, it meant the men had been aboard the sub.

The two men wore civilian clothes. They didn't look as if they had been out in the sun much, which might mean they had been on the *Pilotfish*. It might mean they had been lying around the city, too.

Doc studied the pair, estimated his chances of getting to them, of overpowering them. It would be dangerous.

That had been his idea. Catch one of the men who had been on the *Pilotfish*. Force the fellow to reveal the submarine's location: Simple and direct.

Joney was grumbling again. He said, "We're suckers to fool around Savage. That Renwick doesn't know where the submarine is lying. That fisherman, that Nick, was the only one who knew. Okay, Nick's out of the picture. Nick's kapoot. Why don't we let it lie until the excitement dies down?"

"Pipe down."

"Pipe down hell! We've the same as got the sub in our pocket. We know where it is. We let the noise die down, and in a few weeks or a few months send a diver out to the sub and open that compartment. That was the plan. Why not go ahead with it?"

"The plan," someone told him sourly, "didn't include the noise."

Doc jumped. The third voice!

The third man had spoken, and he sounded so much like Joney's companion that Doc had almost missed the difference. The third man was close.

Joney said, "How do you suppose they came to put Renwick, Mayfair and Brooks on that submarine in the first place?"

The third man swore.

"Giesen," he said. And swore again.

"Yeah, Giesen," Joney agreed. "Giesen smelled a rat, all right."

"You reckon he suspected Clark?"

"Of course not, or he would have clapped Clark in the brig and damned quick. Giesen just had a hunch something was up. So he put Savage's three friends aboard to stop it."

The third speaker, Doc decided, was about fifteen feet ahead, a little in front and to the left of the first two. A thick bush stood at this point. The man must be inside it.

But were they off the submarine? Did they know the

location of the craft? He had to have the answer. The alternative of a mistake now was paralyzing to think about.

It certainly sounded as if they had been on the *Pilot-fish.*

He lay there mentally writhing on the horns of the dilemma, in as devilish a mental spot as he had ever occupied. Then the thing solved itself. Or at least he was suddenly without the necessity of making any choice. The choice was made for him.

XI.

A nesting bird flew wildly from almost under Doc's nose. The bird had been sitting there, unnoticed because of protective concealment, tied to the nest by its protective instinct. Suddenly the bird's patience came to an end. It flew.

Doc never did see the bird. But it was a large one, and made plenty of noise. With a flailing of feathers, hitting bushes, it left.

The man Doc had not yet seen sounded alarmed. He demanded, "What the hell was that?"

"A bird," Joney said.

In the stillness that followed, the distant aeroplane motor spurted. Thunder got loose in the heavens, and the noise of the plane engine was completely lost in the greater uproar overhead.

The earlier rifle shots, Doc thought, must have been fired during the thunder-bursts. That would keep them from being heard. He had this side thought with one part of his mind. The rest of his mind and all his nerves waited for what was coming.

The unseen man said, "A damned funny acting bird, if you ask me."

Joney, not alarmed, jeering, asked, "Who's scared now?"

"Hold it," said the unseen man. "Let's take a look."

He came up out of the bush. He was a long, hungry fellow with leathery hide and water-colored eyes. His blue suit didn't fit him.

Doc Savage had his hat off by now. He leaned it against a grass clump, where there were weeds all around. Then he moved back, to the left.

The long man came forward, walking as if he was on eggs. He had a thin-lipped mouth, as if a slit had been made in a football. His lower lip hung downward and outward.

He said, "God!" He had seen the hat.

He began firing the submachine gun he carried, walking into it as he fired. He did not have the web belt and magazine cases which are military regulation whenever the submachine gun is carried. He had only the gun. It shook and rattled and spouted empties.

The hat jumped around, turning ragged, climbing into the air.

Doc Savage had two rocks in his fists. They were hard flint rocks, not round but nearly enough so for throwing, and somewhat larger than baseballs. He came up on his knees, throwing both rocks.

He threw the left rock first, because he was not as good with his left hand. As it turned out, the throw he made with that hand was better than the other. It dropped the man neatly by grazing his head. The other rock, thrown much harder, hit the man in the stomach pit. He went over backward. The gun, moaning a long burst, cut leaves out of the trees and sprinkled lead over the sky.

Doc went flat again. There were plenty of rocks. He got two more.

He yelled. "Use a grenade on them!"

Then he tossed one of the small rocks. It was dark, and under the circumstances certainly looked like a hand grenade.

The way the other two men flattened out told him one thing: They'd had combat training, at least simulated combat. Whether they were off the sub or not was still a question.

While they were down, Doc moved. He scuttled forward on all fours, keeping as low as he could, and reached the man he had hit with the rock.

He got the submachine gun. He didn't want the fellow shot in the course of whatever was going to happen next, so he kept going. There were large rocks in the weeds and brush. He found one, and hit the dirt behind it. It was as effective as a foxhole, if they didn't flank him.

He had the other rock in his left hand. He threw that. One of the men, Joney, cursed and flattened again.

An uneasy, waiting silence followed.

Doc broke it by calling, "Come in from the right and left, men! Be careful!" He hoped that would worry them. He hoped it would make them think there was a large party surrounding them.

More stillness.

Joney said, "That wasn't no grenade! That was a rock!"

Doc had been inspecting the ammunition supply left in the submachine gun. There wasn't much. About two good bursts. He set the gun for single shot.

Picking out as nearly as he could the place where Joney lay in the weeds, Doc put two bullets through the tall salt-water grass and brush. Apparently he hit nothing. He was not shot at.

"Joney," Doc said.

Joney didn't answer.

Doc said, "Get your hands up, both of you. You haven't got a chance."

No response. Doc watched the grass and low brush alertly. A long time passed. It was about thirty seconds, but it seemed almost that many minutes.

"Joney!" It was the other man.

"Yeah?"

"You going to give up?"

"And stand in front of a firing squad? Hell, no!" Joney sounded hoarse.

Doc lifted his own voice again. He shouted,

"They're going to put up a fight! Come in on them! But be careful!"

Then he picked up small rocks, very small ones, and began flipping them here and there, hoping Joney and the other man wouldn't see them, hoping the sounds the small pebbles made would be mistaken for an ambush party creeping closer.

There was not much of that, about thirty seconds, and Joney said, "Let's get out of here!"

"Okay."

They leaped up and ran. Doc came up himself. It was important that they not get away. But they were sharper than he expected. One was running sidewise, so that he saw Doc instantly.

And the man had another submachine gun. Not a rifle. He'd had a rifle earlier, but he had dropped that, exchanged it for an army model Thompson.

The man swung. The gun put out lead and noise. Doc dived wildly. He got down in time. But there was a shower of twigs, dirt and rock fragments.

He didn't lift his head again. He didn't dare. Not until he had crawled a few yards to reach a spot where they wouldn't expect him. By then, the pair had gotten away.

Their car motor started. Doc sprinted, trying to reach a spot where he could see the car. He did see it, but the machine was going fast through the trees.

He took what seemed the best chance. He put the gun on automatic and emptied it, except for three or four cartridges, into the car motor. The distributor was on the near side of the engine. He should have smashed it, cut wires, shattered spark plugs.

The car left like a smoothly functioning rocket, still hitting on all eight cylinders.

Doc wheeled, ran back to the man he had clubbed down.

The long man had turned over on his face and was mumbling and trying to push himself off the ground. In another minute or so, he would have been on his feet and gone.

Doc seized the man's bony shoulder, jerked him

over on his back, and struck the point of the man's jaw with a fist. Then he shouldered the fellow.

The cab driver was out of his cab. He had the trunk open, had the double-barreled shotgun in his hands.

"You okay?"

Doc said, "Yes. See what kind of a following job you can do!"

He piled into the back seat with his prisoner. The cab began moving, the driver handling the wheel with one hand, repeatedly slamming the door, which wouldn't catch, with the other hand.

They traveled perhaps two hundred yards along the road before there was a squealing noise from underneath. The driver brought the cab to a stop and jumped out.

He pointed. "Ruined a tube, too!" He sounded near tears.

The head of a roofing nail, round and shiny and about the size of a dime, was partly embedded in the casing.

Doc walked along the road, back the way they had come, looking at the blacktop. He found more tacks.

"Better take some branches and rig something across the road to flag down any other cars," he told the taxi driver when he returned. "They dumped roofing nails all over the road."

"My ration board is going to love this," the driver said.

"The navy will take care of it," Doc told him. He got out his billfold.

The driver shook his head. "The twenty you gave me will cover it."

"Whatever you say."

"It's covered."

Doc dragged the long man out of the cab. He shouldered the fellow and walked toward the beach.

Renny Renwick saw his arm signals immediately. The plane approached, motors drumming, dragging a long wedge of wake across the oily, threatening water.

The beach was bad, with partly submerged rocks and sharp reefs. Doc had to wade out into water above his waist. Renny had forgotten to put out a boarding ladder, so that he had difficulty getting aboard with the long man. Renny finally got out of the cockpit long enough to give him a hand. The plane almost drifted on to the rocks. Renny dashed back to the controls, and got them clear.

Doc said. "Take it off. Go over the point and land in New London harbor."

Renny nodded wordlessly. He had seen the long man's face, and he was scowling. "That's one of them," Renny said.

The plane gathered speed, rode the step for a while and climbed off. The rest of the bay fled under them, then a beach and trees, houses, roads. The air was getting rough.

Doc asked, "This fellow was on the *Pilotfish?*"

Renny nodded. "He's one of the sailors who came aboard at the last minute."

Doc leaned back. He knew he shouldn't feel as relieved as he felt. But he couldn't help it. "Then it wasn't entirely a water-haul," he said.

"What happened?"

Doc told him. He explained, "I made a dumb move. The taxi driver would have helped, I think. But I didn't know him and I was afraid to depend on him."

Renny swallowed. "We should kick. We're so damned far ahead of where we were twenty minutes ago that we should complain."

A thermal caught a wing, gave them a nasty heave. The heavy amphibian did a slip that was scary because they didn't have much altitude. Renny did careful coordination with wheel and pedals and got them level.

"He may not know the exact location of the submarine," Doc said.

The long man stirred slightly. Doc went back to him, and began searching the fellow's clothing. Every one of the man's pockets seemed to contain some kind of a weapon.

Renny put the plane in a landing glide, coming down in a diagonal that would set them on the Thames opposite the coal dock in New London.

"He'd better know," Renny said grimly.

XII.

They swung around, taxied the plane out toward the harbor mouth until they reached the yacht club. They picked up a mooring buoy there, and Doc got a line about it. The plane would ride here now without their worrying about watching it.

Not as much thunder was running through the heavens, but what there was of it was louder. There would be a great cannon crashing of sound. The rumbles would die away. Then silence until the next terrific report.

The front, Doc saw, was moving down from the north. It was not far away. Fifteen minutes, probably. It was moving slowly. When it hit, there would be howling winds and turmoil and probably hail and certainly rain. The plane would not be safe here. It would not be safe anywhere except in a stout hanger.

Renny Renwick pulled himself up out of the cockpit. He was ill, exhausted, drained of strength. He moved slowly back in the cabin, keeping hold of things as if he was afraid he would stumble. His long face was not pleasant.

He sank to a knee beside the long man.

"You know where that sub is?" he asked.

The long man looked at him unblinkingly. The fellow had regained some color. There was no sign of fear about him except the perspiration. It was not particularly hot in the plane, but the man was soaked.

Renny said, "Look, I asked you a question."

The man still said nothing.

Renny's face was terrible. He reached out slowly and picked up the man's left hand and dragged the hand to him and seized the little finger on the hand. He broke the finger while the long man suddenly lost his stoicism and began screeching in agony.

Doc Savage had started forward. He stopped. His eyes were on the long man's face.

The long man's face was changing. His expression was altering. Fear. Anxiety, probably for his life. He was suddenly scared stiff of Renny.

Doc retreated. This may be the way, he thought.

Renny hadn't said anything. He was breathing heavily, and his eyes were too wide, his mouth too large and loose, his whole attitude strange. Renny looked like a man who might be losing his mind.

He's just weak and tired and terrified, Doc thought. Just beaten to an emotional pulp by suspense.

Renny got hold of his voice. It sounded as if he had reached into a cage of snakes for it.

Renny said, "I was in that submarine. I was in it just long enough to find out what those others are going through, then I got out. They didn't get out. They've got twelve hours—or they had twelve hours. They've not got much more than two hours now. Two hours. You get that."

He got down and put a hand on each side of the long man's head, put his own terrible face close to the long man's agonized one. He said, "Two hours, pal. We find that submarine in two hours, or Monk and Ham and those other sailors are dead."

The long man looked as if he wanted to shrink down through the cabin floor.

"So I want to know where that submarine is," Renny said.

The long man's answer sounded as if a chain was being dragged out of a box.

"I don't know where it is," he said.

Doc Savage was leaning against one of the cabin seats. He put his weight heavily on it. For a moment disappointment came up and engulfed him. The man didn't know!

Time had come to its end. Time, that was, which would do them any good. Two hours they had to get to the *Pilotfish*, to do what they could do for the men imprisoned in the hull. It was not enough. Not enough to try again to find where the submarine lay.

Renny hadn't moved. He was still on all fours, staring hypnotically into the long man's face.

"Maybe you didn't understand me," Renny said. *"You've got to know."*

The long man dampened his lips. Renny, while the man's tongue was between his teeth, suddenly struck the man's jaw, causing him to bite his tongue painfully. The hurt came out of the man in a low mewing.

Renny breathed inward deeply, fiercely.

"Maybe you heard somewhere that we've never killed anybody in cold blood," he said.

The long man had screwed his eyes shut in pain. He kept them shut.

"Listen," Renny said. *"I've got to know where that submarine is!"*

Doc had never heard Renny's voice the way it was now. Renny was going to kill the man. There wasn't the slightest doubt about it. And the way Renny would do it would not be nice.

Doc restrained an impulse to stop it. Renny wasn't bluffing. Renny was close to the edge of sanity, and he might kill the man in a sudden frenzy. Commit the deed before he could be stopped.

Wildly, Doc tried to think of some other alternative. Truth serum? Truth serum was the only thing he could think of. But truth serum was not always effective, and the efficient employment of it required three or four hours. He could not, he was positive, get results from any truth serum of which he knew. Use of the stuff was illegal. Not that they would worry about that too much, if there had been time. But there wasn't time.

Renny had shut off the plane motors. It was fairly still, except for the loudness of the gathering storm.

Renny's breathing was quite audible.

Fascinated, Doc watched what Renny was doing to the long man. The process was psychological entirely. Renny wasn't touching the fellow, wasn't laying another hand on him for the time being.

There was not more than a foot between their faces. Close enough for the long man to get the benefit of everything Renny was thinking. Hate. Cold perspiration. Intent to kill.

The staring must have gone on wordlessly for three or four minutes.

Then Renny took hold of the man's left arm. Merely took hold of it. The man screamed, hoarsely and as if he was badly hurt, mixing words in with his shriek.

Doc couldn't understand what the man said, but Renny miraculously got it. Renny's face lighted. The black curtains fell.

"You hear that, Doc?" Renny said clearly and rationally. "He knows where the sub is, and he's going to show us."

Doc Savage went forward hastily. There was a chart compartment. He'd been foresighted enough to stuff some marine charts into the case, a New York-to-Boston general scale chart, and smaller detail charts of the water where the *Pilotfish* must be lying.

He put the charts in front of the long man.

"Mark the place," he said.

Then he watched the man. It was important, so important that it was sickening, that they know whether the fellow had lied to temporarily save his neck.

The long man picked through the charts. That was a good sign. He unrolled each and glanced at the area designation. He could be making it look good, though.

He finally selected a chart, eyed it for a while. It seemed to Doc that he was actually picking out bearing points.

"I'll need a protractor and a sharp pencil," the long man said finally. "Parallel rulers, too."

Doc passed him the instruments without comment. He watched the fellow on his knees, marine chart spread out in what clear space there was, squinting, drawing lines with the pencil.

The man looked up finally.

"You can check me on this," he said.

"How were the bearings taken?" Doc asked.

"Clark got them. So did I," the long man explained. "We were on deck with a pelorus and a compass. We shot bearings on Montauk Point light, Fisher's Island light, Little Gull and Watch Hill. Moreover we had clocked off since passing the bell on Southwest Ledge."

"You remember all those figures?"

"Yeah."

Doc thought that unlikely. All those bearings amounted to a lot of remembering.

His doubts must have shown.

The long man looked uneasy. "I had them written down. Then I memorized them. It took about an hour, but I got them pat."

"Why?"

The man shoved out his jaw. "With only one guy knowing where the sub was, there was too much temptation for that guy to double-cross us. To disappear, or something, for a couple of years. He could come back any time. Knowing where the sub was would be like having it in the bank."

Doc said, "Have you some idea of what will happen to you if you are lying?"

The long man nodded. "Yeah. I hope you find the sub there about as much as you hope it is, I ain't kidding."

Doc Savage went back to Renny. He showed Renny his watch. "An hour and fifty minutes, more or less."

"Can the navy get anything out to the submarine in that time?" Renny asked hoarsely.

"Nothing that would do any good."

"What could they get out there?"

"Small surface craft, probably, very small. Nothing in the way of an escape bell."

"Can we do much better?"

"We can try."

"That's all there is to do, isn't it?"

"That's all."

Renny nodded. He went back to the long man. "We're going out to where you say that sub is," he told the man. "One of us will go. And the sub had better be there."

The long man turned the shade of an old newspaper. "God, you don't expect me to drop a diver right on it!" he croaked.

"That's what we expect," Renny said ominously.

"But it may be anywhere within two or three miles of the spot!" The long man sounded ill.

It was daytime. The bearings taken a few moments before the *Pilotfish* was sunk had been taken at night. It was much simpler to get an accurate bearing at night on Montauk Point lighthouse, Fisher's Island, and the others. In fact, it was impossible because of haze to even see Little Gull, which was one of the markers. And Montauk Point, on the tip of Long Island, was not too prominent.

Doc simplified matters somewhat by flying a bearing on Montauk while Renny checked off on Watch Hill, and the other bearing points. At the proper spot, Renny dumped out a little sea trace.

The sea trace was part of the stardard kit most planes carry when working over the ocean. A chemical powder which would stain the water a distinctive yellow.

Doc banked back and landed. There was not much sea running. But there was the inevitable ground swell, greasy and unstable.

When the plane was sloughing through the yellowish sea trace, he called to Renny, "Put out the light buoy. The whistler."

The buoy consisted of an aluminum float which would give out a tweet-tweet sort of a whistle because of the action of the waves. It was anchored by a mushroom weight and a couple of hundred feet of light line. Renny put it overside. He came back to the cockpit.

"What'll we do—work the sound apparatus from the plane or from a rubber boat?" he asked.

"From the plane," Doc said. "You feel able to work the outfit?"

Renny nodded. "I'm feeling better, now that we're getting somewhere."

Doc looked at him sharply. "Don't prop yourself up too high. Maybe we aren't getting anywhere."

The sounding gadget was electrical, and there was nothing new about it. It had none of the hair-raising nearly pseudo-scientific unreality of some of the gadgets which Doc Savage liked to produce to fit a given emergency. This one, in principle, was simple.

A transmitter started a sound wave for the bottom of the ocean. The wave went down, hit the bottom, or any object that was between, and bounced back. The receiver got the bounce, and measured the time-lapse, putting this on a dial where it could be seen.

The thing had one very good quality. It was sensitive to within a couple of feet. It would readily spot the lump of the submarine on the bottom.

Sonic transmitter and receiver were in one unit. The thing had actually been designed for use from seaplanes in this fashion, or from blimps, during the submarine scare early in the war.

Renny adjusted dials. He stuck the stethoscope in his ears.

Doc began to grill the surface of the sea with the plane. Back and forth. Move over a hundred feet each time. Back and forth. The plane crawled up the greasy swells and slithered down the slopes.

The long man occupied a cabin seat. They had tied him there, lashed him hand and foot. He watched Renny listen to the stethoscope and watching the indicator dial. Perspiration had soaked the fellow from head to foot.

Renny let out a howl. "Got it!" He waved his arms. "Holy cow! Here it is!"

Doc swung the plane slowly. "Check it for length," he warned. He sent the plane back a little north of the previous crossing. He watched Renny's face, saw it grow uneasy.

"Must have caught the first sounding near the bow or stern of the sub," Renny muttered.

Doc circled and made another pass over the spot. Renny shook his head sickly. "That's some other wreck," he said, defeated. "It's not over fifty feet long."

They had two more false alarms. Then Renny got one that wasn't.

XIII.

Doc put out a mushroom anchor and a buoy attached to a line. The buoy had a flashing light and a slow-feeding supply of sea trace which would make it easy to locate from the air for twenty-four hours or so. It would hold the plane.

"You going down?" Renny asked anxiously.

"Not until we try the oscillator," Doc told him.

The oscillator was a standard underwater signalling device. This one was portable, not very punchy. But down in the *Pilotfish,* there was oscillator equipment which could send a whining signal a considerable distance.

Provided this was the *Pilotfish.* And provided there was anyone left alive, and that they had electric current for the oscillator.

Doc submerged the oscillator, turned on the power. He keyed slowly.

"Keep on the stethoscope to see whether you can pick up an answer," he warned Renny.

But they were able to get no response out of the sound receiver. They might as well have been holding their ears to a coffin.

They didn't look at each other. They didn't want to exhibit the stark, ill defeat which had fallen upon them.

"Put a knotted line over the side," Doc said.

"Then you're really going down?" Renny demanded.

"Yes."

Doc went back to the large case, upright in the after portion of the cabin, containing the diving dress. The thing was bulky. It wasn't going to be easy to get in and out of the plane wearing the outfit.

The suit was of metal, of flanged construction for

light weight. It was not uncomfortable to wear, not much more uncomfortable than a suit of medieval armor would have been. It somewhat resembled the outfit of an ancient knight.

It was not a terrifically high-pressure outfit. Two hundred feet was probably as deep as it would be safe. But that was enough this time.

Doc stripped off. He put on a special undergarment, something like long-handled underwear, which served mostly as protection against chafing by the suit joints.

"I'll check the air," Renny said grimly.

The suit was self-contained. No necessity existed for a surface air pump and bulky air hose. The absence of the air hose was a particular blessing. There was a tidal current here, and sometimes the pull of the water against a hundred and fifty feet or so of air hose was more than a man could handle.

The regenerating apparatus supplied an unpleasant, but perfectly serviceable air. Its principal parts consisted of compressed oxygen and air cylinders, mixing valves and automatic pressure regulators, caustic soda chamber for absorption of carbonic acid. The process—supplying air to the suit wearer—was entirely automatic and would continue for about an hour and a half.

There was a telephone in the helmet. There was also a conventional bell-ringing button which could be operated with the chin, and this was also connected with an oscillator by which code signals could be sent if the telephone wire became disconnected.

Renny had dropped into a mechanical check-off of the apparatus. He sounded like the co-pilot of a bomber during take-off procedure.

"What about the light and torch?" he asked.

"They're all right."

The light was portable, electric, self-contained. It was rather bulky, and had considerable power. The torch was also portable, an underwater hydro-oxygen which could cut through a couple of inches of solid steel two hundred feet below the surface.

"Check-off seems okay," Doc said.

He found that he couldn't get out through the plane

door with the torch and light slung to the suit. He un-slung them, and with Renny's aid, finally got out through the door. The plane was never meant to serve as a diving platform. In the end, he lost his balance and plunged into the sea.

The water looked blue-green, and because the sky was cloudy, it was intensely dark a few feet down. He had fallen headlong into the sea, which meant nothing because the suit was self-contained. But the few minutes of awkwardness were discomfiting, though.

Over the telephone Renny's excited, "Doc, you all right!" reached his ears. The receiver wasn't working too well; it squawked.

"Hold me up for a check," Doc said.

He was attached to the plane by one line, a one-eighth inch braided airplane control cable. It was light and extremely powerful. It had one drawback—cutting it in case he got hung up. But its advantages out-weighed the disadvantages. The cable was saturated with a paste lubricant which would, under the action of the salt water, create a bright fluorescence for several hours. The cable was like a red-hot wire around him, and it snapped past as Renny stopped his descent by tightening it.

Carefully, Doc checked air and pressure, movement of the suit joints.

He said, "Checks okay. Give me another fifty feet."

He went down by fifty-foot stages, pausing each time for a thorough check.

At a hundred and twenty-five feet, the suit began to grunt and complain, tortured by the pressure. Some of the joints started sweating drops of moisture, but there were no leaks large enough to alarm him. He would, he decided, try working at not much more than atmospheric pressure. If there had been other divers to aid, he would not have taken that chance.

By working at normal atmospheric pressure, he could avoid the dangers when he surfaced. The danger that would come from the blood taking on a great quantity of nitrogen under pressure, then causing bubbles when the diver came to the surface. But there was always a chance the pressure would collapse his armor, and the sudden shock would probably kill him if it did.

He hung there in the blackness. And it was very black. He hadn't switched on the light. It's like hanging in death, he thought.

Into the telephone, he said, "All right. Lower away."

The telephone wire and the thin cable were his only connection with the surface. He sank rapidly. Or he supposed it was rapidly. He couldn't see anything.

The bottom was fairly hard when he hit it. He had known it would be hard. The tide kept it scoured clean. The tidal current sweeping in and out of Long Island Sound.

"On the bottom," he told Renny.

Renny couldn't hold it back. "The sub?" he asked hoarsely. "Do you see the *Pilotfish?*"

Doc worked the light loose from his belt. There was a head clip for it. He decided to plant it in the clip first, and did so, then turned it on.

He was close enough to reach out and touch one of the stern planes of the *Pilotfish*. He reached out and touched it.

"It's here," he told Renny.

Renny did not answer.

"I have my hand on it," Doc said. "Anyway, it's a submarine. And there wouldn't likely be another submarine right here."

Renny didn't answer. Renny wasn't going to answer, he realized suddenly.

Death, black death all around, he thought. The headlamp rammed out fuzzy cone of dirty cotton, which was all there was except the blackness.

"Renny?" he said into the mike. "Renny, what has happened?"

The receiver did not bring Renny's voice.

He was hit suddenly by an awful loneliness. A ghastly emptiness all around him. He screamed, "Ren-

ny, damn it, what happened?" Which was probably
the first time he had lost control in years. He got hold
of himself.

The telephone wires must have broken. He looked
upward. He could see the wires arching upward, near
the luminous cable. They were broken somewhere
above, of course.

It was nothing to get alarmed about. The telephone
wires had just broken.

He began crawling along the *Pilotfish,* doing what he
had come down here to do.

The telephone wires had just broken. But the trouble was that the receiver should have been dead if they
were broken, and the receiver wasn't dead.

XIV.

The pistol was a regulation .45, and Renny knew
quite well that it was loaded.

"You're using," the man told him, "some pretty good
judgment."

The man was Clark. He wore civilian clothes, and
he had dyed his hair and made himself a little trick
moustache with hair and spirit gum. The moustache
was a good job. But it was still Clark.

"Hold it," Clark said. "Hold everything."

That was what he said when the boat came up
alongside.

Renny didn't know how the boat had managed to
get so close without his knowing it was there. He'd
never understand how it had.

But he'd looked up, and there it was. A cabin
cruiser. A big, mahogany fast job. Fast as hell. Not
worth much for anything but speed and flash, which

was doubtless why the navy hadn't taken it over early in the war.

Like a dragon, it had been there. Clark in the bow. Half a dozen other men with him. They were all armed. They had more rifles than commandoes.

They were climbing around now and getting into the plane. The boat's bow had hit the plane. It had gouged quite a hole into the hull, above the waterline. Nobody seemed to care.

"Stand still while you're searched!" Clark snarled.

Renny did it. They relieved him of everything. Every stitch. They tore off everything he wore.

Then they looked at him and someone said, "My God, will you look at the bruises!" Renny looked down at himself. He could understand why he felt so tough. He was a mass of bruises from head to foot. He'd been given them when he was banged around in the submarine during the sinking.

Now that he was naked and helpless, they gave him a little less attention.

The long man got it.

"Well, well," Clark said, looking at the long man. "It's Stickler, what do you know!"

It was the first time Renny had known the long man's name was Stickler.

One of the men started to untie Stickler. Clark halted that with, "Hold it a minute!"

Stickler suddenly looked horribly ill.

"How are you, Stick?" Clark asked.

Stickler swallowed sickly. "Okay," he said.

"Where's Doc Savage?"

"He went down in a diving suit."

"How long ago?"

"Not long. Ten minutes ago, maybe."

"How did they know where the submarine was, Stick?"

"I don't know," Stickler lied. "They just knew."

"Didn't they ask you?"

"They asked me," Stickler said. "But I didn't tell them."

"I was afraid they would beat it out of you," Clark said.

"I was afraid of that too," Stickler lied. "But they already knew."

Clark straightened. He called Stickler a lying son. He shot Stickler once between the eyes.

The man died without hardly jerking. He did not do much but tilt his head forward, and a yarn of crimson strung down on his knees.

Clark went over to the telephone wires, the cable which ran down to Doc Savage's suit.

"Savage on the end of this?" he asked.

Renny lied, "No. That's the anchor cable."

He didn't expect them to believe this. But they did. He was dumbfounded, then quickly hid his surprise.

"Anybody left alive in the submarine?" Clark demanded.

"I don't know," Renny said, telling the truth.

Clark straightened. He told one of his men, "Get the dynamite and lash it all together."

"All of it?" the man demanded, astonished.

"All of it," Clark said. "And hurry up."

Renny said, "If you're planning to lower dynamite and explode it down there and kill Doc Savage—it won't work."

"The hell it won't," Clark said. "I know deep water and submarines and I know it will."

"You don't know that much about them," Renny growled. He hoped in some way to talk them out of exploding the dynamite. The blast, at that depth, would collapse Doc's suit instantly.

Clark was scowling at him. "You found out about me, didn't you?"

Renny's thoughts went back to what they had picked up from the dying man in New York. "A little— Thomas," he said. "Yeah, we learned a little."

Clark swore bitterly.

"I wish to hell you hadn't found that out," he said plaintively. "Now I'll have to hide out again." He scowled. "I want to tell you, it isn't no damn fun, this lam business."

"How did you get in the navy?" Renny asked curiously. "Weren't you afraid of your fingerprints getting you in bad?"

Clark, alias Merry John Thomas, shrugged. "No trick to that. Took some dough. I got to the fellow who took the fingerprints, and just in case he fell down on the job, I got to the fellow who got the cards together for mailing. They had a fake set of fingerprints all fixed up. The fakes went on file instead of mine."

Renny said, "I wouldn't think you would have picked the navy for a hideout."

"Why not? The draft would have got me anyway. The armed forces are about as safe a spot as a man could find for a rest."

Renny nodded. "They told me you were an organizer. But I'm surprised you could get eight of your men aboard the submarine, the way you did."

Clark grinned thinly. "Pal, what do you think I spent three years in the navy for? Hell, I was figuring angles all the time. I kept in practice that way. I was afraid I would go stale, so I kept in touch with a bunch of the boys I could call on and depend on, and I was always figuring angles."

Renny said, "You've figured yourself into the electric chair, that's what."

Clark shook his head. "I'm going to shoot you. You know that, don't you?"

Renny knew it. He didn't know much about who Merry John Thomas had been in private life. But from the way the New York police had reacted, Merry John had been somebody on a par with Capone, Dillinger and Pretty Boy Floyd. The man, of course, intended to kill him.

Renny began talking hastily, hoping to postpone it, hoping to think of some way out.

Renny said, "You know, of course, that the sealed compartment in the *Pilotfish* doesn't contain what you think it does."

Clark jumped visibly. That got him for a minute. Then he sneered. "Kidding me, eh?"

"What makes you think I'd kid you?"

Clark glared at him. "Look, brother, I went to too much trouble to find out the truth. I know what's in the compartment."

Renny saw that the man was worried. That was what he wanted. Renny said, "Better think about it a minute."

Clark, scowling, said. "Garner, my Bank of England connection, couldn't be wrong."

"Garner is in jail right now," Renny said. He didn't know who Garner was, much less whether the man was in any jail.

Clark swore.

"That's like the damned fool law—lock up an innocent man," he said. "Garner is a nice old chump. His secretary was my girl friend, and I got the dope on the gold shipment through her. Garner never knew anything got spilled."

He stopped and watched Renny intently, calculatingly. He began shaking his head. "No, no, bub, you're feeding me a line," he said. "The whole thing was too cute. They wouldn't go through all that finagling on no water haul. The gold is aboard." He leaned forward suddenly. "When do you claim they got wise and pulled a fake?"

"Right at the first?"

"When was that?"

"Before the stuff was brought aboard off the German coast that night," Renny said.

Clark snorted. "Oh, no, it wasn't. My girl friend handled old Garner's dealings with the German bankers. She did the coding and decoding of the messages. All of them. Right from the time the German bankers decided it was too risky to keep all that gold in Germany the way conditions after the war were. She handled the messages all through the thing, the decision to bring the gold to the United States for safekeeping, how it was to be picked up by submarine so nobody would know about it, and the whole thing. She handled it. And there wasn't no faking, or she would have known it."

Facts were getting together in Renny's mind. He

remembered who Garner was. Sir Archibald Rand Garner, financial officer for the British government.

So there was gold from Germany in the *Pilotfish!* He wasn't surprised. Everyone knew the Nazis had quite a supply of gold bullion, largely purloined earlier in the war. And anyone would know also that, with present conditions as upset as they were in Germany, there were safer places for a supply of gold to be.

The secrecy in moving the bullion? That was easy to account for, too. In spite of what the newspaper said, and the diplomats, there was considerable distrust in Europe between interests which were supposed to be friends. The open removal of that much gold to the United States would, Renny could well imagine, raise a fuss. So it had been done secretly.

Clark scowled at Renny. "You're a good liar, big fists," he said sourly. "You kind of worry me."

"You better be worried," Renny assured him. "Your goose is cooked."

"They haven't got any dope on me."

"I'm glad you think so."

Clark grimaced. "Who'd they get it from?"

Renny took a chance. "The girl," he said.

"What girl?"

"Garner's secretary."

"When? Hell, they couldn't have my late plans."

Lying, Renny said, "You dope, I talked to the girl myself not forty-eight hours before the sub sailed."

That did it. That upset the apple cart. Clark laughed. Briefly, explosively, with relief. He didn't say anything.

Clark swung around to the men who were preparing the dynamite. "About ready?" he demanded. They told him they were. The charge was about ready to lower. The stuff had been bundled, the detonators attached, and the charge wires connected. About ready to go down.

Without turning his head, Clark told Renny, "You know why you didn't talk to the girl within forty-eight hours of sailing?"

Renny stared at him. "Why?"

"She met with a fatal accident a week before that," Clark said.

"You killed her?"

"They can't prove it," Clark said, and in the same tone, he ordered his men to start the explosive charge into the depths of the sea.

Renny got a look at the dynamite bundle as it went over the side of the power boat. It shocked him. They had sacked the stuff; there was as much blasting powder as a depth bomb held. Enough, he knew, to crush Doc's self-contained diving gear instantly.

XV.

Delight, Doc Savage thought, can be an earthquake. It can be thunder and lightning, the moon and stars, the complete glory.

He was sprawled out on the deck of the *Pilotfish*, unable for the moment to move. He was having something that a neurologist would probably call a nervous reaction, only using larger words. Another way of putting it was that he was so delighted that he was a little hysterical.

Rapping on the *Pilotfish* hull, below him, asked, "Can you loosen the hatch?"

It was Monk.

Monk was alive.

Twenty-six other men were alive in there with Monk. All of them had survived so far. There had been enough oxygen, enough air pressure, enough soda lime, to keep them all alive.

This information Monk had just tapped out through the hull. He had not gone into detail. He had merely said, *"Twenty-seven alive."*

Unlock the hatch! Or un-block it, rather. They could unlock it from the inside, and they must have done that long ago. Or had they? Maybe they didn't have submarine lungs available.

Doc got hold of himself. He beat against the hull intermittently, asking about lungs.

"Can escape with submarine lung," Monk replied, "if you clear hatch."

Doc crawled to the hatch. Renny had explained earlier that his surmise was that the hatch had been blocked externally.

That was right. Clark's men had blocked the hatch before they sank the *Pilotfish*. The blocking had of necessity been done crudely. But it was an effective job.

He used the light, did some prying. It wasn't effective. He worked the cutting torch out of its bracket, carefully adjusted the valves, and ignited it. He cut through the steel bars they had wedged in place to block the hatch. He extinguished the torch.

"Hatch cleared," he signalled. "Buoy also cleared."

"O.K. Coming out."

Doc stooped carefully, unfastened the midriff weights which gave him bottom buoyancy. He kicked off half of the shoe ballast. He began to rise slowly.

There was no danger in his rising directly to the surface, since he was subject to not much more than atmospheric pressure inside the suit.

It would be different with those in the *Pilotfish*. They would have to come up slowly, clinging to the buoy line. They would have to take not less than five minutes in the ascent.

Procedure inside the *Pilotfish* would now be standard. It would be terrible to undergo, but not necessarily fatal.

The hatch was equipped with a skirt, a tube which extended down a short distance into the compartment. They would open the inboard drain vents, flooding the compartment. The pressure would build up until it reached sea pressure. Then there would be a bubble around the skirt. A bubble of air against the chamber ceiling. They could hang there, clinging to the pipes—the air lines, the conduits, the fuel pipes—while they adjusted the escape lungs.

With sea pressure and compartment pressure equalized, the hatch could be opened. It would probably blow open of it own accord.

Then the men could duck under the skirt. They could find the buoy line. They could follow it to the surface, pausing at intervals to decompress. They would know how to do that. The method was a part of their training.

He had a good feeling. The men in the submarine were as good as safe, he felt.

Then, electrifying. Renny's roar in the headphone: "Doc! They're lowering dynamite! They're—"

Hoarseness and fear ground together in the yell. And violence shut off the cry.

His first instinctive thought was disbelief. Then he began twisting frantically at the ballast weights. He got them off.

Buoyancy shot him upward now. He could tell he was rising. But the water remained intensely black around him. There was not much sensation of lift.

Then there was a paleness about him. A brief glow. He knew that lightning must have flashed in the storm-threatened sky. He was close to the surface. He was on top. He shot out of the water half his length.

He twisted wildly. Trying to get the face-light around. Trying to see what went on.

They shot him twice. The bullets hit the metal suit like sledges. Both went through. The first cut a long rip in the helmet. The second was worse. A hot wire thrust through his left side.

Air, under some pressure, left the suit through the holes. Cold water poured into the helmet, salty, stinging his eyes.

He worked his arms frantically, and sank. More bullets made loud smashing noises against the water.

The suit! He would have to get out of the suit. The suit was designed so it could be removed quickly. He fought with the helmet dogs.

He got the helmet off. It seemed an age. He got the breastplate apart. The hot wire was still in his back, bigger, hotter. The metal suit started sinking as he twisted out of it.

The torch! The cutting torch with its metal gas bottles and connecting hoses! He swam down wildly, got to the suit, and worked with the patent connectors.

He got the torch finally. He could swim up with it.

He couldn't stay under. There was no oxygen apparatus supplying him now. He had to have air. Need for air had become agony in his lungs.

They would shoot at him when he surfaced. They did. But he came up close to the hull, against it actually. They had to lean far over to aim at him. He gave them no time. He got breath, got a look at the side of the boat, then dived.

It was a cabin cruiser with a metal hull. About forty feet. There was a cockpit aft, one designed for deepsea fishing. They were lowering the explosive from that. Three men working with a line and wires.

He swam underwater, made for the wires. He got to them. He was probably six feet under the surface. They could see him. They shot at him. The lead striking into the water made ear-hurting impacts. But no rifle bullet would do much through six feet of water.

He got the wires. He fired the torch. It would, thank God, light itself.

The glare from the torch was incandescent, blinding. But it parted the thin wires instantly. At least there would be no underwater explosion.

The propeller shaft! He swam for it, got hold of the rudder. He knew, then, that he couldn't cut the propeller shaft with the torch. That was what he'd hoped to do. But the shaft was too thick, time too short.

He could stay under a while yet. Actually it had been no more than twenty seconds since he got his lungs full of air. He could manage, he believed, a couple of minutes. He had stayed under longer than that in the past. But not under such conditions as these.

This was a stock model of boat. Gasoline driven, probably. He knew about where the underwater intake for the cooling pumps was. He fumbled along the bottom of the hull and found it, a small protruding scoop and a strainer. It was something to cling to. Not much, but something.

He put the dazzling flame of the torch against the boat hull.

The torch began cutting the hull skin like a sharp knife working on a pie crust. That torch would cut four inches of solid steel underwater in a few moments. It was as efficient under water as the best cutting torches in the open air. This would seem startling to a layman, but it was true.

He moved the torch slowly in a circle. Used about a six-inch radius. The disc of metal broke loose. He felt it. Felt the surge of water into the boat.

The cabin cruiser would sink now.

He kept hold of the torch, pushed himself away from the boat hull, and swam.

The plane had not been on the side of the boat where he'd come up for air. It must be on the other side. He swam in that direction. He needed air badly now.

Suddenly the plane hull was a fat, duck-belly shape above him. He barely made it under the hull. He came to the surface fast, got air, sank. All in one motion. Then he realized he had not been shot at. He came up again, cautiously, and took air into his lungs, watching the plane cabin windows intently, ready to dive again if a hand with a gun appeared.

He heard someone cursing. "Get to the plane!" the man was yelling between profanity.

He heard Monk's voice. "What the hell's going on?" Monk bellowed. Monk! Monk had reached the surface, had come up from the *Pilotfish!*

Doc swam, still keeping the torch, to the stern of the plane hull. He looked around it.

The cabin cruiser was down at the stern already. They were leaving it. Jumping into the sea; swimming toward the plane. No life preservers. But with guns.

The man who had been swearing was now shouting, "I'll pull you aboard! Come here! Grab my hand!"

He was evidently alone in the plane. He had the

cabin door open, was on all fours, reaching downward.

Doc sank quickly. He swam underwater, came up under the man who was reaching. He came up fast, got the man's downstretched arm.

The man screeched. Clark. Doc recognized him from Renny's description.

They began to haul against each other. A wordless kind of a struggle. Then Clark lost the tug-of-war. He toppled out into the water.

Around the bow of the sinking cabin cruiser Monk Mayfair came ploughing.

"Ham!" Monk roared. "Ham, there's a fight!"

He made for the nearest swimmer, flailing both arms.

Ham came around the stern of the cabin cruiser shortly.

More men from the *Pilotfish* followed them.

Clark had dived, Doc kept a grip on the man. Clark tried to stay under. He was fresh, strong, at home in the water.

Doc Savage fought the man, confidently at first, then with terror. Because Doc was weak. He was weaker than he imagined he could be. The wire in his back had become a blazing cable of pain, and everything else was weakness.

He got away from Clark, finally, with the torch. He pulled on the feed trigger, the incandescent cutting flame lashed out, and he was loose. He hadn't burned Clark, just terrorized the man.

Doc lost the torch then. He couldn't hang on to it. He didn't have the strength.

He barely made the surface.

Someone laid hold of him. He clubbed feebly with a fist. "Hey, dammit!" . . . Monk's voice. Anxious. "Blazes, what'd they do to you?" Monk gasped anxiously. Monk was tying a life preserver about him, he thought. He wasn't sure.

He passed out.

There was no darkness. Just a gap in time, and then a glare of white light that hurt his eyes so that he could not see anything. He stopped trying to see, and closed his eyes tightly.

After a while, Monk's voice said, "It was some fight while it lasted. Tough, you missing it. You'd have liked it."

There was a silence.

Very carefully, not opening his eyes, Doc asked, "You get Clark?"

"Commander Wickart did. Shot him. Wickart still had his revolver when he got to the top. He shot Clark and some of Clark's men. Three, I think. Only about half a dozen of the men from the submarine got to the top in time to take part in the fight, and two of them weren't in any shape to be much help. We had us a hell of a time until Ham Brooks took a submarine gun away from one of the gang. A Reising gun. That made it a pushover for our side."

"Where are Clark's men?"

"Those who are alive are being looked after."

"What about Renny?"

"They conked him over the head. He's all right now."

Still very carefully, Doc said, "Use the plane radio. Get hold of the navy. Have them send planes and boats for us."

Monk laughed.

"What are you laughing at?" Doc demanded.

"Where do you think you are now?" Monk asked.

"Eh?"

"In the New London submarine base hospital."

Disbelieving, Doc opened his eyes. After the fireworks in his eyeballs, he decided that he was in a white room with fluorescent lighting.

"What time is it?" Doc asked.

"It's the next day," Monk said.

"What's been wrong with me?"

Monk laughed again. "First time you've been laid up in ages, isn't it? You've got a hole in you from stem to stern, almost. Nothing you won't get over, though."

*   *   *

Ham Brooks came in. He came in bustling, discovered Monk, and stopped hastily. He looked as if he was poised for flight.

Monk scowled at him. "You overdressed shyster!" Monk said bitterly.

Ham ignored this. But he kept a wary eye on Monk. "How do you feel, Doc?" Ham asked.

"I feel fine," Doc said sourly.

"You know yet what the shooting was all about?" Ham inquired.

"No."

"There was gold on that submarine. Tons and tons of it. The Allies were sneaking it out of Germany to keep it out of the hands of the wrong people until things get straightened out. They were bringing it out secretly so as not to stir up a lot of fuss. Just keeping the gold safe in a diplomatic way. Clark found out about it, and he was after it."

"Can the navy get it now?"

"They've got part of it already," Ham said. "The divers are working now. I just saw a radio report from the salvage boat."

Monk was glaring at Ham. "You Judas! You Iscariot!"

Ham grinned. "Smile when you say that," he said.

"You told these nurses I had a wife and several half-witted children, you stinker," Monk said bitterly. "That's the same thing you always tell them. You might at least think up a new fib."

A constellation of stars floated into the room. A blonde in a nurse's uniform. A gorgeous dish, lovely to behold.

The lovely smiled at Ham, eyed Monk coldly, and asked Monk, "How is the little wife and family today?"

Monk said to Doc, "You see what I mean." He sidled toward Ham. Ham retreated through the door. Monk sauntered after him. The last heard of them, it sounded as if they were both running.

Doc sighed pleasantly. Monk and Ham in a fuss. Things were back to normal again.

He smiled at the blonde job. She smiled back. He

said, "Ham has a wife and I don't know how many dim-witted children, too."

The blonde job seemed startled. She came over and plumped his pillow. She smelled of gardenias. She was distinctly a destroyer. She was a blonde bomber.

"Me, too," Doc said hastily.

OUT OF THIS WORLD!

That's the only way to describe Bantam's great series of science fiction classics. These space-age thrillers are filled with terror, fancy and adventure and written by America's most renowned writers of science fiction. Welcome to outer space and have a good trip!

FANTASY AND SCIENCE FICTION FAVORITES

Bantam brings you the recognized classics as well as the current favorites in fantasy and science fiction. Here you will find the beloved Conan books along with recent titles by the most respected authors in the genre.

☐	01166	URSHURAK	
		Bros. Hildebrandt & Nichols	$8.95
☐	13610	NOVA Samuel R. Delany	$2.25
☐	13534	TRITON Samuel R. Delany	$2.50
☐	13612	DHALGREN Samuel R. Delany	$2.95
☐	11662	SONG OF THE PEARL Ruth Nichols	$1.75
☐	12018	CONAN THE SWORDSMAN #1	
		DeCamp & Carter	$1.95
☐	12706	CONAN THE LIBERATOR #2	
		DeCamp & Carter	$1.95
☐	12970	THE SWORD OF SKELOS #3	
		Andrew Offutt	$1.95
☐	14321	THE ROAD OF KINGS #4	$2.25
		Karl E. Wagner	
☐	11276	THE GOLDEN SWORD Janet Morris	$1.95
☐	14127	DRAGONSINGER Anne McCaffrey	$2.50
☐	14204	DRAGONSONG Anne McCaffrey	$2.50
☐	12019	KULL Robert E. Howard	$1.95
☐	10779	MAN PLUS Frederik Pohl	$1.95
☐	13680	TIME STORM Gordon R. Dickson	$2.50
☐	13400	SPACE ON MY HANDS Frederic Brown	$1.95

Bantam Book Catalog

Here's your up-to-the-minute listing of over 1,400 titles by your favorite authors.

This illustrated, large format catalog gives a description of each title. For your convenience, it is divided into categories in fiction and non-fiction—gothics, science fiction, westerns, mysteries, cookbooks, mysticism and occult, biographies, history, family living, health, psychology, art.

So don't delay—take advantage of this special opportunity to increase your reading pleasure.

Just send us your name and address and 50¢ (to help defray postage and handling costs).